JUST UNTIL THE WEDDING

EMI HILTON

Published by:

5 Prince Publishing and Books, LLC

DBA 5 Prince Publishing

PO Box 865

Arvada, Colorado 80001

Digital ISBN: 978-1-63112-434-1

Print ISBN: 978-1-63112-435-8

Cover design by Marianne Nowicki

Interior design by 5 Prince Publishing

First Edition

F02162026

For more information about this title, visit: www.5princebooks.com

For the dreamers

ACKNOWLEDGMENTS

As always, a huge thank you to my readers. Thank you for supporting me on my writing journey, for purchasing my books, sharing my novels with a friend, and leaving five-star reviews. Each time you read and share my books with others my readership grows. Thank you, thank you, thank you.

To my marvelous editor Cate Byers, it was a joy to work with you on this manuscript. You find a unique way to bring my vision to light. I am thankful for your patience with me as I learn to improve as an author. With each novel I work on with you, I grow in some way. So, thank you for your guidance.

To my publisher, 5 Prince Publishing, thank you for believing in me and my work. Your belief in me and my words has turned my dream into a reality. Thank you for giving my stories a home, and my heart a reason to keep writing. From the bottom of my heart, a million thanks.

To my husband Tyler, it's only with you by my side that I have the ability to write. Our love story is what continues to inspire and guide me. I would be lost without you. I love you to the moon and back.

To family and friends, thank you for supporting me and my dream. Thank you for believing in me and helping to share my work with the world. You are my biggest cheerleaders. If I don't say it enough, this is me saying it, my life is better with you in it.

Finally, my faithful Father in Heaven, God, my heart is full of gratitude for the guidance and inspiration thou grants me. I know every good gift comes from thee. Every door that has been opened, every dream that I have achieved, has only been possible because of thee. Thou art my source of strength and creativity. I know I am nothing without thee. I humbly devote this book to thee. In all things, may the glory and honor be thine forever.

ALSO BY EMI HILTON

Just Until the Wedding

New to Newport

Keeping Kama

Picking Pismo

Leaving Cloverton

Come to the Cape

JUST UNTIL THE WEDDING

CHAPTER 1

Brooke stared at the package of hot French bread. A minute ticked by, then two. Did she dare purchase the loaf? She pinched the sleeve of it, and the plastic window on the package crinkled under her fingertips. Then the tantalizing aroma of fresh bread hit her nostrils. She salivated. Ugh, she wanted the bread more than anything. But if she knew anything about carbs, it was that, magically, no amount of cardio could offset eating it.

Another minute passed, and Brooke's gaze remained glued. If she bought the loaf, she was eating the whole thing, game over. She inhaled another whiff of the warm, carb-loaded goodness. Gosh, she imagined how good it tasted. The melt in your mouth, eat until your stomach aches kind of deliciousness. Best part, this particular bag of joy would only set her back a mere three bucks. But the echo of her mother's old saying, 'a moment on the lips is a lifetime on the hips' vibrated in her psyche again and again, back and forth, like she was on a child's teeter-totter.

But breakup calories did not count, right?

It was practically written in stone.

A perfectly formed forearm came around her shoulder and

snatched a packet of the French bread. After all, she was being an aisle hog.

"Just buy it." He tossed the sleeve of bread into his hand-held basket like any man would. No thoughts about how it might make them bloat or add an uncomfortable inch that made their jeans too tight. "You know you won't regret it." He smiled, making his blue eyes pop.

Brooke peered up at the cool drink of water and allowed her ogling gaze to travel the length of his chiseled biceps and broad shoulders. His full head of not-quite-curly dark brown hair made him attractive in a boy next door look. Inwardly, she cringed as she glanced down at her ragged, disheveled appearance. *Ah, come on now.* She never met hot guys when she looked put together. Never.

Brooke blinked. "No, I know I will— regret it, big time. I'm just trying to decide how much I care."

She knew she looked bad. Her dirty hair hadn't been washed in days. To make matters worse, she had thrown it up into a haphazard bun on her way out the door. A mustard stain she needed to wash out shone brightly on the front of her hoodie. After her back-to-back shifts at the hospital, her eyes burned from lack of sleep. The dark circles which stared back at her in the mirror made herself flinch. If she wasn't so bone dead tired, coupled with her gut-wrenching sadness, she might have cared.

"Ahh," he replied.

"I'm a woman," she countered.

Gosh, his eyes were intriguing, a perfect match of turquoise and aqua. She'd read somewhere that the blue-eyed and dark-haired combo was a dying breed. Then and there she cast a prayer, it wasn't true.

"I noticed." His lips twitched like he found her a bit amusing.

"If you didn't hear, carbs are the woman's enemy."

"Are they now?" His eyes glinted with humor. "I thought a

woman's enemy was men who didn't pay on dates and people who don't put their cart away after they visit the grocery store."

"Wrong." She made a buzzer sound. "Carbs, it always was and always will be carbs. This is why I'm trying to decide." Brooke forced her gaze away from the hot guy back to the bread rack. "Do I care I will polish off the entire loaf by myself on my way home?"

"Did you want me to answer that?" he replied.

"No."

His gaze roamed her body. "Bad day?"

Bingo, genius.

Brooke shifted back to take in the boy next door with his five o'clock shadow. He looked like he was on his way to a casting call for a Hallmark movie, and she wanted to hate him for it. He probably dated women who hated bread and drank green smoothies on their way to yoga. Most definitely he didn't date women like her.

"You have no idea," Brooke muttered.

She scooted closer to the bread rack and pinched the bag of French bread again. The aroma seeped out of the top of the open bag, hitting her again with its intoxicating scent. It screamed 'buy me, buy me'. Brooke planned to as soon as Mr. Hottie moved it along. She preferred to make unhealthy food choices alone.

"Oh," he stammered.

His gaze slid up and down her a second time in a less than obvious manner. She wondered if he thought she looked as bad as she appeared. *Wait, she didn't want to know the answer.*

"I'm sorry to hear that." He stepped back and widened the space between them like she was a loose cannon. "I hope it gets better. Maybe the bread will help?" Slowly, he moved further away.

"Not likely." Brooke picked up a package of the bread, then added, "But thanks."

It looked like Brooke had dinner.

"Hey," he smiled and revealed his dazzling white teeth. "You're going for it." He nodded his head toward her loaf of bread. "Good for you."

"Yep, I can't resist." Brooke forced herself to straighten her shoulders. "I guess you could say I no longer care about—anything." She laughed nervously as she fought back the tears working toward the corners of her eyes. With a forced smile, she continued, "So, why not eat my sorrows away on a loaf of bread?"

"Ahh—" he rubbed the back of his neck and shuffled his feet.

He suddenly looked very uncomfortable. Word to the wise, do not share your mess of a life with a stranger. Deep discomfort will follow for you and them. Keep those emotions packed in tight until you find yourself alone again.

He scrunched his nose. "Sorry."

She shrugged. "My life is falling apart."

"I gathered that much." He stumbled a step back and his hip hit the end of the aisle shelving.

"This," Brooke shook the package of bread, "will help."

Stop talking. You are scaring him.

"I see." His lips pursed together, forming a tight line. "Good luck—with—that." He tried to back up more but his body was pinned between her and the aisle.

"Nothing I can't handle." She laughed.

"Okay," His eyes dilated a smidge, just enough that she thought he might think she was a total weirdo.

But luckily, she lived in Chicago. Her chances of seeing this guy again were pretty much zilch. The beauty of city living.

"Okay," she repeated.

With nothing left to say, she brushed past him and shuffled over to the checkout lines. Brooke didn't care what Mr. Tall, Dark, and Handsome was doing, but she planned on high-tailing it out of this grocery store before she managed to have even more awkward conversations with innocent people.

So, she weaved through the store and arrived at the checkout lanes. But she found every line ten people deep. She groaned. Maybe this wasn't worth it? She gnawed on her bottom lip as she contemplated abandoning the bread. A whiff of it filled her lungs. No, she needed this more than anything, bad choices and all. A cashier opened the self-checkout machines on the section past the normal checkout. Bingo.

This forced Brooke to duck and dive around the crowded lines and crawl her way to the self-checkout. By the time she arrived, the line for self-checkout weaved down the cookie aisle. She dragged her feet to the end of it.

As she waited, the beautiful cookies in plastic packaging taunted her. She ran her finger along the row of cookies. The double stuffed Oreos called her name. *Eat me, eat me, eat me.* Quickly, she checked the back of the package for the nutrition content. Terrible idea. She placed the package back on the shelf. The line didn't budge, and the Oreos stared back at her.

"Fine," she muttered to herself way too loud. "I'll buy you too."

If she was going down, she planned on doing it in style.

So, there she stood, hot bread in one hand and Oreos in the other, with her ugliest and grungiest clothes on. Her blood pressure rose with each passing minute. One customer had twelve coupons, another tried to ring up gift cards which wasn't allowed in the self-checkout, and another tried to purchase alcohol. This required a worker to shuffle on over and approve the purchase. She peered down at her two items.

Was this worth it?

Yes.

"Oreos, too," the familiar voice from earlier interrupted her thoughts. "Excellent choice." He spoke from behind her.

Her jaw clenched. Something about his upbeat tone made her grip both items tightly in each hand. The package of Oreos crinkled under the clutch of her fingertips. Sure, she knew she was headed down the path of destruction, but she wanted to do it alone.

"Are you," Brooke swiveled to face him then hissed with far too much gusto, "following me?"

"What?" He took a large step back, widening the gap between them. He looked around the aisle then back at her. "I'm sorry. I just got out of a twelve-hour surgery. I tend to be a bit chatty afterwards. I'm not following you. I thought we had a moment back there," his voice softened, and he placed a hand over his chest, "I guess I was wrong."

"Surgery?" She rolled her eyes. "Please."

Brooke had met plenty of men like him at the hospital where she worked. Men who loved to use their profession as bragging rights to be a total turd. Well, too bad, she was not taking the bait. Guess what, news flash, she was a doctor too. Pediatrician.

"Um, sorry. Huh?"

"I get it, you're a surgeon." Brooke dramatically waved the hand with the package of Oreos around. "I should be drooling and throwing myself at you to get the chance to be with such a total catch."

"That wasn't what I was—"

She interrupted and said, "Save it."

The line shifted forward.

He pursed his lips together then he curtly nodded.

She swung back around and shuffled up. The surgeon followed too, but kept a huge gap between them. If the situation was reversed, she would have done the same thing. But she told herself he wouldn't think about her ever again after tonight.

Five agonizing minutes later, she found herself at the front of the line. A self-checkout machine opened up. She strode over and quickly scanned the Oreos and bread. Then she tapped her credit card against the screen to complete her transaction, but it failed.

With a groan, she muttered to herself, "This can't be happening." She tried a second time, convinced it scanned it wrong. It made an embarrassing loud beep that would've woken the dead.

The cashier running the three checkout registers came over. "Is everything okay?" Their wrist had a dangle of keys and cards hanging from it.

"No." Brooke tapped her credit card again. "It's not accepting my card."

Beep. Beep. Beep. It blasted back at her, loud enough that a few other customers peered in her direction. Brooke tapped it again and again against the screen. *This will work. The card is active.*

"Let me see." The cashier moved closer.

Brooke held up the card then slowly attempted to tap her credit card against the machine. It failed again. "See? This shouldn't be happening. It's your machine, not my card. I used it earlier today."

"Oh." They pointed to the big sign above the check-out screen. "We don't accept American Express."

"You don't?" She wanted to shrivel into herself. "Since when?"

"Since last week, it's too expensive. American Express charges exorbitant fees, too much for a little corner grocery store like us. The owner finally made the decision to not accept it anymore."

"I see." She squinted at the sign for a moment letting the realization that she had no other way to pay sink in.

The cashier's forehead furrowed. "Do you have any other form of payment?"

"No." Brooke stared down at the bread and Oreos. "I sure don't."

She had only left the house for a quick walk around the block, and she'd brought one credit card with her as an afterthought. The walk had been to lift her spirits. When she returned from her long shift at the hospital to her empty and lonely apartment, she knew she needed to get outside for a minute. She had read somewhere that exercise helped lift a person's mood, so she decided to give it a try. The stop at the grocery store really hadn't been planned. The call of bad food choices had pulled her through the doors.

"Okay, then." The cashier rubbed their hands together and uncomfortably rocked back and forth on their heels. "I'm not sure how to help you then."

"Forget it." Brooke slid the credit card back into the pocket of her sweatpants and moved the items to the side of the machine. "I don't need them anyways." Then she walked away leaving the unpurchased items for the cashier to deal with.

It was for the best. She took it as the universe's way of keeping her off carbs and stopping her from eating away her heart full of sorrows. Though the whole situation completely mortified her. Repressed memories from her childhood trekked up to the surface. No matter how hard she tried to splat them away, they broke through her protective layer.

Her mom never had enough money to pay for her things at the store. She wasted all her money on drugs and booze. Often, they'd ring everything up only to discover they had maybe a fourth of what was needed to cover what was on the conveyer belt. Then her mom would ask the cashier to remove items one at a time until the bill was low enough for her to pay for it. It didn't help that the cashier always eyed her dirty face and ratty clothes with pity, making her feel small and insignificant in the world.

Sometimes her mom would beg the random cashier or the person behind them in line to spot them the difference. It worked sometimes. Other times, they left the store with only an item or two. Then Brooke knew she wasn't eating until she received the free school lunch the next day. So, she promised herself, way back as a child, that someday she'd earn enough to never have to bear the shame again. And there was no chance she'd ever do drugs or drink alcohol. Living the nightmare of her childhood kept her far away from those things.

In this moment, Brooke reminded herself she wasn't ten, and she wasn't her mother. It wasn't her fault the grocery store stopped taking her type of credit card. The grocery store stop had been a terrible idea, anyway. Brooke wasn't a person who ate bread or Oreos, nor was she a person who hissed at unsuspecting nice guys. Usually, people thanked her for being kind and considerate. Her patients and their parents loved her quiet and calm demeanor. And she always received high reviews at the hospital where she worked. But today, this evening, was out of character for her, she wished she could close her eyes and start over.

Only this morning her world had lit on fire and burned to the ground. She woke up to a text from her boyfriend, Justin, dumping her. He didn't even think she was worthy of a phone call. Apparently, Justin met the woman of his dreams, who, newsflash, wasn't her. He didn't explain how they met either or the shady timeline.

Somehow, Brooke managed to pull herself together enough to get to work. But work, well, it wasn't too great either. A pair of twins vomited all over her at the hospital when she was examining them. She had to change into the extra set of clothes in her locker to rid herself of the vomit chunks. Then she had an itch between her shoulder blades she couldn't reach. Back at home, her kitchen sink had a leak that made the most annoying dripping sound. And now, this.

Inside, she felt dead.

Empty.

Alone.

The glass electric doors swung open, blasting her with the frigid Chicago winter air. She shivered and crossed her arms to try and warm herself as she passed through the doors. The L train ran overhead. A gust of dingy air replaced the earlier aroma of bread. Slowly, she made her way to the crosswalk and pounded the button with a closed fist. The dark sky matched the color of her heart. She wondered if it would snow overnight, making the sidewalk a slushy mess on her way to work tomorrow. Then she thought of Justin and how he wouldn't spend the night alone. Her shoulders drooped.

"Hey, wait up," the now-familiar voice from the grocery store called out.

Brooke peered over her shoulder as the man from earlier jogged out of the store and over to where she waited. He had a brown paper bag in each of his hands. It looked like he didn't only have American Express. The crosswalk light flashed walk, but she remained glued in place.

She rubbed her arms with her hands. "Yeah? What's up?" She sounded like a teenager.

He landed in front of her. "Here." He held a bag out to her. The loaf of French bread stuck out of the top. "This is for you."

Blankly, she stared down at the bag. Her jaw slackened a little. *This guy bought her things. She hadn't even been nice to him.* Tears tickled the corners of her eyes. Kindness from strangers wasn't something she experienced too often.

When she didn't move or answer, he said again, "Here." He shook the bag. "Take it." Then he pressed it against her arms.

Brooke kept her arms folded. "Did you buy my bread and Oreos?" Her voice softened as their gaze caught. All that stared back at her was a sincere and earnest desire to help her.

"Yes, so please take it."

Slowly, she uncrossed her arm and hooked her hand around the top handle. He let go.

"I can't believe you bought me my things." She forced her gaze away from him and down to the bag in her hands. "Why?" The worry lines on her forehead eased. "I wasn't very nice to you back there. I'm really sorry by the way. I'm normally not ill-mannered." She gnawed on her bottom lip, trying to find the words. "So, why would you buy food for me?"

"Because you said you were having a difficult day." He rubbed the back of his neck with his free hand. "And if you went into a store only to buy those two items, I figured you do need them, for whatever reason."

Then she blurted out the first thing that came to her mind. "Are you a murderer or something?" She cautiously brought the bag tight against her chest and cradled it between her arms. "Buy me bread to butter me up then I end up as a story on Dateline."

He laughed. "No—geez. Do I give off that vibe?" He shuffled his feet then ran his free hand through his messy dark locks. "I hope I don't look like a murderer. But I think you've managed to give me one more thing to be self-conscious about."

She chuckled. "Sorry, I'm not used to men being nice to me for no reason." A crooked smile cracked her lips. "Also, I just watched this documentary about Ted Bundy. He was attractive and used his charm to lure women. You seemed too good to be true buying my bread and Oreos."

"Ha." He shifted his own brown bag from one hand to the other. "Trust me, I'm not charming any women."

"I don't know." She held up the bag. "This certainly could've worked on women who are into that type of thing." A tiny smile attempted to make the ends of her lips curl.

"But not you." His eyes crinkled around the edges while the streetlamp overhead made them shine brightly. "Right?"

"Correct." She shook her head. "Not me."

The crosswalk light came and went again. Another L train ran overhead making the street vibrate. Brooke pressed the crosswalk button again.

"Thanks." She peered out at the cars on the street piling up as the light turned red. "It was incredibly good Samaritan of you."

"I try."

"Well," she swung her gaze from him to the crosswalk and back, "thanks—sorry I didn't catch your name."

"Logan." He straightened himself. "And you?"

"Brooke."

"Enjoy your Oreos and bread," he smiled, making his eyes

twinkle. The knots in her stomach loosened. "It was nice meeting you."

"Thanks again for the food." The crosswalk light lit up, and she pointed at it. "I'd better go. Have a nice life, Logan." Then she genuinely smiled.

"You too."

Swiftly, she entered the crosswalk and left Logan standing on the corner. She wondered if he lived nearby, and what hospital he worked at. If this was a romcom, he would've jogged after her or at least asked for her number before she disappeared. But it wasn't, not even close. If anything, her life was one of those awful dark comedies where everyone else laughed but her. The highlight of her day would be to eat bread and Oreos, alone.

Her skin itched to peer back over her shoulder to see if Logan still stood on the corner, but she forced herself to keep walking. The aroma of bread wafted out of her bag. Her hand dipped inside the warm bag, and she ripped a piece off and bit into it. When the perfectly warm bread hit her lips, she sighed. It tasted heavenly. Why did it taste this good? She polished off the piece she had and tore another chunk to eat.

Another L train raced above her, making her body tremor as it passed. Bitter air nipped at her exposed skin, and she wished she had remembered a jacket on the way out. Despite it, her insides were warm and full of bread. Instead of crying on her walk home, she thought of Logan and his simple act of kindness. She knew she would find a way to pay it forward and purchase someone else's groceries when their credit card didn't work.

She ate and walked then ate some more. Her apartment wasn't far, only a few blocks from the grocery store. Despite the close distance, by the time she rounded the corner to her building, she had managed to polish off half her loaf of bread. In front of her apartment building was George, her friend, and the building security guard. He lived in the building with his wife.

Brooke tucked the loaf back into her brown bag and waved.

George waved back and held the door open as she approached. "Good evening. You're back fast. I thought you said you were going on a long walk," he teased.

"Long enough to get some much-needed essentials." She shook her bag as she entered the building. "I lost my desire for a long walk as soon as I entered the grocery store."

"Oh, okay." George chuckled as he followed her inside the building and closed the door behind them, but he lingered in front of the door. "At least you managed to buy dinner?" He raised an eyebrow.

"Yep," Brooke beamed. "Exactly."

"Did you have a long day at the hospital?" George readjusted his leather gloves.

Brooke enjoyed his company and appreciated his friendly greetings when she came and went. George knew she lived alone and that she didn't have any family to speak of. Her mom had died a while ago, and her dad up and left one day when she was a kid and never came back. Brooke asked about her dad a few times after he left, but then her mom told her he died, and she knew enough to not ask any more questions.

"So long." She hesitated. "Also, Justin and I broke up. If he stops by do not let him up to my apartment."

"Did you finally give him the boot?" George buttoned the top two buttons of his coat.

Over the three years she had lived in the building, they had developed a camaraderie she enjoyed. George was about thirty years her senior. With the age difference, he became a sounding board for her different life experiences. He always managed to give her good advice when she was faced with some sort of obstacle.

"I wish. It sure would make for a better story." Brooke sighed making her shoulders droop. "He left me for someone shinier, brighter, and younger."

The sting of saying it out loud made it feel like a quick swift kick to the gut. The bread in her belly churned and made her nauseous.

"Ahh, then you dodged a bullet." He spotted another resident coming inside, and he opened the door and held it for them. Brooke lingered, because she needed to talk this entire thing through with someone. George waited until the resident crossed the lobby to the elevators to continue, "Nobody should be saddled with an idiot."

Brooke laughed. "I think the patients at the hospital would beg to differ. Justin is well-respected among our colleagues, and the patients love him. I mean he has that dreamy doctor persona down."

George shook his head. "I don't care what the patients or your co-workers say about him, the guy is an idiot." He cupped his gloved hands together. "Didn't he try to blame you when all his whites in the wash turned blue? And it was only because *he* threw a pair of jeans in with his socks and underwear?"

"I can't believe you remember that." Brooke cradled her brown paper bag to her chest. "I had completely forgotten that happened." Then she laughed, making the tension in her chest ease a bit. "I guess he does lack what people call street smarts."

Justin grew up privileged while Brooke grew up in total dysfunction. Her desire to become a doctor was part love of medicine and part desire to create stability for herself. The moment she turned eighteen and graduated from high school, she left. When she packed up her stuff, her mom never even asked where she was going. Not once did she call to find out if she was safe. Brooke knew her mom was probably never sober long enough to notice her absence.

For years, she managed to be alone in the world. She grew accustomed to not having a safety net, a loving family or parents. But when she met Justin, through her best friend, Aubrey and her fiancé Ian, suddenly she wasn't alone. She was part of a pair, and part of a friend group. This meant Brooke wasn't eating

Christmas dinner standing up in her kitchen. Thanksgiving she found herself around a table with nice linen, real china, and people who knew how to say an entire sentence without a long string of swear words.

When the red flags with Justin started to pop up, Brooke looked past them. Being with him certainly beat being alone. Sure, she didn't like his arrogant attitude or his condescending tone when he explained things to her. But who didn't make some compromises when it came to relationships? So, she accepted their relationship with all its flaws, because for once in her life she belonged somewhere. Then she never expected in her wildest dreams, Justin would be the one who didn't choose her, because she thought she was the one making all the concessions.

"And didn't he try to get his money back after he ate a whole cherry pie, but the label on the packaging said it was peach," George said as he raised an eyebrow.

"Stop it." Brooke laughed again, grateful George wanted to cheer her up. "Ok. You have a point. I'm better off without him. He did have a tendency to act entitled."

"Yes. You're better off." George peered out the front door, double checking for any residents on their way inside.

She wished she felt better off.

Instead, she only felt more alone.

"But one big problem, I have my best friend's wedding coming up." Brooke shuffled her feet. "And Justin is going to be the best man, and I'm one of the bridesmaids. I can't wiggle my way out of it, and now I need a plus one."

The detail seemed minuscule, but it haunted her, nonetheless. Her best friend, Aubrey happened to be marrying the man of her dreams, Justin's best friend, Ian. And being dumped this close to the wedding meant she needed a date. To add salt to the wound, she'd no doubt have to endure an entire day watching him cuddled up with his new girlfriend.

"Last I checked you worked at a hospital with tons of doctor friends roaming the halls. Ask one of them to go with you. Better yet, ask one of them to go and pretend to be your new boyfriend, which will make Justin green with envy. Suddenly, his new shiny and bright thing won't look so sparkly."

"Wow, don't you have all the answers tonight?" Brooke moved toward the elevator. "Thanks for the advice. I probably won't take it, but thank you, nonetheless. I'll talk to you later."

"Have a nice evening." George went back to his post outside of the building.

Brooke clutched the brown bag to her chest after she hit the elevator button and waited for it to arrive at the lobby. The doors dinged then swung open, she crawled into the elevator and hit her floor button.

Maybe she could call in sick tomorrow? But she knew slinking away wasn't her style. Instead, she planned on eating her Oreos while she cried. Come tomorrow, she'll dust herself off, square her shoulders and go back to work. If things became too unbearable, she could always relocate. She wasn't married to this place, maybe a new hospital in a new city was just what she needed.

Brooke moved to Chicago after medical school and took a great job offer at the hospital here. The city's lower cost of living made it more attractive than the other big cities on the East Coast. Then shortly after her move, she made friends with Aubrey, met Justin, and she thought she'd live here forever. Chicago was a great city. It had enough of everything to keep her around.

But if seeing Justin every day at work became too much to handle, she'd apply for a new job in a new city and leave. She let the idea settle in her mind, helping her regain control. Today she wouldn't spiral. One always had choices, you only needed to give yourself permission to see them all.

Once she made it into the comfort of her apartment, she settled onto her brown leather sofa and didn't even bother removing her shoes as she kicked her feet up onto her coffee table. Then she dug back into her grocery bag and retrieved her packet of Oreos. She peeled back the top of the plastic film top and ate five in rapid succession. The taste of chocolate didn't even register. Brooke turned on a true crime show to keep from thinking and reminded herself breakup calories didn't count.

At some point, she drifted to sleep.

Her dreams were a mixture of bread, Oreos, and Logan. The guy she would never see again.

CHAPTER 2

After returning from the grocery store, his tiredness from work hit him. Hard. Logan put away his groceries and chugged a protein shake standing up in his kitchen. The earlier adrenaline from getting off work had dissipated, and exhaustion took over. He turned on a basketball game, plopped on the couch and fell asleep within seconds. Then he slept for seven hours fully clothed with his shoes still on.

An annoying ring woke him from his deep sleep. Groggily, he swiped his eyes and patted the couch for his cell phone. He eventually found it. The hospital's number flashed across his screen.

He clicked accept, putting the phone to his ear. "This is Dr. Schofield." Logan swung his legs over the side of the couch and sat up.

"Hey, Dr. Schofield. This is Tamara at the hospital." She sped forward without taking a breath. "We need you to come in for an emergency appendectomy. It's an eleven-year-old boy. I know you worked yesterday, but the hospital has been swamped with emergency surgeries. And you're the closest to the hospital."

"No problem." He ran a hand down the length of his face to

further wake himself up. "I'll be there in fifteen minutes." He hung up.

Logan made quick work of washing his face with cold water to wake himself up. Then he changed into a clean pair of scrubs. He headed out of his apartment to the hospital. His apartment was located right on the Magnificent Mile, a few short blocks away. After finishing his residency, he had then spent two more years in Boston specializing in pediatric general surgery. This was the first job since starting medical school where he would make actual money, which felt foreign after living for so long off student loans and his meager residency salary.

Due to his fast walking pace, he breezed through the doors of the hospital twelve minutes later. Being a general surgeon meant the surgeries he performed were often urgent. A patient might come in with severe stomach pain and an hour later they might find themselves prepped for gallbladder removal. With his on-call obligations, Logan purposely selected an apartment within walking distance of the hospital. Plus, he liked living in the city.

Chicago was home. He grew up in Naperville, a suburb thirty miles away from downtown Chicago. His parents still lived there. His sister had married her high school sweetheart, and now they had twin baby girls and lived in the same neighborhood as his parents. Being the youngest, he'd spent the past years in a never-ending state of FOMO but not anymore. He joined his sister and her family at his parent's house for the weekly Sunday dinners any time he wasn't working.

As he rode the elevator up to the general surgery floor, Logan's mind wandered to his brief encounter with the bread woman from the grocery store. He wondered if the bread helped her bad day. But then he entered the operating room, and his thoughts of Brooke dissipated. His instincts and years of medical training took over.

Luckily, the appendectomy was straightforward. After he performed the surgery, he went to his office to finish the required paperwork. Then he decided to check on the patient's recovery before going home. He knocked on the door of the patient's room and announced his arrival.

He waited for the anticipated *come in* and entered once he heard it. In the room, he found Dylan in the hospital bed with his parents by his side. To his surprise, the anesthesiologist who administered the anesthesia was next to his bed side. A nurse checked his vitals and pointed out something to Dr. Moreno on the computer screen. This made his blood pressure rise a notch.

Dylan's parents glanced over at his arrival.

"Hello, everyone." Logan strode across the room to Dylan's bedside. "I'm stopping by to check on Dylan before I head out."

Dylan's eyes were glazed. He appeared groggy.

He swiped Dylan's medical file off the wall next to the door then leafed through the first few pages. Then he forced a smile at Dylan's parents and came up next to Dr. Moreno and leaned in closer. "How's he doing, Dr. Moreno?" he whispered.

Dylan mumbled some nonsensical words and rustled around in his bed.

Dylan's mom gnawed on a fingernail. "Is he going to be, okay?"

"Anything we need to be worried about, doctor?" Dylan's dad wrapped a comforting arm around Dylan's mom's shoulders.

Dr. Moreno exchanged a quiet look with Logan. Then he spoke up loud enough for Dylan's parents to hear. "Oh, Dylan's doing fine." Dr. Moreno checked his blood pressure then uncuffed the sleeve from his bicep. "He's taking a little longer than normal to come out of the anesthesia, but he's becoming more coherent with each minute. I'm checking his vitals a second time."

Dr. Moreno asked Dylan a few questions. Dylan responded to half of them. The nurse assisted him as they continued through the necessary precautions to ensure Dylan was stable and recovering.

Time ticked by and Logan made himself useful by answering Dylan's parents' questions about their son. He hoped to ease their nerves and keep their attention off Dr. Moreno and the nurse taking Dylan's vitals. Dylan's condition improved. The grogginess in his eyes cleared, and his earlier slurring of his words disappeared. According to his file, Dylan had a history of taking longer than normal to come out of anesthesia and had a similar incident when he had surgery to remove his tonsils.

Dr. Moreno made eye contact with Logan and nodded. Then he swiveled on his bedside chair to the computer and entered some information.

"Dylan, I put in a request for a pediatrician to check in on you too as an extra precaution." Dr. Moreno wiggled the mouse at the computer and entered the vitals into it. Then he closed out the program and stood. "The pediatrician, Dr. O'Connor, will be by soon. She's one of our best." He sidestepped around the hospital bed.

"Ok." Dylan's mom chewed on her thumb nail. "This has been an eventful day. We went to a movie last night, and we thought his stomachache this morning was due to him eating too much popcorn. Little did we know he'd have to have his appendix removed."

"I'm glad you brought him in when you did." Dr. Moreno glanced at Logan then the nurse. "And I hope the next few days for you all is a lot less eventful."

"As for me," Logan placed a hand on his chest, "I wanted to report that the surgery was straightforward with no complications." He then squeezed Dylan's shoulder. "And you earned your way out of school for at least a week."

Dylan mustered up a half smile.

Dr. Moreno chuckled and moved toward the door to leave. A knock at the door sounded before he left, and Dr. Moreno opened it.

Then bread woman, Brooke, from last night breezed through

the door. For a brief moment, she stalled. Then she straightened her back and lifted her chin. "Dr. Moreno." She continued further into the room.

Logan paused thinking he might be seeing things. Her appearance was completely different than the night before. Today, she wore a lab coat over her black pencil skirt and a vibrant blue button-down blouse tucked into it. Her brown hair was down and curled into loose beach waves that danced around her shoulder blades.

The sight of her all put together and in control made him suck in a breath and simply stare back in awe. This couldn't be the same woman from last night, could it? The woman he met last night was vulnerable and down on her luck. This version of Brooke knocked him off balance with her squared shoulders and confidence.

Then she stopped by the foot of Dylan's hospital bed and peered around, and her gaze landed on Logan. Her eyes dilated a smidge, but she quickly regained her composure. "We meet again." She stared back at him.

Logan grinned. "I guess so."

Her lips twitched in the corners like she was fighting off the forming of a smile. "Is that the patient's file?" She nodded toward the chart in Logan's hand.

"Yes," Logan stretched his arm out to offer it to her, "it's all yours."

"Thanks." Brooke accepted the chart and opened to the first page.

"How—" Dr. Moreno wagged a finger between them. "How do you two know each other? He only started here a week ago." He furrowed his brow.

Brooke's back stiffened, and she continued to flip through the chart. "We go way back—" She snatched a pen out the top pocket of her lab coat and made a note on the chart. "Not that it is any of your business." Rapidly, she snapped the file closed. It made Dr. Moreno flinch.

Oh, these two had history. Logan only hoped Dr. Moreno wasn't the reason Brooke was eating bread and Oreos last night. But the inkling in his gut told him he was one hundred percent the guilty party.

"Can I talk to you for a minute outside, Dr. O'Connor?" Dr. Moreno asked.

"Nope." Then Brooke strode across the room over to Dylan's bedside completely ignoring Dr. Moreno's request. "I'm Dr. O'Connor, a pediatrician here. I understand you had your appendix taken out," she smiled warmly.

Dr. Moreno shuffled his feet then let out an audible huff. "Dylan, I'll be sending a nurse in again in twenty minutes to check your vitals."

"Thanks," Dylan's mom replied.

Brooke kept her back to him. Dr. Moreno rolled his eyes then left. With Dr. Moreno gone, Logan noticed how Brooke's shoulders loosened.

Logan didn't really need to stay, but he wanted to talk to Brooke again. This time he hoped to get her number. He lingered.

"So, I heard your appendix was giving you some trouble." She smiled as she patted Dylan's arm.

"I'll say," he replied. "I thought my stomachache was from all the popcorn I ate at the movies last night. I don't think I'll ever eat popcorn again."

"Ever?" Brooke tsked. "Now, that's just not right. What other food can you pour a stick of butter over and eat to your heart's content?"

"None?" Dylan offered.

"Bingo." Brooke made a few notes on his patient file. "I hope this experience won't ruin an entire food for you. It's the best part of going to the movies. Promise me, you'll at least try to eat popcorn one more time. For me?" She flashed a brilliant smile.

Dylan shrugged. "Ok, I promise."

Then she asked Dylan and his parents some follow-up questions and jotted a few more things down on the patient's file and dropped it back in the holder on the wall.

"I think you're going to be fine." Brooke clicked her pen closed and slid it back into the front pocket of her lab coat. Then she plopped herself down on the swivel chair Dr. Moreno had occupied. She entered some information into the computer. Then twisted to face Dylan, she wagged a finger at Dylan. "But no dodgeball for a few weeks."

Dylan half smiled. His parents agreed to make him rest and recover properly.

"Well, I'm off." She stood. "I wish you a speedy recovery."

Logan wished Dylan the same then followed Brooke back out to the hallway.

He closed the door to Dylan's hospital room. Nurses walked by them at a brisk pace. Random machines ticked and clicked. Brooke shifted to face him.

His heartrate racked up without his consent. "How was the bread?" Logan raised an eyebrow while simultaneously telling himself to simmer on down.

Act normal. Breathe.

Being around Brooke made forming coherent thoughts difficult. He found her more attractive than anyone else he had ever met.

"Delicious." Brooke shoved her hands into the pockets of her lab coat. "Unfortunately, you were a witness to my rock bottom." She gave him a tight smile. "I, now, plan on actively avoiding you anytime I see you, so I don't die from the humiliation. If you see me again, I give you full liberty to completely ignore me." Her eyes crinkled at the corners.

"I—" Logan placed a hand on his chest, "for one, enjoy a woman in sweatpants."

Brooke scoffed while she managed to roll her eyes. "Have a nice life." Then she brushed past him down the hallway in the opposite direction he needed to go.

Okay, humor and his weak attempt at flirting wasn't going to cut it. But he always enjoyed a challenge. Logan jogged to catch up with her as she rounded the corner to the nurses' station.

When he was two feet behind her, she whipped back and said, "Why are you following me? I wasn't kidding when I said I'm going to try my best never to run into you again. It's one thing to go to the store without a usable credit card, another to buy only two totally unhealthy items, and an entirely different animal to look like the cat dragged me in. Then to top it all off, the guy who helped me in my moment of pure misery is in fact my new colleague." She narrowed her gaze. "I have no choice but to actively dodge you until the day I die."

"Well, where's the fun in that?" His lips twitched.

"Stop." Brooke held up a hand. "I'm not kidding." Then she pinched the bridge of her nose. "I'm not someone who does those things. You happened to be a witness to my total demise. A demise I want to never remember." She dropped her hand and met his gaze.

"Oh, I could never forget you even if I tried."

"Ahh," she groaned. "This can't be happening."

Logan laughed.

"I'm glad you find my life amusing."

He shrugged. "I'm only relieved it isn't me for once. But for your information, my rock bottoms happen to include spicy Thai food."

Her lips curled a smidge as the tight lines of her forehead loosened. "Pad Thai noodles?"

"Extra spicy."

"Fine." Brooke lifted her chin. "I'll acknowledge your presence with a hello when I see you again."

He placed his hand over his heart. "I'd be honored."

She smirked. Her eyes danced with mischievousness.

"Now, tell me—did last night have anything to do with Dr. Moreno?" Logan tilted his head to the side. "Are you trying to avoid him, too?"

She crinkled her nose and gnawed on her bottom lip. "Was it that obvious?"

Logan rolled his hand back and forth. "No, and yes."

"Geez," she muttered. "Absolutely, fantastic." She continued to the nurses' station.

"If he was the reason your world was falling apart, what did he do?"

"Though you've seen me in sweatpants, I don't think our fresh, day-old friendship is at that level."

"Fair enough." He pursed his lips together.

They arrived at the nurses' station. He still needed to head in the other direction, but he hadn't found a way to make himself leave.

Brooke smiled at one of the nurses sitting behind the station's computer. "Hey, Aubrey."

Aubrey stopped typing and glanced up. "Oh, Brooke," her voice oozed with compassion. She quickly pushed out her swivel chair and rounded the station, holding out her arms in a hug to her. "Ian told me what happened." Brooke stood stiffly as Aubrey hugged her. "Why didn't you call me? I would've come over." They broke their embrace.

Logan wondered if he should slip away. This clearly was a conversation that wasn't any of his business, but he'd bet good money, it was about Dr. Moreno.

"I know, but I wanted to be alone." Brooke flashed a glance over her shoulder and confirmed Logan hadn't left. "I'm still not ready to talk about it." Then she leaned in closer and lowered her voice, "Let's go out this weekend, and I'll fill you in on the details."

"Sure." Aubrey nodded. "Sounds good."

Brooke motioned toward him. "Aubrey, this is Dr. Schofield. He's a new surgeon who recently started here."

"Well," Aubrey smiled, "hello."

"Aubrey," Brooke continued, "is a nurse here and also happens to be my best friend."

"Really," Logan held his hand out to Aubrey, "nice to meet you."

Aubrey shook his hand in return. Then both women stared at him. With the introductions out of the way, Logan realized he was staying way too long.

"I was only called in for the one surgery, so I guess I'd better go." He shuffled his feet and glanced between the two women. "It was nice seeing you again. I'll see you around?" His brow lifted.

Brooke flashed Aubrey a glance he couldn't decipher. A buzz went off indicating a patient had pushed their call button.

Aubrey tapped the button off. "That's for me. I better go." She readjusted the stethoscope around her neck. "Some of us are meeting up after work tonight at Robert's Pizza and Dough. Dr. Schofield, you're invited too. Please come. It would be a great chance for you to meet some of the other doctors and nurses who work here."

"You can call me Logan."

"Okay—Logan. Ian will be there, that's my fiancé. He works here too as a cardiologist. Please come, the more the merrier," Aubrey said.

"What about Justin?" Brooke inquired.

Who's Justin?

Aubrey flipped her hair over her shoulder. "He'll be there."

"Then nah, I'm good. Let me know when you can meet up—alone."

"You're going to have to learn to do stuff with him there."

Aubrey fiddled with her loosened hair then tucked it behind her ear. "Sorry, that came out way harsh, but I think you have to rip this thing off like a band aid. You won't be able to avoid Justin. Plus, Logan will be there." Aubrey peered past Brooke to Logan. "You'll come, right?"

"He doesn't want to come," Brooke interjected.

Logan grinned. "I'm free, and I'd love to come and meet some new people."

Brooke pinched the sleeve of Aubrey's scrubs and directed her away from him. They walked a few paces until they were out of ear shot. Logan could only imagine what she was saying. And who was Justin? Was Justin and Dr. Moreno the same person? He didn't get a good look at his name badge earlier. He watched as they chatted with their heads close together. Finally, Aubrey left, and Brooke slowly dragged her feet back to where Logan stood.

Once in front of him, Brooke rocked back and forth on her heels. "So, I guess I'll see you tonight?"

He wanted to quiz her about Justin, and if his suspicions were that he was in fact Dr. Moreno. But he knew he had a lot of ground to cover before they were on such familiar terms with one another. Plus, according to Aubrey, this Justin character would be there tonight so he wouldn't have to wait long to get to the bottom of it.

"I wouldn't miss it." Logan grinned.

"Ok, then." Brooke unnecessarily adjusted the collar of her lab coat. "I have to finish my rounds."

"And I'm headed home." He stepped away. "I'll see you tonight."

"Tonight."

"Oh, Brooke—"

"Yeah?" she furrowed her inquisitive brow.

"Do you need me to bring you another package of Oreos? I don't think they have those on the menu at the pizza place?"

Brooke rolled her eyes, but her lips curled. "I'll manage." She scrunched her nose. "I only ate half the pack last night. I might have to polish off the rest of it after this evening. So, another stop at the grocery store might be on the agenda afterwards."

Logan rubbed his thumb down his jaw. "Hey, you have a plan." He tried to think of something smooth to say but he came up blank. "See you soon." Then he left.

His entire walk home he thought about Brooke eating Oreos on her couch, and he thought he wouldn't mind sitting next to her, eating them too.

CHAPTER 3

Brooke didn't get off work until a little past six. Technically, Aubrey said the meet up for pizza and drinks started at six, but there was no way she was headed there straight from work. If she had to face Justin with a new woman on his arm, then she needed her most protective armor. Meaning, a dress that wasn't business attire, a face that didn't have smudged makeup, and hair that wasn't ratty.

With a quick stop at home to change her clothes, fix her makeup, and double-check her hair, Brooke walked into Robert's Pizza and Dough a mere forty minutes late. She spotted the long table with about fifteen doctors and nurses from the hospital. The table already held a variety of pizzas, food, and drinks. They appeared to be halfway finished eating.

One chair was open next to Justin and his new leggy blonde. Nope. Aubrey and Ian sat across from them. In the middle were doctors and nurses she knew. Then on the other end sat Logan with a free chair next to him. Her pulse raced. He had on slacks and a long button-down checked shirt tucked into them. Dang, he looked good. It almost made her forget about how she wanted to punch Justin in the face.

For a second, Brooke stared at everyone eating and chatting. Justin had dumped her and nobody, including her best friend, seemed to care how the entire thing had rocked her to her core. Yeah, she couldn't do it. She stayed frozen in place, willing herself to be strong and appear undeterred. This was a bad idea. She wasn't ready to see Justin in a social setting with someone new on his arm. It stung too bad.

Her legs remembered how to move. She pivoted to leave, but Aubrey spotted her and called out to her at an unearthly volume. Everyone at the table peered over at her. Fresh heat splashed her cheeks. Justin straightened his back and wrapped an arm around his new woman's shoulders while lowering his gaze to avoid eye contact with her. She wondered if the new lady even knew about their relationship or if he had painted himself as an image of chivalry.

Logan's cup paused midair when their eyes met. The cup hovered inches from his lips. Then his gaze flickered down her frame. He shook his head the smallest amount, took a drink and twisted back to face the doctors across the table from him. Aubrey ran over to her.

"I'm glad you came." Aubrey hugged her while she stood stiffly. "I was worried you'd be a no show." She broke their embrace.

"I can't do this." Luckily, those at the table went back to talking and eating, except for Justin whose gaze remained glued on her. "Why did you suggest this? You know I'm not ready to be around him." Her words sounded like a hiss.

Aubrey put a hand on her hip. "You were around him today at work."

"That was different. I had no choice." She forced herself to take a deep breath and settle the quiver in her voice. "This—this feels like I've been karate punched. I mean look at her." Brooke tilted her head in the general direction.

"Yeah, I know." Aubrey leaned in closer to her, and added, "But for the record, she is completely wrong for him."

Her shoulders drooped. "But she's gorgeous." Then her bottom lip trembled. She blinked rapidly to fight the tears threatening to spill over.

Aubrey squeezed her forearm and found her gaze. "You're gorgeous." She squeezed again.

"You have to say that because you're my friend." Brooke shot her a crooked smile. "It doesn't count."

Aubrey let go. "I'd say it even if you weren't my best friend." She flashed a glance over her shoulder back toward the table. "I wish Justin wasn't such a total nimrod—but he's Ian's best friend. What am I supposed to do?" The worry lines on her forehead tightened. "We both chose our best friends. I wish I wasn't in this situation, but you have to see how I'm in a tight spot."

Anger seeped into her veins, and she hated Justin even more for putting them in this situation. If he had been so unhappy with her, why hadn't he broken up with her months ago. Instead, he strung her along like a fool and only kicked her to the curb when he had another lady secure and ready. Her blood simmered near boiling point. Now, he got to sit down at the end by their friends while she was left to feel like the odd one out.

"Well—" Brooke stared at the table of people. Logan caught her gaze again and waved. The knot in her gut loosened and brought her mounting blood pressure down. Her brain managed to clear enough for her to think straight. "I'll stay, but I'm not sitting over by you guys. I'm headed to the opposite end of the table."

A look of relief washed over Aubrey's countenance. "I understand." Then she leaned in closer. "And Logan is easy on the eyes." Then she winked.

"Really?" Brooke straightened her back and pulled back her shoulders. "I hadn't noticed."

Aubrey cackled. "Yeah, okay—"

They made their way over to the table. Aubrey slipped back into her seat next to Ian, and she headed to the opposite end. The crowded space meant she had to shimmy sideways to reach the chair next to Logan.

When she arrived, she gripped the back of the empty chair and pointed at it with her other hand. "Is this seat taken?"

"Nope." Logan peered up at her and smiled brightly, allowing his dazzling whites to practically blind her. "It's all yours."

Brooke dragged the chair out and flopped herself into it. She greeted Dr. Salsburg and Dr. Hernandez, who both worked in radiology. They exchanged a few pleasantries before they returned to a conversation with one another.

"I'm glad you made it." Logan tapped his shoulder against hers. "It's nice to see a familiar face. Everyone has been nice, but you're the main reason I came tonight."

"Then I guess you're lucky I stayed. I almost hightailed it out of here." Brooke snatched the menu left behind in front of her seat. Her stomach rumbled. She flipped it open. "I'm in a bit of an awkward situation. My ex is sitting down at the other end with his new girlfriend, and we broke up yesterday." She pretended to peruse the menu and didn't dare look over at him.

"Dr. Moreno is Justin and is your ex, right?" Logan inquired with a low voice. "He introduced me to his girlfriend when he arrived. I didn't—I mean, yikes. He already brought his new girlfriend. Wow, what a jerk move."

Dr. Salsburg and Dr. Hernandez on the other side of the table talked about the hiring of a new head of Radiology. Brooke nodded as she half listened then flipped to the next page of the menu. Food, she needed food to face tonight, and quick.

"I know. It's terrible." Brooke peered over at his plate. "What did you order?"

Logan looked down at his plate like he forgot what he ate. "Some kind of pizza that a few of the doctors ordered together. I'm sure there is still enough to share."

"No, that's okay. I'm hungry." Brooke flipped back to the page with the pasta pages. "But I don't know what for."

Logan picked up his piece of pizza and took a bite. After he wiped his face with a napkin, he inquired, "I'm assuming you and Justin parting ways wasn't up to you?"

"Nope." Brooke whipped the menu shut. "Which is why I'm over here alone, and he's over there with the new woman he started dating before he even broke up with me."

Brooke twisted in her seat to catch a server's attention then waved them over. The server approached. Brooke ordered a plate of chicken pesto pasta and a side salad. She hoped everyone didn't leave before her food arrived. Then the server left to put in her order.

"Well, I'm glad you're here." His lips twitched in the corners. "Thanks for suffering so I didn't have to be alone." Their eyes locked, and heat flooded her core.

She broke their gaze first. An untouched glass of water sat in front of her. "Do you know if anyone has drunk out of this?" She pointed at the cup.

"I spit in it earlier." Logan winked. "But, besides that, it's free game." He smirked, making the flirtatious energy weaving between them go up a notch.

Brooke fought off the smile. "Do you always spit into random glasses of water?" She faked caution as she took a small sip of water.

"I knew you were coming, and it was my only defense to keep anyone else—" he tilted his head to her chair, "from sitting there. I figured if I mentioned the spit water, they'd sit elsewhere." He cracked his knuckles then leaned back against his chair. "And it worked like a charm."

"Ahh." Brooke sipped again then set the glass down. "Thank you? How very chivalrous of you," she teased.

"I know, right?" Logan tapped his shoulder against hers. "My mother would be proud."

An eruption of laughter from the other end of the table interrupted them. They peered past the doctors in the middle. Justin, his new girlfriend, Aubrey and Ian laughed hysterically at some video on Justin's phone. Her back stiffened and jaw clenched tight. Then she forced herself to shift back and for good measure twisted her back to them so she had zero chance of seeing them.

"Sorry." Logan lowered his voice and picked up another slice of pizza from the platter in front of him. "But if it makes you feel any better, you're prettier than her." He shoved the end of the pizza into his mouth.

Heat splashed her cheeks.

"You shouldn't say things like that." Her throat grew tight. Brooke sipped on her water again. "Comments like that can get you into trouble."

He finished his bite and shrugged. "But it's true. And I'm not trying to date her. I find you attractive and not her. She isn't my type." He ate another bite of pizza, then added, "Plus, you're way more interesting than her."

"How would you know?" She fidgeted with the silverware in front of her. "You don't know either of us."

"I know that you like Oreos and bread. That means you have good taste." He wiped the corners of his mouth with a napkin then ate another bite of his pizza. "And you're an incredible pediatrician which means you're ambitious and driven."

He chewed. Brooke watched him. Slowly, he swallowed, and she watched the gentle glide of his Adam's apple bob. A primal urge made her want to run a finger down the length of his neck. For a solid three minutes, she hadn't thought about Justin once. Progress.

"That makes me sound—" She caught her fidgeting and leaned her forearms on the table, "I could say the same about you."

"We aren't talking about me. We're talking about you." He polished off the rest of the slice of pizza. "I think being a pediatrician is incredible, and I've always been unable to resist a woman who knows how to snack. And I already know that you happen to love two of my favorite foods."

Brooke rolled her eyes. She appreciated Logan's weak attempt to lift her mood even if he was completely full of it. Though his method did work, because she hadn't tried to sneak glances at the other end of the table, not even once. It was the little victories at this point. Plus, she liked talking to Logan. He put her at ease and seemed genuinely interested in her. Justin always acted annoyed when they chatted like he had somewhere else to be, and she constantly found herself trying to prove to him she was a person worth sticking around for. In hindsight, she knew the relationship never had the legs to go the distance, but the feeling of abandonment shook her to her core.

Dr. Hernandez interrupted them when he abruptly stood. "I have to head back." He smoothly retrieved his wallet from his pocket and tossed some money onto the table. "That should cover what I owe. It was nice meeting you, Dr. Schofield. I'll see you both again soon."

"I need to head back to the hospital too." Dr. Salsburg pushed her chair back. "I'll walk back with you if you don't mind." She also placed money down on the table.

Dr. Hernandez smiled at her. "Great. I'd love the company."

Brooke swore she saw a spark in Dr. Hernandez's eyes. No wonder they hadn't spoken two words to them the entire time. But then again, Brooke had partly forgotten there were other people at the table besides Logan, too.

They left. The other doctors in the middle gathered up their stuff as well. Brooke's food still hadn't arrived. Justin and his lady pal were still stationed at the far end with Ian and Aubrey. Geez, she hoped they didn't try to get them to shuffle on down to their spot to merge their conversations.

"You can go," she peered around again for the server, "I

arrived late, but I'm going to wait for my food. I'm starving, but please don't let me keep you if you have someone to get home to."

She partly cringed at her weak attempt to find out if Logan was in fact single. Suddenly, her break up with Justin appeared miles away.

"I don't have anyone to get home to." Logan sipped his soda. "And if that was your sneaky way of asking me if I'm single then — I am by the way, single." He smiled smugly.

She unnecessarily fidgeted with her silverware again. "I—I—wasn't asking," Brooke stammered.

He shrugged. "But now you know," he said matter-of-factly.

"I guess I do." Heat flushed her cheeks, and she attempted to cool herself off by waving her hand in front of herself.

Why did she feel flustered around Logan? They had only met yesterday, and she was in no position to jump into something new with another guy. Her heart still beat for Justin, didn't it? She peered over at the other end of the table. Justin wrapped his arm around his new girlfriend's shoulders then kissed her lovingly on the temple. Ugh, he never kissed her that way.

Her server came by to refill drinks, and Brooke inquired about her food.

The server replied, annoyed, "Look around, this place is slammed with orders. It will come out when it comes out."

"Okay, well— I guess bring it out in a to-go box," she instructed the server.

"No." Logan interjected and waved the idea away. "That won't be necessary. Bring it out as planned."

Brooke fiddled with her hair then swept it over one shoulder. "Really?"

She recognized how hopeful it made her feel.

"No, I've got all night." He wiped his face with a napkin then crumpled it up and tossed it on his plate. "I'll stay until you're finished eating."

Deadpan, the server muttered, "What do you want me to do?"

"I guess," she threw up a hand, "bring it out once it's ready and forget about making it a to-go."

"Fine." The server melted into the crowded beast of the restaurant.

He wagged his eyebrows. "Oh, they *like* you," Logan teased.

Brooke punched him in the arm. "Thanks a lot." She fought a smile. "I might not be able to come back here again until there is a turnover in employees."

What was she doing? Justin dumped her like ten minutes ago, and now she threw herself at the first guy who flirted with her. Wait, was Logan even flirting? Maybe this wasn't flirting. Maybe she didn't even know how to date anymore. Maybe this was the start of a beautiful friendship, she certainly could use a few more friends. Could guys and gals be friends with one another without one of them wanting more? Her head spun more than she wanted.

Logan smirked. "I guess we'll have to find a new restaurant to frequent."

She found him annoyingly cute. "We?" She raised an eyebrow.

"You heard me correctly," he countered.

Aubrey caught her attention then waved at them to join them down at the other end. Brooke shook her head and shifted her back, to block seeing Justin and his girlfriend. She was enjoying this flirtatious and fun conversation.

"Okay, why did you pick to work at a hospital in Chicago?" Brooke leaned in closer. Their shoulders grazed one another a few times but never landed.

She placed her forearm on the table.

Logan leaned in closer, too. "Why did *you* end up here?" Their arms nearly rested against one another, but a stubborn inch kept them apart.

"I asked you first." Her skin itched, and she didn't know why.

She couldn't ever remember feeling this sort of electric pull toward someone. And she had no idea how to act normally.

Logan stared back at her for a moment. He rubbed his jaw with his thumb and forefinger. She wondered if he would even answer, or if she should speed forward.

But then he said, "It was an incredible opportunity, and I grew up outside the city. My family is still there. I can make it home for Sunday dinners when I'm not working. Chicago is home. And what about you?"

Out of nowhere her pasta and salad arrived along with the group check. Logan took it from the server and set it on the other side of him.

Aubrey came over and plopped a wad of cash down. "This should cover our portion for the four of us." She nudged her head in their direction.

They were putting their coats back on. Justin held out a jacket for his new woman then gently adjusted the lapel once she had it on. A solid gut punch gave Brooke a stomachache. The guy never did that for her. The woman stared up at him with goo-goo eyes. Geez, had Brooke ever looked at Justin like that? Maybe their relationship had been a total façade.

When she and Justin had hit it off at a small get together with Aubrey and Ian, Brooke hung onto him for dear life. In a new city, with no other friends to speak of, she had been vulnerable to his attention. Sure, Justin had bugged her in small ways, but with both of their chaotic work schedules they didn't see each other too much. The breaks of time in between gave her enough breathers to handle him and look past his annoying habits. It probably wasn't the most glowing recommendation for relationship goals that one wanted, but at the time it beat being alone. Had Justin done her a favor by showing his true colors before she pledged her life to him?

Maybe.

"Okay." Brooke snapped her attention back to Aubrey. "Are you headed home?"

"Yeah, Ian has an early shift tomorrow." Aubrey buttoned up

her jacket. "Are you guys staying? I can hang a little longer and send Ian on his way if you want." She gave her a look like *what do you want me to do*.

"Brooke's food just arrived." Logan opened the bill folder and stuffed the cash inside from Aubrey and the other amount left on the table. "I can stay until she finishes. I'll make sure she makes it home okay. You don't need to stay behind, unless Brooke wants you to." He peeled open his own wallet and put more cash inside the bill folder then shut it closed.

"Umm." Brooke picked up her fork for her salad. "Are you sure I won't be keeping you?" Her stomach fluttered as she waited for his reply.

"Nah, I have no life besides working." Logan leaned in closer. "I'm in no hurry to go home to an empty apartment."

"Great." Aubrey smiled.

Brooke stood and gave Aubrey a parting hug. Then Aubrey shimmied sideways through the crowd to the other end of the table where Ian, Justin, and the new woman waited for her return. Soon, they exited the restaurant. The tension spot between her shoulder blades finally loosened.

Logan brought his ankle up and rested it on his opposite knee. "So?" He raised a curious brow.

Her stomach growled. "Yeah—" She speared her salad and shoveled a bite into her mouth and chewed. Once she finished, she said, "Go on." Then she went in for another fork full of salad.

"You now know why I'm here." His lips twitched. The wrinkles around his eyes deepened as he held her gaze. "What about you? Why Chicago?"

She shrugged and finished her bite. "Why not?" She picked up her water and drank. Then she set the glass back down while acutely aware that Logan seemed to be tracking her every movement. "I figured it was as good a place as any."

The messy town of her youth in middle-of-nowhere Virginia was a place she wanted to forget. A dead alcoholic mother and dead deadbeat dad she hadn't seen since her childhood anyway, meant she didn't care where she landed as long as it wasn't where she came from. A big city meant lots of people and great ability to start over. Plus, her highest job offer was in Chicago. Brooke didn't even hesitate when she was offered the job, she simply said yes.

"What about your parents?" Logan prodded. "Where do they live?"

"They're dead." Brooke speared another piece of lettuce then shoveled it into her mouth.

She hated talking about her parents. If anything, she avoided all personal conversations about her past. Her childhood was riddled with abuse and horrible memories. People didn't want you to unload that on them. Instead, she learned to say the bare minimum about her less-than-ideal childhood and turn the conversation back onto the other person. It always worked like a charm.

"Ahh." He placed his hand lightly on her forearm. "I'm sorry to hear that."

Brooke shrugged. "I'm not." She moved onto her pasta, taking a bite.

A look of confusion skated across his face. "You're not sorry they're dead?" Logan dropped his raised foot back onto the ground and leaned in closer.

"Nope." She ate more of the pasta.

Her hunger made her mind muddled. She stretched to think of a way to change the conversation, but she came up blank. Instead, she remained quiet and ate pasta while Logan studied her.

"Umm—" Logan ran a hand through his hair. "I'm assuming they weren't the greatest people."

Brooke smiled. "Ahh," she patted his shoulder, "you're sharp."

The tips of his ears-tinged pink. "Touché." Logan leaned his back against his chair. "I'll shut up now."

"My family history is definitely not first date material—" Brooke's eyes dilated at her misstep. "I mean not that this is a first date. I know it's not." She rambled on and on. "I'm not some girl who makes things into more than they are. We are only enjoying a meal together. You were being nice by staying behind—"

Logan placed a steady hand on her forearm settling the tightening of her chest. "Hey, I'm having a nice time, whatever this might be. And for what it's worth, I think you're pretty amazing. And the fact that you came from I don't know—less than ideal family circumstances only makes me admire you more."

"Really?" Brooke hated how hopeful and desperate her voice sounded. She straightened her back and found her confidence again. "But, you barely know me." Brooke dabbed her napkin at the corners of her mouth.

"I know enough."

She tossed the napkin down on the table. "Yeah, what do you know?" Brooke raised a skeptical eyebrow.

"That I'd like to become your friend."

Friend?

Her stomach dropped.

Why did she hate the sound of friends?

Then she quickly reminded herself she was fresh off of a breakup. Friends, she could do friends.

Brooke ran a finger around the rim of her glass. "Why do you want to be friends with me?"

Logan chuckled. "Because I told you I like hanging out with women who snack."

She rolled her eyes while she fought the urge to smile. "That's ridiculous."

"No, it's not. I like snacks too." His gaze danced across her face. "And I promise as a friend to always bring the snacks." He fiddled around for a moment then shoved his hand into his jacket which hung off the back of his chair. Finally, he pulled out a personal size pack of Oreos. "Here." He held them out to her. "I figured you might need these, now you don't have to stop by the store if you polished off the rest of your pack at home."

The guy bought her Oreos. She couldn't remember the last thing Justin had bought her, but she knew for sure it wasn't anything he put that much thought into.

"Fine." She grinned as she took the package and tossed it into her purse. "We can be friends."

Logan beamed. "Awesome."

She finished up her meal then said, "Okay friend, let's start by you telling me how much I owe for the check." Brooke tried to reach for the bill folder.

He blocked her hand with his own. "It's on me. I already put in enough for both of our meals."

"Oh." She sat back. "That seems very nonfriend like to me and more into the date material while we both established this is not a date."

"I know it's not a date, but I hate to admit this out loud," Logan smirked, "I have to buy my friends."

Brooke laughed. "I highly doubt that."

"It's true." He pushed the bill folder far away from them.

"I should've known with the Oreos," Brooke teased.

"See? I came prepared. I knew I wanted to be your friend, and I needed something to butter you up."

"It started in high school didn't it," Brooke offered as she gathered up her purse and jacket.

He shoved his arms into the coat he'd left on the back of the chair. Once he had his jacket back on, he replied, "Clearly." Logan pushed back his chair and stood.

She stumbled to her feet and put on her jacket. "Did you have to pay people to sit with you at lunch?" Brooke jested.

"Still do." Logan motioned for her to go first. "So, nothing has changed."

She snatched up her purse and pushed through the throngs of

people who squeezed in every nook and cranny of the tight space. Logan followed behind her, close enough she caught the scent of his woodsy cologne. Gosh, the man smelled good. *Friends, friends, friends*. They finally made it outside.

"Which way?" Logan shoved his hands into the pockets of his peacoat.

Brooke nudged her head in the direction of her apartment. "I'm this way." It wasn't far, only a few blocks past the hospital. "I can manage to get home on my own if you live in the opposite direction."

"I'd like to walk you home," he stated, without revealing if it was an inconvenience or not.

"Okay." She twisted on the sidewalk toward her apartment. They meandered at a comfortable pace side by side. "Is that how you win over your friends?" Her lips twitched again. "You buy them off and do nice things for them."

"It's usually a good place to start." The light ahead changed and forced them to stop on one side of the crosswalk. The familiar sound of the L train passing over their heads made him speak louder. "And my mom would never forgive me if I promised to walk a woman home, and I didn't."

The idea warmed her heart. She didn't have any clue what it would feel like to have someone teach you things like that. For a second, she tried to imagine having a parent who cared about her well-being rather than treating her like the worst thing that happened to them. If her parents taught her anything, it was what not to do. She hoped someday she wouldn't repeat their mistakes.

"Are you close to your mom?" Brooke inquired as she hit the crossing walk button.

"Yes." Logan popped the collar of his peacoat. "I'm close with my dad too. And my sister loves to be in my business as well. I try to remind her I'm a grown man only two years younger than her, but she conveniently forgets that part. But I don't mind, she's given me the cutest twin nieces a guy could ask for." His eyes shimmered at the mention of them.

It made her like him even more.

"How old are the twins?" she asked.

"Nine months." The crosswalk changed. They stepped off the curb and walked to the other side. He continued, "They're still snuggly and warm when you hold them. The best is if they fall asleep in your arms. I have to soak it all up now, because I know once they start walking it'll be all over."

"True." They turned the corner. Brooke spotted her apartment coming into view. "I'm only a half a block away." She pointed out her building.

"Oh, do you live at the old boiler factory?"

"I do. It was converted to apartments a while back before I moved here."

"I looked at an apartment there too, but they didn't have anything available." He scratched his chin then shoved his hand back into his pocket. "I love how the old factories and buildings in the city have been converted into apartments. The city managed to keep the beauty of the architecture. It's what makes Chicago special."

"I agree." Brooke spotted George at his usual guarding spot outside the front door and waved. "I love my apartment, and my doorman, George." She pointed him out. Logan glanced in his direction then she added, "He's like the dad I never had. He listens to me then imparts his wisdom when I ask for help with my problems."

He studied her for a moment then commented, "Then I'm glad he's in your life."

She appreciated he didn't press her further about her dad.

They made it to the front of her building and halted.

George greeted them. "Good evening." He opened the door to the inside. "Who's your friend?" He raised an eyebrow and exchanged a quick look with her.

"George, this is Logan." Brooke motioned toward him. "He's a surgeon at the hospital."

Logan held out a hand. "It's nice to meet you." George shook his hand in return.

"Likewise." George smirked. His eyes shone with delight. "I see you didn't waste any time taking my advice."

Heat splashed her cheeks. "Umm— that's not—"

"What advice?" Logan's gaze skidded between George and Brooke.

"That I'd quit walking around alone at night," Brooke blurted out before George further explained.

"Oh." Logan nodded in agreement. "Good advice."

They stood in a beat of awkward silence.

George gripped the door. "Are you coming in or what?"

"I'm going in." Brooke shifted to face Logan. "Thanks for walking me. I'm sure I'll run into you again at the hospital."

Logan slid his hand into his pocket and removed his phone. "Can I get your number?" He rubbed the back of his neck with his opposite hand. "I need friends, remember? And I'd like to hang out with you again."

Amused, Brooke smiled. "Friends, right—" Her voice trailed off with her eye roll.

"I need someone to show me around the city," he quickly added.

Brooke was all too aware that George stood only a few feet away, listening to their entire exchange. She wondered what he thought about it.

She ignored George for a second and replied, "I thought you grew up in Chicago."

"Outside of the city, in the suburbs, it's completely different." If she knew him better, she'd daresay he was nervous. The thought that she made a guy nervous made her heart soar a tad. He continued his rambling, "I need a friend to teach me the best places to eat, shop, that type of thing. Are you up for it?"

For a second, she stared back at him. He flashed her a cheesy smile. She wondered if she wanted to be friends with Logan or if she cared for something more. Either way, her calendar was suddenly bleak and free. There wasn't a need for her to skip a thousand steps ahead to whatever the future held for her.

Brooke made a *give me* motion. "I've taken mercy on you." He handed over his cell phone. Without looking up, she said, "We can be friends," as she typed in her contact information. Once done, she handed it back to him.

Logan glanced down at his phone for a moment before he shoved it into his pocket. "Ok, then." He pedalled backward two feet. "Brooke, I'll be in touch when I need you to educate me on the inner workings of Chicago." Then he motioned toward George, "It was nice meeting you."

George nodded.

"You both have a nice evening." Then he pivoted and walked in the opposite direction.

Brooke watched him walk away and wondered how far out of the way her apartment was from his.

George's voice startled her when he said, "Not bad." He whistled to himself. "I'm impressed. I gave you the suggestion to find a guy at work, and you had a surgeon walk you home in a snap. You work fast. Is he already on board to go with you to the wedding?"

"What?" She stared at him while her brain played catch up. "Wedding—" Ding, she still needed a date to Aubrey and Ian's wedding. "It didn't come up."

"Ahh," he waved the idea off, "you still have time to ask him." George shuffled her through the door into the lobby.

The warmth of the lobby enveloped her.

"He did say he wants to be my friend." Brooke unbuttoned her jacket as she moved further into the lobby. "Maybe he'd be willing to go with me."

It wasn't a horrible idea. Logan was easy on the eyes, and she enjoyed his company. Maybe the wedding wouldn't be a total bust if he came. She let the idea simmer.

"I have a feeling Mr. Surgeon wants to be more than friends." He stalled in front of the lobby desk. "I think if you ask him to go with you, he'll go."

"Really?" The thought pleased her more than it should. "I think you're reading it wrong."

"I don't think I am." George continued, "That's how it always starts—the classic friend to lover trope."

"Trope?" Brooke raised a skeptical eyebrow. "Since when did you read romance novels?"

"I don't, but my wife does." George adjusted the sleeves of his jacket. "Then she drags me to those romcom movies when the books she reads are made into movies."

"You're a good man, George. Other men could take notes from you." Brooke continued to the elevator bay. She pressed the button and turned to face him. "But nothing is going to happen between me and Logan." Her voice made the space vibrate with her declaration.

George cackled. "Those are fighting words."

The elevator opened. "Bye." Brooke rolled her eyes and waved him off, entering the elevator and riding it up to her apartment.

Friends, she could be friends with Logan. George had it wrong, and she planned on proving it to him. Because they would only ever be friends.

CHAPTER 4

Logan peeled off his jacket and plopped himself down on his couch. His mind reviewed the entire night's interactions with Brooke. *Friends?* It sounded weak even to him. He groaned. If he could go back, he would've asked her out. But no, he chickened out, blamed her recent break up with Dr. Moreno as an excuse. And snap, he single-handedly placed himself in the dreaded friend zone. Ugh.

He leaned forward and raked his hands through his hair. Surely, one could bridge the gap, right? Did any of his friends manage to parlay their way from friends into dating? Maybe they could offer him much-needed guidance to fix this. He came up blank. He'd dug himself into a hole.

His phone rang. He fetched it out of his pocket. His sister's name, Danielle, flashed across the screen. Logan smiled to himself as he leaned back on his couch and kicked up his legs on the coffee table. At least he could count on her to take his mind off the fiasco of his dating incompetence. He tapped the screen to answer and put it to his ear.

"Danielle," Logan cupped the back of his head with one hand, "are my cute nieces keeping you up again?"

"Yes," she huffed. Danielle continued, "It's a good thing they're cute, because I swear—" Her voice was interrupted by a wail, soon another crier joined.

The twins cried in almost unison. The sound made him move the phone six inches away from his ear to keep from having permanent hearing damage.

"Have they been crying a lot today?" Logan spoke over the loud ruckus in the background with the phone still far from his ear. He hit the speakerphone and set his phone down on the coffee table.

"Off and on. I might lose it." He heard Danielle try to soothe the twins. Logan waited, knowing his sister only needed someone to complain to. He heard Danielle speak calmly to them. A minute later the crying stopped. "There, I should be good for a minute or two."

"What did you do?" He rested his forearms on his knees and leaned closer to his phone's mic.

"I'm currently holding a pacifier into each of their mouths. Luckily, there was this invention of air pods to allow me to keep my hands free while on a call."

"True." More silence. Logan cleared his throat. "As much as I love to shoot the breeze with you, I know it isn't what you do. Please ask whatever it is that you want to ask me."

"Can't a sister call to talk to her brother?" Danielle asked.

"Some sisters do, mine doesn't." He cradled his hands together. "Spit it out. What did you want? Free babysitting? Maybe going in on a group gift for Mom's birthday? Or do you need me to get Mom and Dad out of your hair?"

Danielle groaned. "How do you know me so well?"

"I think living in the same house for half your life does that to people."

A cry escaped. Danielle rustled around and then the crying stopped.

"Can you make it to dinner next Sunday?" she asked.

His stomach twisted. Danielle was up to something. She knew he would come if he could, but the dangling inquiry told him to tread lightly.

"Why?" he replied.

"Just answer the question," she countered.

"Tell me what you are up to and then I'll answer."

Danielle huffed. "I ran into Shelby—"

"No," he interrupted her. His jaw tightened while his neck stiffened. The mention of his ex-girlfriend made sweat tickle his brow. He never wanted to see her again. "Absolutely not." He stood and paced the small length of his living room.

"Why not?" Her voice eked out of the speakerphone. "She's back in town. Apparently, she's single and working as a nurse at the dialysis center on Seventh Street. She kept asking about you, and Logan she looks good, like time hasn't aged her one bit."

Maybe time hadn't aged her, but it had aged him. He couldn't and wouldn't see her. Even after all these years, she still held this grip on him. He wondered if first loves were like that with everyone. He swore he would never agree with anyone more than Sheryl Crow singing about the first cut being the deepest. And the cut from Shelby managed to paralyze him.

The woman had broken his heart when she dumped him right before they went off to college. It took his first year of college to learn how to function without her in his life. Then it took another year to even have the courage to ask another woman out. Shelby tossed him aside and never looked back. He didn't care how good she looked because being attracted to her had never been the problem.

Sure, he'd seen her a few times since they broke up. He ran into her in between college and medical school, and he asked her out to grab lunch. Bad idea. He fell back in love with her once again after a simple conversation. When they made plans to meet up again, she ghosted him. It unraveled him even more.

No. No. No. He didn't have it in him to get over her *again.*

She'd always be the one who got away, and he knew he wasn't strong enough to see her again. Because three years ago, during Christmas he ran into her at the grocery store. They chatted for a half hour in the cereal aisle. She was as beautiful and intriguing as always. Then for the next six months, Logan had to will her away from his psyche as he replayed the conversation over and over again hoping to find a glimmer of hope that she felt what he felt. Nope. Sometimes you needed to leave the past in the past, which was exactly what he planned to do. No family dinner dates with Shelby.

"I don't care." He raked his hair and practically shouted in the direction of his phone. "I'm not seeing her again. I can't do it. She messes with my head too much. You know she does, why would you even bring her up?"

"I think she's different now." Danielle paused, "Plus, I invited her to dinner. It's the perfect chance to either reconnect or close that chapter of your life for good."

His jaw clenched. "Uninvite her." His hands drew into fists at his sides while his heart rose to an astronomical level.

"Why would I do that?" Danielle asked with a voice laced with fake innocence. "I've already invited her, and it would be rude to take back the invitation."

"But I've met someone, that's why," he blurted out without thinking.

It came out of left field, but somehow deep down he knew it was his only shield of defense. When Danielle had an idea, she stopped at nothing to see it to fruition. Though he knew she'd back down if she thought he had a chance with someone else.

"What? When?" A stray cry sounded through the speaker, and Danielle hushed the baby for a moment. When the crying subsided, she added, "You've barely moved to Chicago. How in the world have you had time to meet someone?"

She called his bluff. But the idea of seeing Shelby made him dig in his heels and burrow himself deeper in the lie he set up.

"I guess chalk it up to fate." He dropped back down on his sofa and swiped the phone off the coffee table. "I don't tell you everything. Besides, the relationship is new, and I wanted to see where it went before I told you about it."

"I don't believe you. I think you're making this up," Danielle hissed. "You're trying to get out of seeing Shelby which I don't understand. The timing was never right between you two, but you're both back in Chicago permanently. This is your chance to be together."

"No, it's not our chance to be together." Logan closed his eyes for a moment and tried to find his equilibrium again. "She dumped me. End of story. She didn't want me then, why would she want me now? If she somehow agreed to date me, it would only be until somebody better came along. Then she'd leave me high and dry again. No, thank you." He forced himself to take a deep settling breath in an attempt to lessen the pounding behind his ears.

"Ok."

"Huh?" He scratched his head.

"Bring your new lady friend to dinner next Sunday, and I'll uninvite Shelby. I'll text her and apologize and tell her I didn't know you were dating someone."

He liked that idea. He liked Shelby feeling the sting of rejection versus the other way around. It was a thousand percent childish of him, but sometimes past relationships did that to a person.

"I'll find out if Brooke is free."

"Oh, she has a name," Danielle said.

He cranked his neck in each direction to loosen the tightening of it. Why, oh why, had he opened his mouth? *Because you don't want to see Shelby. And your sister has it in her mind that you two are going to have some fairy tale reconnection.* "Yes, her name is Brooke. She's a busy pediatrician, and I'm not sure about her work schedule—" Logan let his voice fade.

He never lied, but here he managed to create a lie deep enough he already needed to find a way to get out of it. But why Brooke? Wishful thinking? Either way, a fake girlfriend with a busy job meant he had managed to buy himself a few weeks before he revealed he broke up with her. Danielle would be none the wiser, and he'll have avoided a dinner which would have sent him into an unraveling tailspin.

"Pediatrician, you say."

"Yep."

This could work. Mentioning Brooke's name meant it was easier to keep track of these lies.

"I'm assuming you met her at the hospital."

The spot between his shoulder blades pinched.

Admit the truth. You still have time to fess up.

"I did."

"Then find out if *Brooke* can make it next Sunday for dinner at Mom and Dad's."

"I can't make any promises," Logan countered.

Meaning, Brooke would never be going to dinner at his parents' house. A long span of possible excuses for her absence rattled off in his brain. Whether or not he liked it, he'd have to see this thing through. Danielle could never know he lied about having a girlfriend.

"Because Brooke isn't real," Danielle scoffed.

"No—"

A loud eruption of blood curdling cries interrupted him.

"Dang," Danielle muttered. "I let their pacifiers slip out of their mouths right when they were dozing off. I need to go—" She continued to speak but the babies' wails made it hard to hear what she said.

"Can you repeat that?"

"It's not important," she shouted. More screams, more cries. Logan heard Danielle attempting to soothe the twins. "I can't wait to meet this mysterious Brooke."

"She's fantastic. You'll love her."

It wasn't even a lie.

"Fine."

"Fine." Logan hung up and tossed his phone on his couch.

He rubbed the length of his jaw raw as he contemplated his predicament. If he didn't bring Brooke around to his parents eventually, Danielle would scheme and find a way for him to see Shelby again. Sure, he could bow out a few times, but Danielle had a knack for sniffing out a lie. He had a month, tops, to show up with Brooke. An idea sprung into his head, and he smiled to himself. Something beneficial for him and Brooke.

Brooke rounded the corner to the nurses' station. Aubrey sat behind the computer. When Brooke arrived, she placed the stack of patient files in her arms onto the top of the counter. "Hey, there." She let out a long exhale.

Aubrey cocked an eyebrow. "Bad day?" Her fingers stalled in place over the keyboard.

The dinner with Logan last week had been a bright spot in the lackluster life. Because last night after work, she spent the evening stalking Justin and his new girlfriend on social media. After a wasted hour, she forced herself to close the app and delete it from her home screen.

"You have no idea."

Ten minutes ago, she had run into Justin again. They both mumbled their hurried hellos before he booked it in the opposite direction. She wondered how long his presence would invade every part of her life. Would it ever get easier? Then she reminded herself, he should be the one who was embarrassed, not her. He cheated on her. "I bumped into Justin a few minutes ago. Awkward," she grimaced.

Aubrey scrunched up her nose. "I'm sorry. I'm sure dinner the other night wasn't great either."

"Yeah, please don't remind me." Brooke forced herself to open the top file of her stack. "I don't think I can do another thing socially with him there for a while, at least until I'm in a better head space."

"I understand." Aubrey nodded. "I hate that he's put you in this position, but I hope with time you might feel more comfortable around him." She leaned back in her chair.

"Maybe, someday." She forced herself to make a note on the open file.

Aubrey typed again then stopped. "It seemed like you and Logan were hitting it off. How did it go after we left?"

"Logan is nice." Brooke popped a hip and rested it against the station. She gnawed on the inside of her cheek. The fact he asked for her number and had yet to text her made her realize the guy had taken pity on her. He mentioned multiple times he wanted to be friends, aka, I'm not attracted to you, you're a bread-and Oreo-eating weirdo. "He says he would like to be friends."

"Oh," Aubrey popped an eyebrow, "friends, you say."

"Yes," she practically hissed back.

Aubrey held up her hands in defeat. The subject of Logan dropped.

They worked in tandem. Aubrey clacked the keyboard of the computer. Brooke filtered through her stack of patient files. As she made a note on a file toward the end of her stack, Brooke kept her gaze on the paperwork when she asked, "What did you think of Justin's girlfriend?"

The keyboard clacking stopped. Aubrey paused. Brooke clocked her back stiffen.

"Umm," Aubrey cleared her throat, "maybe we shouldn't talk about Justin and his new relationship. It might be for the best."

"Okay, if that's how you want it." Brooke forced herself to make a note on the chart, but a tremor ran through her hand making it shaky. "I'm assuming this is because you think his new relationship is more than a fling for him?"

Her mind flashed through a series of important life events. Ones where Justin was there with the new girl, and Brooke was nowhere to be seen. She was losing everything, not just Justin, but her entire circle of friends. As Aubrey sat in front of her, she saw the gap between them widen. Boundaries were being created where neither could venture outside them and stay friends.

"I—I—" Aubrey stammered. "I think it's better this way."

Her world crashed down. Not only had she lost Justin, but she was losing Aubrey and Ian too. This was only the beginning. Her mind quickly cataloged every worst-case social scenario, all the ones she would no doubt be left out of. Their friendship had worked because they were both part of a couple, and their boyfriends were best friends.

Loneliness engulfed her even though Aubrey remained a few feet away. Years of friendship which centered around a dynamic that no longer existed, meant maybe they weren't as close as she once thought. Maybe she needed a new friend. If Logan ever contacted her about doing something, she would say yes.

A buzzer sounded. Aubrey tapped it off. "I need to go check on this patient. Let's try and meet for lunch soon." She stood and pushed in her chair. "Text me your schedule, and I'll figure out mine too."

A weird undercurrent hovered right below the surface. Tangible and real.

"I'd love to meet for lunch," Brooke replied in her most genuine and upbeat voice she could muster. Aubrey rounded the station, and Brooke squeezed her arm to stop her in place. She found her gaze. "Hey," she paused, letting her voice soften, "I'm sorry. I know this is tricky, but I would like to find a way for us to stay friends."

"We will," Aubrey smiled but it didn't reach her eyes, "stay friends. Don't you worry."

Brooke wanted to believe it was possible but a nagging feeling lingered.

"Okay, then it's decided," Brooke said like her words set everything in stone.

Aubrey left and headed down the hall to check on her patient.

Brooke finished her patients' charts then tossed them into the pile to be updated into the computer. Then she shoved her pen back into the pocket of her lab coat.

"Hey," a familiar voice called out to her. Brooke pivoted toward it. Logan jogged down the hallway opposite the direction Aubrey disappeared. He arrived in front of her out of breath. "I'm glad I caught you," Logan leaned forward and gripped his knees as his breathing evened out.

"You okay?" A half laugh escaped her. "Or did you finish running a marathon I didn't know about?" She scrutinized him.

"Haha." Logan rolled his eyes then straightened himself. "I can't help it if my only workouts involve walking to and from work. Then I spotted you, and I didn't want you to disappear before I could talk to you."

"You could've texted me." She leaned her hip against the nurses' station and fully faced him. "I mean you gave me that I want to be friends hard sell but then promptly ghosted me so—"

"It didn't save," he blurted out then Logan rubbed the back of his neck. "I have no idea what happened, but the contact did not save." His labored breathing evened out. "I don't want you thinking I ghosted you, because I do want to be your friend. I heard from another doctor that you were on shift today. I booked it here after my surgery."

"Uh, huh." Skeptically, she raised an eyebrow. "Okay."

"It's true." His beautiful blue eyes glinted with mischievousness. He snatched his phone from the pocket of his lab coat. "I did want to see you again, but your number really didn't save. Here—" holding it out to her, "can you reenter your number?"

An unfamiliar zing traveled down her spine. "I guess." Their fingers brushed as she took the phone from him. Slowly, she entered her phone number and double checked to make sure it was saved as a new contact. It didn't look to be a duplicate. "There you go." She held it out for him, and he snagged it back.

"Thanks." Logan pulled up his contacts then tapped on her name. He turned the screen to face her. "I have it now." Then he put it back in his pocket.

"You do." Then they stared at one another. The air quaked with a palpable tension, and she wondered if he felt it too. When he didn't speak, Brooke filled the void. "I guess text me when you want to hang out, friend." She took one step in the direction of her patient's room, but she slowed her step in case he cared to prolong their conversation.

"Another thing before you take off—"

Brooke twisted back to face him and folded her arms.

Logan rocked back and forth on his heels, "I have a favor I needed to ask of you."

"Are we already to the favor part of our friendship?" She laughed. "I don't know, this might be going a bit fast for me."

His face fell. "Oh, okay." Logan waved a hand. "Forget about it. I'll see you around." Then he shifted to leave.

Brooke pinched the sleeve of his lab coat. "Wait." She let out a long breath. He traced the length of her hand up to her face. She dropped her hand and straightened herself. "I was only giving you a hard time. What was the favor?" Then she shoved her hands into the pockets of her lab coat.

He rubbed the back of his neck. "I need you to come to my parents for dinner and pretend to be my new girlfriend. I need them to think I'm not available, because my ex is in town and my sister is determined to play matchmaker." The words came in rapid succession.

Taken back by his proposal, Brooke let the proposition simmer in her brain. "You need a pretend girlfriend?"

"Yes." His shoulders drooped a little bit more. "I most definitely need exactly that."

"To avoid your ex thinking you're available?"

"You're hitting the high points." He shook his head then peered down the hallway past her with a glazed-over look. "I know it sounds pathetic, and it probably won't work. But I can't let my family think I'm available. I need my ex to believe I've moved on. It's pitiful and childish, but aren't we all like that when it comes to broken hearts?"

Brooke knew loads about broken hearts not only from romantic relationships. Her heart still broke a little when she saw families out with their kids, parents doting on them with love in their eyes. Her mom never once looked at her with an ounce of compassion. So love, yeah, Brooke wasn't sure she'd ever have the privilege of experiencing it. It seemed like an intangible thing just outside of her reach. People like her learned to continue with the constant voice in their head making them question their own worth. Seeing Logan wearing the face of defeat did something to her.

"I'm in," Brooke quickly said. "I'll do it."

"Really?" His face brightened and light entered his eyes again. "You will?"

"Yes." This was a terrible idea. "But—" her voice trailed off.

"What?" He stepped closer, close enough her breath hitched. "I'll do anything, just say the word."

Brooke exhaled. "You have to pretend to be my boyfriend for Ian and Aubrey's wedding. I can't go alone. I might die from the humiliation. Justin is Ian's best man. I'm a bridesmaid. Let's just say, I think this proposition could be mutually beneficial for us both."

"Done." Logan smiled and pulled back his shoulders. "I'll text you and let you know the details of this dinner with my parents. My sister will be there too with her family. It's a whole thing."

"Meaning—" Brooke shifted her weight from one foot to the other, "what exactly?"

"My sister Danielle will ask you a bazillion questions." Logan ran a hand through his hair. "My parents will act far too thrilled to have you there. Someone will make it awkward by saying something off base then asking when the wedding is. You know, normal family meddling."

She didn't know, but it sounded interesting, maybe even a little fun.

"I can't wait." Brooke couldn't help it, she smiled. "If I'm faking a romantic relationship to an entire slew of people, I better start brushing up on my acting skills. I did take some improv classes back in high school but that was mainly comedy."

"Unfortunately, my life is comical to everyone else but me." Logan grinned. "You'll fit right in."

Her gaze locked with his and a tingle rushed through her. She cleared her throat. "How long do we have before this family dinner?"

Logan's lips twitched. "My sister wants us to go next weekend, but I'll push her off as long as possible. I can buy us a bit more time." He scratched his jaw. "We'll probably need to meet up beforehand to do a rough outline of our relationship timeline. I need my family to believe this is real."

"They will, don't worry. I think hashing out the details of your whirlwind romance is a good idea though." Her phone buzzed, and she fished it out of her pocket. An email from the head of pediatrics flashed across the screen. He needed to discuss a patient's case with her. "I need to go address this email." She peered up at him while she tapped her phone against her palm. "Text me, Logan, and we'll figure out when to meet up." She paused then added, "This will work."

"I sure hope so." A gloomy look danced across his face, and Brooke wanted to reach out and hug him but knew it wasn't appropriate.

A doctor Brooke knew walked by, and she waved then turned back to Logan and said very professionally, "I look forward to collaborating with you on this issue." The doctor waved back, then continued down the hallway until they were out of earshot.

Logan plunged his hand into the front pocket of his lab coat and yanked out a personal size package of mini Oreos. "Me too. Here," he slapped the package into her hands, "I told you I pay off my friends. Here's something for the road." Then he winked. "I'll be in touch." Then he left.

She smiled and slipped the package into her pocket and headed to her office to address the email waiting for her.

CHAPTER 5

Three weeks whizzed right on by. Logan learned the ins and outs of his new job. His time became consumed with long surgeries and being on call. The best part of his day, though, became his fun late night text exchanges with Brooke. After they came to their agreement in the hospital, Logan started texting her in the evening under the guise of getting to know her. He promised it was research to sell their fake relationship to his family and her friends.

But before he even knew what happened, Brooke became the bright spot in his day.

He'd managed to keep his sister and parents at bay about his new girlfriend, but he knew it was tick tock. If he didn't materialize at Sunday dinner soon with Brooke on his arm, he didn't know what Danielle would plan without his knowledge.

One evening after a long work day, Logan returned to his apartment, kicked off his shoes and brought his take-out to his couch. Before he even sat down, his phone dinged. He smiled, grappling it out of his pocket expecting a text from Brooke. Instead, tension gathered in his shoulders.

Admit it, this Brooke woman isn't real.

He groaned and lowered himself onto the couch and set the to-go bag on the coffee table. Logan wondered how best to respond. He found his disposable fork from the to-go bag and removed the to-go box. His stomach growled so he ate half of the orange chicken before he responded.

She's real. But even you must admit our family is a lot, and I didn't want to scare her off by bringing her home to meet everyone if the relationship fizzled and died out before it became anything real.

According to my calculations, you've been dating this mystery woman for at least a month.

The words dangled like a month was a year. Logan wiped his face with his napkin then picked his phone back up.

EXACTLY! One month is nothing in the land of dating.

Just admit you're lying so I can invite Shelby over. I ran into her again when I took the girls for a walk in the stroller, and she was looking extra cute in her leggings and beanie.

I don't care. You have to drop this. I don't want to see Shelby.

Give me another month.

Two weeks.

Fine.

Honestly, Logan would've settled for a week. Two weeks was more than enough time to finalize the details of their fake relationship. While he finished eating, he put on the game but muted it.

Once full, he bit the bullet and called Brooke instead of texting.

She picked up on the third ring and answered, "Is everything okay?"

"Everything is fine." Logan kicked up his feet and readjusted a pillow behind his head. "I thought calling would be easier so we could talk instead of trying to hash this out over text messaging. My sister is hounding me to bring around my new girlfriend. I bought us two weeks which I know isn't much."

"I'm up for it. I've always enjoyed a good challenge."

It made him smile. He enjoyed her sassy confident side.

"I hoped you would say that, but I do think we should meet up in person and go over everything. Make a cheat sheet of sorts, hash out our timeline, memorize the details about each other, you get the idea. What night are you free this week for dinner?"

"Um, give me a second to check." The phone went silent besides some rustling around. Finally, she popped back on and said, "I can do Thursday night or Saturday morning."

"Let's do Thursday night." He swung his legs around and sat up. The thought of seeing Brooke made him perk up. The woman was easy on the eyes, and he did enjoy her company. Even if they were only fake dating, it didn't mean he couldn't enjoy himself. "I was recommended a restaurant around the corner from the hospital. It's on the Magnificent Mile."

"What's it called? Maybe I've been there before."

Logan panicked. He had no clue what restaurant to eat at, and he had no idea why he said he received a recommendation. But he planned on scouring the pages of Yelp later to figure it out.

"Umm," he raked his hair, "I'll text you the name once I secure a reservation. I don't want you to get your hopes up if I have to book my backup place."

"Wow, okay." Brooke paused, "You've really thought this through. I wish all my fictional dates put this much time into where they took me to eat."

"You know me, just playing the part."

What in the world? Logan shook his head and muttered to himself about his blabbering.

"I see."

Logan tried to think of a clever response but came up dry. "I'll text you the details when I've confirmed everything. Do you want me to pick you up at the hospital or your apartment? Or should we meet at the restaurant?"

"Umm—I'm not sure yet when I'll be off work." Her voice trailed off then Brooke continued, "I'll let you know. I'd prefer to go home and change first. I'll either have you pick me up from my apartment or I can meet you there."

"I don't mind coming to get you. It gives me an excuse to exercise." He should've stopped talking but the nervous energy pulsating through his veins made him ramble on. "And you don't need to dress up for me. I think you look good no matter what you wear. I mean you can if you want, but you don't have to. You'll look fine in anything." He snapped his mouth shut.

Boy, his game was rusty. Good thing this whole relationship was fake.

"True," Brooke groaned. "But I'm not going to go out with you to a nice restaurant wearing sweats. I do have some standards. They are remarkably low, but they do still exist."

"Gotcha, you only wear sweatpants to buy bread and Oreos," he countered, hoping she understood his comment as fun flirting and not a dig.

"Yes, and then I take them home to eat them alone in the comfort of my own apartment."

Logan's lips curled into a smile. "Same."

"Really? I figured the French bread you bought was to take to some sort of dinner party, at least that was the story I made up in my head," Brooke said. "I figured you as a CrossFit, I only eat clean, type of guy."

"I'm glad I give off that vibe. Can you share that with your single friends you want to set me up with?"

Brooke laughed. Her laugh vibrated through every cell of his body, invigorating him more than it should. "I'm never setting you up with anyone. Nice try."

"Noted. I'll text you the details of our dinner."

They said their goodbyes.

Then Logan spent the rest of the evening researching where to take Brooke on their fake date. He knew it wasn't a real date, but he felt hopeful and excited in a way he hadn't for a long time. After careful research, he decided on The Purple Pig and was able to secure a reservation. Though he planned everything immediately, he waited another day to text Brooke the details. He didn't know why, but he didn't want to appear overly eager. They agreed he'd pick her up at seven from her apartment then walk the few blocks to the restaurant.

Thursday came before he knew it. As he neared Brooke's apartment that evening, his hands shook with nervous energy. The winter air nipped at his skin making the tips of his ears sting. He tightened the scarf around his neck and buttoned his peacoat jacket up to his neck. The doorman, who he remembered as George, stood stationed outside of the apartment building.

"Good evening, George," Logan greeted as he halted in front of the building.

For a second George studied him, then his face lit up and he remarked, "You're Brooke's new doctor friend, right?"

"That's me." Logan shuffled back and forth on his heels. "She told me to text her when I arrive, and she'd meet me in the lobby." He texted her quickly.

George opened the door to the building and motioned for

him to enter. "Go right on in and wait in the lobby where it's warm. Brooke mentioned she had a friend coming by."

"Thanks." Logan slipped inside and loosened the scarf from around his neck as the cozy warmth of the building enveloped him.

George didn't enter the lobby but remained outside at his post.

Five minutes later the doors to the elevator opened, and Brooke sauntered out. His jaw dropped. The woman looked like a knock-out in her black dress and heels. Her hair hung loose in soft beach waves which danced over her shoulders. A part of him wondered how her hair would feel between his fingertips. She had a small sparkly clutch in one hand and a long peacoat jacket slung over her arm. Suddenly, he wondered why he hadn't put more of an effort into his own appearance. Though he had on a checkered button-down shirt and slacks, he couldn't even remember what color it was or if it was new or old. Nothing about the pounding in his chest felt fake. His attraction to her was one hundred percent real. He choked back on his saliva and forced himself to find his center.

"You look beautiful," he remarked as she arrived in front of him.

She smiled shyly at him. "Thank you." The air dripped with the aroma of her perfume. It wasn't too spicy or too sweet, but it made his heart hammer harder.

He swallowed. "I'm glad we could do this."

"Me too." Her eyes dazzled with the lights of the foyer. "Even if this is fake, it was nice to have an excuse to dress up."

"Well, you nailed the part." His fingers itched to take her hand. He clutched them into a fist and forced them into the front pocket of his peacoat. "Are you okay to walk?" His gaze dropped to her magnificent heels with a strappy back.

Gosh, her legs looked fantastic.

"Oh, these." Brooke lifted the heel of one foot. "They are more comfortable than they look." Then she winked as her face filled with amusement.

Heat flooded his core while his heart took a few liberties.

"Okay," he stepped closer, and a pack punch of her tantalizing perfume nearly did him in. He cleared his throat. "Can I help you with your coat? It's chilly. You won't last long without it on."

"Yes." Brooke handed him her coat. Their eyes danced with one another for a moment, before she added, "I'd appreciate it."

He held it out for her to slip on. She twisted her back to him then weaved her arm through one hole then shifted her clutch to the other hand and then slipped the other in. Gently, he lifted her hair out of the collar of the jacket where it tucked in. The silky strands sifted through his fingertips while her womanly aroma filled his lungs. He wanted to stay there forever and breathe in the perfect scent, but he forced himself to remove his hands and step away.

He managed to say, "Ready?"

"Yes, I'm starving." They walked across the lobby to the exit. "I haven't eaten since this morning. My day was slammed. How about you?"

He grasped the door and held it open for her. Her body brushed against him as she passed through to the outside. He wondered what she would feel like pressed up against his body, but he shook the thought off and reminded himself to listen.

"It was good. I had to perform kidney stone surgery this morning." They made it outside, and the door shut behind them. "The worst I've ever seen, the person had stones that were centimeters, not millimeters."

"Kidney stones, huh?" Brooke waved goodbye to George. George exchanged a smirk with Brooke that Logan caught. They strode on the sidewalk toward the restaurant. She continued, "Luckily, I've never had the pleasure of experiencing kidney stones, but I've heard they're incredibly painful."

"Consider yourself blessed." Logan plunged his hands into the pockets of his peacoat to keep himself from reaching for her hand. "I've had the unfortunate experience of kidney stones. I thought I was dying. I survived, but I required heavy medication to pass them."

"Yikes." Brooke winced. "That sounds terrible. How old were you?"

"Oh," he tried to remember, "I was in high school—I think it was my senior year. My mom slept on the floor of my room, because I wrung in pain and threw up the entire night."

"Wow." She slowly nodded and gazed out at the sidewalk before them. "Your mom sounds great. I don't think my mom ever did something like that for me." Brooke leaned in and clutched his forearm and squeezed. "But I'm glad you had your mom." She dropped her hand.

He wondered how to respond. He wanted to ask her a million questions about her past, but he knew it wasn't appropriate, not if they weren't really together. Not before she offered the information and wasn't prodded for it.

Logan smiled. "I think you'll like her when you meet her."

"I am sure I will," she remarked. "What is she like?"

"Oh, you know, besides being way into my business?" he teased.

She nodded.

"She is kind and thoughtful. Patient." A flood of happy memories from his childhood came to the forefront of his mind. Ones where Mom sprinkled in her goodness at every turn. He never realized what a blessing it was to have good parents until he came to hear the sad and hard upbringings of others. "I'd do stupid things, and she'd always find a way to help me learn and desire to do better the next time around. I loved that she'd tell me again and again that no matter what I did, or how much I messed up, she'd be there for me and love me."

She smiled. "I can't wait to meet her."

They arrived at the restaurant. After they checked in with the host, they were led to a table in the corner pocket of the place. It was loud and crowded, but Logan liked the vibe. His day to day was quiet, and during surgeries his mind went blank and silent. Being out in the vibrant city night life made him remember why he wanted to live in Chicago and not in one of the surrounding suburbs.

They removed their jackets and hung them on the back of their seats.

Brooke opened her menu first. "Besides your mom being wonderful what else do I need to know about your parents? I need the basics." The small candle in the center of the two-top table provided enough light to read the menu and create a more intimate atmosphere.

"My dad is a surgeon too." Logan opened his menu too.

"Ahh, the family business." Brooke flipped to the next page in the menu. "What type of surgeon?"

"Heart."

"Wow, okay." She glanced up and tilted her head to the side. "And you didn't want to be a heart surgeon too?"

"I didn't place in the specialty." Logan ran his finger down the list of entrée selections. He hated how his stomach still twisted when he revealed this to someone. "I tried. I really did. It's a sore spot with my dad, please avoid bringing it up when you meet him." His back stiffened, and he cranked his neck back and forth to loosen the tense feeling.

"Hey," the softness of her voice made him pause and peer across the table at her. "I would never bring up something like that. I understand more than anyone how complicated families can be."

And with every fiber of his being, he believed her.

"Thanks." Logan forced himself to look back down at his menu. "My dad was disappointed. Honestly, it was a huge blow to me too. But I'm happy where I ended up even if it wasn't the original plan."

"I understand." Brooke shut her menu and fidgeted with the silverware in front of her. "I always wanted to specialize in internal medicine, but when I did the rotations, I didn't connect with it as much as I would've liked. Being a pediatrician wasn't ever the plan. I honestly didn't have any experience with children, but it's where I placed. I'm happy with how it worked out."

Logan smiled. "Thanks for telling me that."

Brooke nodded. "Is your mom a doctor too?" She took a sip of water from the glass in front of her.

"Heavens no." He shook his head. "She's a retired school librarian. A quiet gentle person who loved to spend her time among books."

From the outside, his parents seemed like an odd pair, but their marriage was one that Logan admired. They evened each other out. His mom was steady while his dad was loud and fierce. Each parent helped to shape him into the person he became.

"I wish I had more time to read than I do." She traced a finger over the edge of her glass. "Usually, when I get off work, I'm too beat to do anything other than eat and binge true crime stories on TV."

"Hence your Ted Bundy reference," he smirked.

Her lips twitched. "You know me too well."

The server came by. They ordered a selection of tapas, meat and cheese, and grilled vegetables. After the server left, Brooke didn't waste time getting down to business.

"Besides hashing out the details of our relationship timeline," she placed her folded hands-on top of the table, "I think we need to make a list of rules for our fake relationship. Rules will ensure neither of us gets confused about what's real and what isn't."

"Umm," Logan leaned his forearms on the table, leaning in closer to her. "Could you give me an example?"

Brooke unfolded her hands and fished for her clutch. She unsnapped the front of it and retrieved her phone. After she opened up a note saved on it, Brooke slid it across the table toward him.

She motioned at it. "That's what I came up with."

Slowly, Logan picked up her phone. The lengthy list included every possible scenario of physical touching. Rules-like when hand holding or arm around the shoulder were okay. A hand on the knee was allowed when it was visible to others. Possible kissing had so many addendums that it made his head spin.

He slid her phone back to her. She snatched it. The list doused whatever had or hadn't been building between them. It wasn't lost on him that this wasn't a date, not even close. To Brooke this was a business deal, a mutually beneficial exchange. The realization depressed him more than it should. After all, he was the one who had suggested it. But then Brooke showed up looking the way she did.

"I'm not sure any of this is necessary." Logan found her gaze. "I promise not to do anything to make you feel uncomfortable. If I do, simply tell me to knock it off." Unnecessarily, he adjusted the ends of his sleeves. "I'm a good listener and take directions better than most."

"I like to be prepared." Brooke scrolled through the list again. "And I don't want to be confused on what's real and what isn't. We'll have to touch. We can't avoid it." She placed the phone face down on the table. A seriousness settled on her face. "We need people to think we're really dating, and you're into me. Like head over heels, I'm so in love I can't remember anyone else who came before type of performance."

Logan knew he wouldn't need to fake anything. He already found Brooke beautiful.

"Text me the list. I'll review it tonight." Logan took a sip of his water. "And I'll make people believe I'm in love with you. I promise."

"Great." Brooke's stiff posture loosened. "I'm glad we're on the same page."

"I know it's hard to believe," he shifted and leaned back against his chair, "but I have dated before."

"I never said—" She almost made her hand graze his but she clenched her hand into a fist and brought it back to her lap. "I only know we both need the people in our lives to think we're in love."

"I can play the part."

"I believe you now," she muttered. A plate dropped three tables away. They both twisted in their seats to look toward the commotion. When they confirmed the situation was under control, they faced each other again. She continued, "I—I—"

"I understand." He placed a firm hand on her forearm. "I'll memorize the list. I'll play the part. I'll be the perfect doting boyfriend."

"Ok." She gnawed on her bottom lip. "But we're in agreement, right? No kissing me unless it's absolutely necessary." The intimate lighting of the restaurant made her face glimmer and eyes shine brightly.

"The same rule applies to you." He removed his hand and wagged a finger. "No kissing me no matter how bad you want to. Kissing is for audiences only."

"Don't worry," she locked eyes with him, "that won't be a problem."

He hated how disappointed her declaration made him. Meanwhile, his fingers itched to touch her. Her thighs and his were only a foot apart, and their knees kept grazing each other every time she uncrossed and crossed her legs. And it nearly did him in. Every. Single. Time. Brooke appeared oblivious to the tight quarters under the table while his heartbeat remained a tad too high.

The server brought by the first of the tapas, a hummus plate with pita bread. They each served themselves.

He broke off a piece of the pita bread and spread hummus on top. "Let's circle back to the kissing rules."

Brooke rolled her eyes. "We never really left the topic," she raised an eyebrow, "but okay, go on."

"When you want to make Justin jealous," he ate a bite of his bread and hummus then continued once he swallowed, "is that a good time to kiss you?"

Brooke smothered her pita bread with hummus. "Yes, that's exactly what I want you to do." She ate a bite then wiped her face with her napkin. "The same in reverse. I'll kiss you when we need to convince your family we're really together."

"Hmm." Logan polished off the rest of his hummus bread. "We might need to practice the kissing thing a few times to make sure we get it right."

"I think we'll be fine." She paused and shot him a skeptical look. "Unless you're a terrible kisser."

"I haven't heard any complaints." He smirked as he bit into his bread. Her cheeks splashed with color. "And like I mentioned before, I'm an excellent listener. If on the off chance you find my kissing repulsive, you can tell me how to fix it."

"Then it's settled," she muttered. She shoved her phone back into her clutch. "I'll send you the list, commit it to memory before we go to dinner with your family."

"I will." Logan forced himself to smile.

His insides twisted. He needed to change the tide, push them back into the realm of fun like their text message exchanges over the last few weeks.

The server dropped off their cheese and meat plate.

"Enough about the list of rules." He speared a piece of bruschetta and cut off a bit of the gouda. "I propose we play the game of twenty questions in preparation."

Brooke used the fork to spear cheese and meat for herself. "Good idea." She placed it on her plate. "You go first since it was your idea."

"What's your most embarrassing high school moment?"

Her eyes widened and cheeks flushed. "Wow, you're jumping

in feet first." She patted the corners of her mouth with her napkin. "I'm trying to decide if I should tell you the truth or make something up, because technically you would probably not be able to know the difference—"

"Ahh, come on." He ate a bite of his meat and cheese. "Please don't hold out on me. I want to know everything about you and keeping everything else real will be much easier to track."

A long pause.

"I'm waiting," he prodded.

"Fine." She scrunched up her nose. "In high school, on a rainy day, I slipped and ripped the entire back of my jeans. Like sliced them open right along the seam. Not only had I fallen, but I also managed to moon everyone who saw me get up. It was horrifying."

Logan winced. "Ugh."

"The guy who I nicknamed the Teen Dream saw it and then proceeded to call me Split Pants for the next two years. I called my mom to bring me another pair of pants, but she never picked up her phone. I'm sure she was probably passed out drunk or high on her latest concoction of drugs. She never even knew what happened. I didn't have a lot of clothes. I had to babysit the neighbor's kids for four Saturday nights to earn enough money to buy new ones to replace them." Brooke bit her bottom lip. "I shouldn't have told you that." She glanced away and out at the crowded restaurant. She shook her head and tapped her bottom lip with her pointer finger. "I try my best not to talk about my mom or my childhood. It's better that way." She blinked then shifted to face him again. "Forget I mentioned it."

"Hey," he placed a hand over hers. Logan wished he could wrap his arms around her, drawing her close to his chest and help her feel safe. "I won't tell anyone about the pants or your less-than-ideal childhood. It's not my information to share."

"I—" She paused then finally said, "Thank you."

"You can tell me anything." And he meant it. He hoped to

bring lightness back to the conversation. "I'm a lock box." He made a zipping motion across his lips. "Now, I need to tell you my most embarrassing moment. Are you ready?" Logan cocked an eyebrow.

She smiled and leaned in closer. "I'm listening."

"Junior year, I was homecoming king—"

"Of course you were," she rolled her eyes, "I've only been around you a handful of times, and I pegged you as one who had his way with the ladies."

Logan grinned. "I know, I'm awesome." He winked. "But enough about my greatness, I'm about to tell you the most humiliating moment of my life."

Her eyes sparkled. "I'm on the edge of my seat."

"While I was crowned homecoming king my fly was all the way down. Like gaping open with the little zipper hanging sideways type of open. I wondered why people were pointing. It wasn't until I started dancing with the crowned queen that she politely let me know it was open for everyone to see."

"Was the queen the woman your sister wants you to see again?"

"Hey," he stilled. "How did you know?"

Brooke took a long sip of her drink then said, "Because she was the queen. The queen always has her king waiting in the wings."

His jaw hardened. "She dumped me on graduation night."

The memory of that night still stung years later. A night full of celebration became his darkest low. Shelby revealed after the graduation party, she wanted to end things. According to her, she had wanted to dump him midyear but knew she needed a date to prom and breaking up earlier would've ruined her senior year. Now it seemed to only have ruined him forever.

"I'm sure that was hard but remember you were practically children. People change, grow. They become better versions of who they were back in high school." Brooke tilted her head to the side, "Doesn't the king in you want to see if you and the queen could give it another go?"

"No." Tension tightened his neck.

"You're lying." Brooke patted his forearm then shrugged. "I get it. I've lied to myself too. Sometimes it's easier than seeing the truth."

"I am not— there's nothing there."

"There is," she firmly said. "I'll be your fake girlfriend. I'll help make your queen jealous. And who knows, maybe you and the queen will find a way back to each other."

He ran a hand down the length of his face. "No way, it would never work. It isn't like that for me."

"We'll see." Brooke picked up the knife to cut off another piece of cheese. "We'll see."

CHAPTER 6

Brooke smoothed out the front of her blouse and studied her appearance in the mirror. Her black slacks were freshly pressed from the dry cleaner. She wondered if her outfit was appropriate to meet her fake boyfriend's parents. Logan had reassured her anything she wore would be fine because they were a casual family. Big problem, she didn't know the first thing about casual gatherings. Family gatherings of her own were nonexistent and she had no point of reference. And Justin's family were an uptight and formal bunch, think two forks and two spoons dinner.

Her stomach twisted, reconfirming her nerves. She reminded herself she didn't need to be anxious. This didn't mean a thing. To Logan's family she'd simply become a random woman they meant once.

An Amazon delivery made her phone buzz. Brooke checked the time and confirmed she had enough time to hustle on down to the lobby to pick it up from George before Logan arrived.

When she entered the lobby, George whistled. "It looks like someone is headed somewhere special."

Her cheeks warmed. "I know I need to step it up, I normally

wear sweats if I'm not working." She arrived in front of the lobby desk.

"Hey," George held his hands up. "You said it, not me."

"Amazon let me know I have a package waiting." She leaned her hip against the desk.

"Oh," George scuttled out of his chair. "Let me check what is here, but you didn't answer my question. Where are you off to?" He walked to the table which held the packages delivered for the residents.

"I'm meeting Logan's parents today." Brooke watched George still.

He furrowed his brow. "Already? This is more serious than I thought."

"It's not serious. We're friends, nothing more."

"Hmm." George found the package and placed it on top of the desk. "Are you sure about that? In my day and age, meeting someone's parents— well you didn't do that unless you really cared about the woman."

"Times have changed." Brooke scrutinized her nice fresh coat of nude nail polish. "It isn't like that with him." Brooke plunged her hand into her pocket and retrieved her phone. Then located the list of rules they had agreed upon for their fake dating relationship in her notes. "See?" She whipped the screen around to let him see it. "It's right here in black and white. We have an agreement. The entire thing is fake."

George tipped up his hat a bit then took her phone from her. "Geez, I'm getting old." He patted the desk and located his readers. Once on, he scanned the list. "These are the rules?" He looked up at her over the top of his glasses. "Seems like a lot of nonsense for two people who are fighting real feelings."

"We're friends who need to make other people jealous."

He cleared his throat then peered back down at the phone. "Rule one, hand holding will only be done in the presence of

Justin and/or Shelby. Huh?" George scratched his head. "You've got to be kidding me."

"We had to establish the rules. I didn't want to really fall in love with Logan."

"And why," George scrolled through the list, "would that be such a bad idea?"

"Because I'm not over Justin," she countered.

"Wrong." He scrolled more. "Try again."

"Because," she thought for a minute then added, "I need time to be single."

"Stop spewing a bunch of malarkey." George finished reading and handed the phone back to her. He removed his glasses and tossed them onto the desk. "I really like the addendums about kissing. Tongue can only be used if and when Justin or Shelby are staring." He laughed and shook his head. "Nice try. It's not going to work, because you're playing with fire."

"I don't think we'll ever get to kissing." She slipped the phone back into her pocket. "It probably wasn't necessary to include it."

"Maybe."

She stared back at him. "I guess I'll run this package up to my apartment before Logan arrives."

"Okay, I'll make sure to keep your fake date company when he arrives."

"Please don't." Brooke balanced the box in her arms. "In fact, please don't talk to him at all."

"Sorry," George smirked. A glint in his eyes made Brooke uneasy. "It's my job to greet the guests of the people who live here. I can't shirk my duties."

"Fine." Brooke whipped around and walked across the lobby to the elevator bay. "Have it your way." Her voice vibrated across the tile floors. She used the corner of the box to hit the elevator button.

"I usually do." Then George chuckled and sat back down behind the lobby desk.

She entered the elevator and went up to her apartment to drop off her package. A few minutes later, Logan texted letting her know he had arrived. She shot him a quick text, gathered her purse and went back down to the lobby. When the elevator opened, she heard the laughter of Logan and George.

Logan leaned over the desk, looking much too dapper in his jeans and navy henley tee under a Carhartt jacket. She questioned her outfit. For a second, she wavered. Too late, they turned in her direction when she stepped off the elevator. George whistled, making her cheeks warm. Logan straightened himself and walked toward her, meeting her halfway across the lobby.

"You look nice," he said as his hungry eyes ran down her, making her skin tingle. "I like your hair that way."

"Oh," Brooke fluffed her hair. She actually washed it this morning, which she hadn't done in almost a week. Her schedule at the hospital had been a bit chaotic. So, this morning she enjoyed the luxury of lathering thick shampoo into her locks. It lifted her own mood immensely. "Thanks," she managed. "I like that blue on you, it makes your eyes pop."

"This?" Logan smiled and peered down at her his T-shirt. "I've never had anyone tell me that but thanks."

With a nod, she shifted and placed her purse over her shoulder. "Should we go?"

"Yes." Logan clapped his hands together then rubbed them back and forth dramatically. "Let's do this. Let's get our fake date on."

Brooke's lips twitched with amusement. "Alright."

They walked the rest of the lobby, passing George as they headed outside. They said goodbye.

George yelled at the back of them, "Fake dating— yeah right."

She waved him off, but his comment made her stomach swim. Her palms sweated. Even though this arrangement was beneficial for both, she wanted Logan's parents to like her. She tried to remind herself she'd never see them again so it didn't matter, but her jittery hands begged to differ.

They wandered around the side of the building to where Logan had parked in one of the designated guest's spots. He held her door open to his sporty sedan, and she climbed in.

When on the expressway toward his parents' house, Brooke shifted in her seat to face him. For a moment, she found herself distracted as she stared at his sharp jaw and broad shoulders. The inside of the car swirled with his spicy aftershave. *Geez, this guy smelled good and looked even better.*

"So," Brooke leaned over the middle console. "Tell me what I need to know to impress your family. I remember their names from our study session, but I'm still worried they won't like me."

Logan glanced over his shoulder and changed lanes. "I already know they'll love you."

"What about Danielle?" Brooke adjusted her seat belt where it dug into her. "Shouldn't I be worried about her since she wants to see you back with the queen?"

"Shelby."

"Shelby," she repeated. "It does sound like a queen name."

He shrugged but didn't comment.

"Danielle—how do I get in her good graces with so many things stacked against me?"

His gaze darted quickly to her then back to the road. "You have nothing to worry about. Danielle is easy to win over. If you show some love for her twins, maybe ask to hold them and play with them, I think she'll warm up to you in no time. And acting head over heels in love with me would help too."

"Ok." Her stomach twisted. She wondered if her acting skills were up for the challenge. "I'll try my best."

"Hey," Logan lightly touched her forearm, "you don't need to be nervous. I know everyone is going to love you. Just be yourself, and it should be fine."

Brooke tilted her head away and stared out the passenger

window, watching the mile markers as they passed by. If only he knew how many versions of herself, she had to be over the years to survive. Growing up, she learned to be invisible. Her main goal was to move undetected to avoid her mom's alcoholic rages and drug-induced abuse. In college, she learned talking about her less than perfect family life made people uncomfortable. People didn't want the nitty gritty. She once again molded herself into a version that made her likeable. Survival. Only those who lived with no safety net, knew what it was like.

"Justin's family never approved of me. Honestly, I don't even think they liked me a little," she stated. Her revelation vibrated in the space between them. The sting of rejection was a fresh wound even now. "That's why I'm worried. Parents usually don't like me." Tears tickled the corners of her eyes. She blinked rapidly to keep them at bay. Her gaze focused at the mile markers drifting on by.

Logan squeezed her forearm. "Hey, I'm sorry to hear that." He squeezed one more time before letting go and repositioning his hand on the steering wheel. "How could anyone not like you?"

Brooke shifted back to face him. "I know, right?" she joked.

The car grew silent. She leaned her head back against the head rest. Logan didn't speak, which she appreciated.

"Justin's family was old money, like his ancestors came over on the Mayflower. His mom was part of some group… what was it called?" She tried to think of the name. Then she snapped, "Daughters of the American Revolution."

"Ahh," Logan nodded.

"I clearly did not come from the same stock. They didn't approve."

He raised an eyebrow. "But you're a pediatrician for crying out loud." He shook his head and merged over a lane. "What did they expect? A Rockefeller?"

She laughed, loosening the tension in her chest. "Probably."

She ran a finger over the console between them. "I, certainly, didn't fit the bill."

Logan scratched his jaw. "You'd fit my bill."

"Oh." Her cheeks reddened. She continued on, "Justin's mom took one look at me and managed to make me feel like complete trash. Her dismissal of me was painful. She often made loud sighs and critical remarks which didn't help either. All I've ever wanted was a family, and I had been hopeful to join his and make them my own. I was wrong about that, too." Brooke stared out the window again.

"I think you could still find that," Logan interjected. "Not every family is like that. I think normal families would be thrilled if their son came home with you."

She wondered if his words were true. What she came from clearly wasn't functional, but what was normal? Would she even recognize when she saw it?

"I hope you're right," Brooke offered.

"Me too."

The car grew quiet again. Sounds from the radio whirled around them. They continued in comfortable silence for a few minutes.

Brooke scrunched up her nose. "I'm sorry I just unloaded on you. You didn't need to know all that information about me."

"Hey, we're friends." He shot her a smile as he changed lanes. "You can tell me anything."

The words vibrated through her.

She believed him.

Friends.

His words managed to loosen the knot in her stomach. Soon, Logan merged over and exited. After the exit, the landscape changed. They weaved down a nice and well-kept neighborhood with large oak trees lining both sides of the street. Snow from their large storm two nights earlier still dotted the front yards of the houses. Yards displayed handmade snowmen and made her smile. She imagined the families outside at the first sign of snow, the children squealing with delight as they rolled the big balls to make them. Maybe some people were normal. Maybe some people did have it all. But would she ever be one of them? Doubtful.

Minutes later, he parked his car in front of a stately brick house with a massive front yard and white shutters. The house had a long walkway which led up to it. Despite its regal appearance it somehow still looked cozy and welcoming.

Brooke peered out the windshield. "You grew up here?"

"No." Logan unbuckled his seatbelt. "My parents bought this place after I went to college. They wanted to be part of the local country club. They've become golfers in their later years."

"Gotcha." She unbuckled her own seatbelt and sat back in no move to leave. "And your sister, she lives in this neighborhood too?"

"She does. I should've mentioned that before. Danielle moved here with her husband after they married. My parents bought in the neighborhood to be close to her. But I grew up across town."

"I see."

She wondered if this home was an upgrade or a sensible downgrade but either way it intimidated her. Sure, someday she hoped to own her own home, but with her heavy student loans she knew it was far off from becoming a reality.

"Come on." Logan opened his door and climbed out. "Let's get this over with."

The moment Brooke made it out of the car, the front door swung open and a woman around her age came barreling down the walkway toward them. She had Logan's same dark hair and blue eyes. Even from far away, she looked stunning.

"She is real!" Danielle exclaimed as she continued the rest of the way toward them. "I thought for sure my brother had made you up, and I was ready for him to turn up empty handed and blame your absence on a break up." She halted in front of them and put a hand on her hip. Her hungry eyes roamed over Brooke.

Brooke gulped. "I'm real, I promise."

Logan wrapped an arm around Brooke's waist and inched her closer until their hips touched. Warmth spread down her body. His strong arm seemed to communicate to her they were in this thing together. It managed to dampen the pounding of her heart.

He tsked. "I can't believe you thought I had made Brooke up." Protectively, he tightened his arm around her waist. His fingertips dipped into her skin. She loved the feeling of him pressing against her. It almost felt real. "I don't know whether to be embarrassed or insulted." He narrowed his gaze, but his lips twitched mischievously.

Danielle rolled her eyes and shooed off his comment. "Come here." She held her arms out to her. "We're huggers in our family, so you'll need to get used to it."

Logan released the grip around her waist. "It's true, sorry." He furrowed his brow at her.

"I can't argue with that." Brooke stepped into her open arms and hugged her back. "I've never been one to turn down a hug."

It was warm and inviting. For split second, Brooke believed the things Logan spoke about in the car: normal families with love which was unconditional. It was no wonder Logan was as terrific as he appeared to be, he had the safety of love.

They broke their embrace. Then Danielle hugged Logan.

His parents appeared in the doorway, each with a baby in their arms. "Come out of the cold and stop hogging Brooke. We want to meet her too," Logan's mom hollered.

"Coming," Logan said.

He snatched up Brooke's hand and led her up the walkway to the front door.

As they walked, Danielle said, "Everyone is very excited to meet you. You've been a bit of a mystery. We're glad Logan finally brought you around."

Danielle's bright vibrant smile confirmed her sincerity.

"I'm glad to be here too," Brooke replied.

And she meant it.

Her heart melted as she thought of what a family could be; all warmth and happiness. Unfortunately, it was a far cry from the world she grew up in where dysfunction, addiction, and fighting reigned. This feeling was worth coming home for.

They made it to the front stoop.

Logan's mom thrust the baby in her arms off to Danielle. "Here, take Lily. I want to give this beautiful girl a hug too."

Danielle smiled and scooped Lily up into her arms. "Of course." Once the baby was safely in her arms, she bounced her and tickled her tummy until the baby squealed with delight.

"I'm glad you're here." Logan's mom smiled. "I'm Amy."

Brooke embraced her. Amy smelled like warm bread and cinnamon, and immediately Brooke sensed her goodness. They broke their embrace. Amy stepped closer to her husband and nudged him, "and my husband is Paul."

"It's nice to meet you." Paul bounced the other twin in his arms. "I would give you a hug too, but I'm holding Amelia."

"Now that we have introductions out of the way," Amy linked her hands around the crook of Brooke's arm. "Come on in and tell me everything about yourself." She led her to the front door.

"Oh." Brooke flashed her gaze to Logan for help. "I'm kind of boring. There isn't much to tell. I'm a pediatrician. I met Logan at the hospital where we work."

The doorway was too tight to pass through side by side. Amy dropped her hands from her elbow and let her go through first.

"Mom—" Logan shot Amy a warning look. "Let's at least feed Brooke first before the interrogation starts."

They passed through the threshold. Cherry wood floors and an impressive staircase greeted them. A formal living room had crisp cream-colored carpet that practically blinded her. Next, they passed a formal dining room with seating for ten. Finally, they arrived at the kitchen with an eat-in breakfast nook and family room attached. The table was set with two high chairs pulled up to it.

A man stationed at the stove peered over at them as they entered.

"She does exist," he teased. He shot Danielle an unreadable look. "I knew Logan wouldn't make her up." He turned off one of the burners. "I'm Michael by the way. Danielle's husband." Michael flipped a kitchen towel over his shoulder.

Brooke smiled. "It's nice to meet you."

"You guys," Logan came up next to Brooke and wrapped his arm around her shoulders and squeezed them, "make it sound like it's a miracle anyone would date me."

"It is a marvel," Michael teased. "I mean look at him."

Brooke grinned. "I know, right?" She cupped his cheek with one hand. "I have to look at his face all the time, poor me." She made a pouty face.

"Hey," Logan smiled against her hand. His cheek shifted under her palm. The scratchy surface of his stubble rubbed her skin. "I haven't heard any complaints until now." He winked.

With a smirk, Brooke lightly patted his cheek before she dropped it.

Danielle deposited Lily into one of the high chairs while Paul strapped Amelia into the other one. Amy snatched a canister of kid puffs cereal out of the cupboard and peeled back the lid. She walked over and dumped a pile on each tray in front of the girls. Their little chubby hands hungrily clutched them and shoved some into their mouths.

"Even you can admit you never bring women over." Danielle scuttled around the high chairs and moved across the kitchen to where Paul stood. She removed a lid to one of the tall pots. "At least not since Shelby." She placed the lid back on the pot and peered over her shoulder. "So, Brooke, you can't blame us for being a bit excited."

Brooke replied with a crooked smile, "I understand. Thanks again for the invitation."

The mention of the woman who broke Logan's heart made her stomach twist.

"I'm glad you're here too." Logan nuzzled her neck. The feeling of him intimately close startled her at first, she tilted her chin up to meet his gaze. He dipped his head near her ear, close enough his breath tickled her neck. "I'm trying to sell this thing. Work with me," he whispered sending a zing through her.

How was he this good at pretending?

This is fake. This is fake. This is fake.

But part of her wished it was real. And the thought terrified her.

Amy puttered around the kitchen then opened the oven and pulled out a beautiful loaf of sourdough bread. Then she set it on the empty burner next to the large pot.

"My, that smells delicious," Brooke commented as her stomach rumbled loud enough for everyone in the room to hear. "I do have a thing for bread." She smirked at Logan, and his lips twitched mischievously like they shared an inside joke.

Everyone laughed, but she joined in too.

"I hope you like it. Logan didn't give us a heads up on any food allergies." Amy rubbed her hands together. "Do you have any?" Then she twisted her fingers into a knot. "I should've asked to double check."

"No food allergies."

The tight lines of Amy's forehead loosened. "That's a relief."

"I'm not a picky eater either," Brooke quickly added.

"Great." Amy directed Paul to carry the pot to the table. "Paul here made his famous Bolognese sauce. His mom was Italian."

"But my dad was Irish." Paul lifted the large pot with two pot holders and carried it to the table. "That's why these twins here have their strawberry blonde hair." He set the pot in the middle of the table on top of a pad.

Logan still had his arm around her shoulders. Warmth tickled down her spine, and Brooke leaned a bit of her weight against his firm chest, allowing herself to pretend for minute he really wanted to have his arm around her.

Amy sliced the bread and placed it on a wood platter. "Where is your family from, Brooke?"

"Yeah," Danielle piped up. "Did you grow up in Chicago?" She tossed some more puffs onto one of the twins high chair tray.

Brooke stilled. "No, I'm not from here." Logan squeezed her shoulders ever so slightly.

Her heartrate sped up. Flushed, she paused as she tried to figure out the best way to respond. She did not want to talk about her messed up family, drug addict and alcoholic mother or the dad who abandoned her before she ever really knew him. Logan's family obviously lived in another universe where people were kind and stable.

"She's from Virginia, a small town." Logan kissed her gently at the temple. Her skin sang from the touch of his lips. Part of her knew the feeling would last past the evening, while Logan wouldn't think about it another second. "And enough with the cross examination, you're making Brooke nervous." He dropped his arm. "Where do you want us to sit?" He peered over at Paul.

Gosh, Logan saved her. It made her like him even more.

Paul directed them to sit next to each other while Danielle and Michael sat across from them with a twin on each side of them. Amy placed the bread and salad down next to the pot of pasta. Then Amy and Paul took the seats at the heads of the table.

They passed the food around in a circle, family style. Danielle broke the bread and pasta into small pieces and placed it on the twins' trays. Brooke ate bits of her pasta.

"Brooke," Danielle said as she buttered her slice of bread. "I know you're a pediatrician, but please don't judge me when I let my girls have a little bit of the chocolate cake."

Brooke speared another pasta noodle. "I won't." She ate a bite of pasta. Then she wiped her face with her napkin. "I've seen the whole gamut of parenting in my line of work. I think there's nothing wrong with giving them a bite of cake. I can already tell you and Michael are great parents." Then she set her napkin back down on her lap and squeezed Logan's thigh. "And I can see why Logan is such a fantastic person. He had wonderful parents who supported him too." She tilted her chin toward Logan and caught his gaze and smiled.

Logan returned her smile then brushed her hair over one shoulder and kissed her right there on the tip of it. It was sweet and endearing and seemed much too real. The guy could act, because when she twisted back to face those at the table, Amy beamed back.

"We do have great parents," Danielle commented.

"The best," Logan added.

And although Brooke had thought that Amy's smile couldn't get any bigger, it did.

Paul cleared his throat. "Thank you. But I'm sure you have great parents too."

Brooke stared down at her plate and forced herself to start on her salad. Her lips pursed together as her shaky hand speared some lettuce. Heat smeared her cheeks. She shoved the salad into her mouth to keep from responding.

These situations never became easier. How much do you reveal about your past without making others look at you with pity? She chewed and wondered how to respond.

"Umm—" Brooke attempted to explain.

"Brooke's parents are—" Logan jumped in.

Brooke cut him off and said, "My parents are no longer living. And I don't really like talking about it."

Amy placed a hand on her forearm. "I'm so sorry to hear that. How terrible for you. I hope you at least have a sibling—" Her voice trailed off.

"No." Brooke ate another bite of her salad. "I was an only child."

"Wow, that's rough," Paul added as he set his water glass down. "How tragic."

"Yep." Brooke darted her gaze to her plate and shoveled another bite of salad into her mouth.

Logan piped up, "Have I told you yet how I met Brooke?" He peered over at her with a glint in his eyes. The attention made her stomach flip on itself.

There he went again, saving her like they were coconspirators.

"You said you met at the hospital," Danielle said with a look of confusion. "Did you lie about that?"

The twins squealed with delight as they made a mess of the pasta. Danielle swiped up some pasta the girls had tossed onto the floor though it was fruitless. Sauce smeared across their faces as they fisted food into their mouths.

"No, we did run into each other at the hospital," Logan added. "But we originally met at the grocery store."

Her lips twitched as she fought a smile. Logan wrapped an arm around her shoulders. He smirked.

"Please don't tell them about the bread," Brooke only half pleaded, and half teased. "I'm trying to make a good impression here."

"What bread?" Amy inquired.

He ran a finger down the length of her nose. "Not just any bread. French bread," Logan said.

"They'll never look at me the same after this." Brooke shook her head and grimaced. "I can't believe you're telling them this."

"Ooh," Danielle leaned forward and rested her elbow on the table to cradle her chin. "You have to spill now. We want details."

Logan shifted closer. His face hovered only inches from hers. She wondered if he might kiss her, then she reminded herself how ridiculous that would be.

He studied her for a moment. "Can I tell them?" Logan asked.

She didn't love the story of her rock bottom, but this had shifted the conversation away from her dead parents and sad past. If it kept his family from asking more questions, then she figured it wouldn't hurt.

"I guess," she exhaled the breath she didn't know she had been holding. "Go ahead."

Logan ran his hand down the length of her hair. It made her feel his touch everywhere. He shifted to face his eagerly waiting family and quickly rehashed how they met in the grocery store.

"I might have accused him of being a serial killer when he offered me the bag," Brooke heard herself reveal. "I watch a lot of true crime documentaries." She shrugged.

"I love true crime too," Amy said. "Paul watches them with me."

"But I'm not," Logan said. Then he motioned at the table filled with his family. "Right?" He raised an eyebrow.

"No." Brooke smiled and leaned her head against his shoulder. "You're not. You might be the best thing to ever buy me bread."

"Ahh." Amy cupped her hands together. "That might be the sweetest thing I have ever heard." Then she wagged a finger at them. "You can keep her, Logan. I approve. You two are meant for each other. I mean the woman loves bread."

Brooke chuckled. "And I love men who buy it for me."

"My secret weapon." Logan tightened his arm around her shoulders. It sent a tingling sensation down her spine, making the whole dinner feel real. Like this wasn't a fake relationship. Like Logan felt the sparks flying between them as their mutual attraction mounted. Like maybe someday she could find someone like him and have it all. "And it worked. I found you." He held her gaze far longer than normal.

She gulped. Her throat was raw and dry. The line between real and pretend muddled a bit more. For a moment, she forgot about everyone else in the room. Sweat gathered at her temples as her body fully flushed. A fiery glint filled his eyes. How could Logan fake this? Did he feel this mounting attraction too?

Paul cleared his throat, snapping her out of the weird trance she found herself in. Brooke looked away first and forced herself to pick her fork back up. The rest of dinner passed in an easy back and forth with less heat and less confusion.

With the main course and dessert done, Amy pushed her chair back. "We have a rule in our house whoever cooks doesn't clean up." She tossed her napkin onto her plate. "So, Brooke, let's leave the dishes to the men. Then we can go into the family room and visit for a while."

"Umm, last I checked I made the sauce." Paul raised an eyebrow. "Since when is this a rule?"

Amy whacked Paul on his arm. "Hush." Then she waved him off.

"Hey," Michael chimed in. "And what about me? I helped wash the tomatoes and cut them."

"But that doesn't count dear, you only assisted Paul with a little prep work, and Paul," she narrowed her gaze at him, "I cook almost every night, the least you can do is both tonight." They exchanged a look with one another.

"I'm happy to help with the dishes." Brooke gnawed on her bottom lip. The last thing she wanted to do was to be left alone with Amy. "I didn't do any cooking either. I should be the one to help."

"Nonsense." Amy stood and pushed in her chair. "The rule doesn't apply to guests, but to Logan who needs to learn to do the dishes. Come on. Let's leave the men to it." She waved her over.

Logan leaned in. His lip hovered near her ear. "I think you can't get out of this." His breath tickled her neck, "And Mom is about to grill you. I'm sorry," he whispered.

Brooke whispered back, "I know, you owe me. And remember this is just until the wedding."

A look of confusion crossed his face. "What wedding?"

She squeezed his forearm. "The one you have to go with me to as payback. Aubrey and Ian's, remember?"

"Right, right." He smiled back at those staring at them. He whispered. "You're doing great." He kissed her at the temple. "Only another thirty minutes then we're in the clear. Can you manage that long?"

His expression was open and sincere. Brooke knew if she said the word, he'd leave right then.

"I can tough it out another half hour." She squeezed his thigh. "I'm having a nice time."

"I am too." Logan pushed back his seat and grasped Brooke's plate stacking it on top of his own before he stood.

Danielle and Amy made quick work of wiping down the twins and lifting them out of their high chairs. They each carried one of the babies into the attached family room. Baby toys were shoved into every available corner. The sight made Brooke smile, because the space looked lived in and enjoyed.

Brooke settled onto the loveseat.

Danielle set Lily into a wide saucer thing while Amy put Amelia into a jumping chair which hung in the doorway which she assumed led to bedrooms. Faint noises came from the kitchen, running water, bustling of pots, and laughter. Brooke peered over at the men busy cleaning then reverted her attention back to those in the family room.

With the girls occupied, Amy and Danielle sat opposite of her on the couch. For a minute, they watched the babies bounce and play.

"Do you want kids?" Danielle asked out of the blue.

"Oh," Brooke shifted uncomfortably in her seat. "I—I—well." She didn't know how to answer. Sure, in a fantasy scenario where she married the perfect guy, she'd want kids. But she knew the consequences of having kids with someone who wasn't ready or didn't want them. She'd never put herself in that position. "Maybe, if I found the right person to have them with."

Amy whacked Danielle on the arm. "You're coming in a little strong there. Let's not scare her off."

Danielle rubbed her arm where Amy had whacked her. "I need to know, because Logan wants kids." She caught Brooke's gaze. "He's great with the twins by the way."

Brooke crossed then uncrossed her legs. "I would imagine he is."

"I think what Danielle is trying to say is—" Amy shot Danielle a pointed look. "If you and Logan continued to date, just know he'd be a good dad someday."

"Okay. I'll certainly take that into consideration."

Lily started to fuss. Danielle lifted her out of the saucer then placed her on the floor with a selection of toys. Amelia whined to be freed from her contraption. Danielle retrieved her too and set her down next to her sister. She let out a heavily tired sigh then brushed back some loosened strands of hair with the back of her wrist.

"I can only imagine how tired you must be," Brooke heard herself comment. Danielle plopped herself down on the floor next to her babies. "Whenever I see new mothers at the hospital, being around them for even minutes, I can sense their exhaustion. How is it going with not one, but two babies?"

"Honestly?" Danielle asked.

Brooke nodded.

"It's the hardest thing I've ever done. I'm always tired, always running on empty. Luckily, my parents have helped me a lot. Michael is a great dad too, so that is a bonus. But sometimes it feels like I'm drowning, and I wondered if I'll ever get to come up for air."

Suddenly, the dark circles under her eyes seemed more noticeable. Brooke wondered when the last time Danielle had a full night's sleep was. The twins crawled around on the floor then up and down on Danielle's outstretched legs. They clawed at every part of her, her pants, shirt, and necklace. Twins, wow, she was exhausted from only watching them. One crawled off of her first then the next. They scampered across the carpeted floor. Brooke tried to remember who Lily was and who was Amelia.

"I'm sorry. I've heard it gets better, at least that's what the moms who I see say," Brooke offered.

But her heart pinched tight, and she sincerely wanted to give help to Danielle, but she didn't know how. After today she'd drift away from this family's life never to be seen again. The twins moved on and fought over books then blocks. The three women watched the twins play and chatted about nothing of consequence.

Eventually, Logan came into the room. A few seconds later, Michael and Paul appeared behind him.

"Done already?" Brooke lifted her eyebrow.

Paul walked over and sat down next to Amy, wrapping his arm around her shoulders.

"Logan here," Michael came up and clapped his back, "managed to clean up in record speed. I think it might have been due to him wanting to see someone."

"Guilty. Brooke is my number one girl." Logan winked at her but then went over and plopped himself down next to the twins. He picked up Lily and held her high up in the air. She giggled with delight. Then he brought her back down and snuggled her against his chest. "But I needed to see my other girls before I have to leave, too."

Lily wiggled out of his embrace and crawled out of his lap. Danielle scurried off of the floor due to Logan occupying up so much space. To her surprise, she came and sat next to Brooke on the loveseat. Michael lowered himself into an accent chair. Logan stretched his legs out then twisted onto his side, propping himself up with one elbow. The twins quickly crawled over him. Up and down, they went over his body like it was a wonderful jungle gym. He laughed and tickled them. Love radiated in the room. Brooke watched in awe. She'd never seen a man interact with children in such a natural and easy way. Her pulse raced. If Logan didn't become a father someday, the world would be deprived of his goodness.

"See," Danielle whispered. "I told you he was good with kids. I'd hate to see his fatherly instinct wasted."

"I—I—" Brooke swallowed. Perspiration tickled her temples. She hated lying to these kind unassuming people. His family wanted the best for him, and he deserved it. He deserved anyone but her. "I agree."

Danielle patted her on her forearm. "Then we are on the same page."

What page?

Marry and have a couple of kids page?

If only they knew this was a lie, a lie that would only carry on until her friend's wedding.

Her skin itched. "Logan," her voice cracked. She swiped at the perspiration on her temple and cleared her throat. This evening must end, immediately. When he didn't appear to hear her, she repeated louder, "Logan—"

He glanced over his shoulder and met her gaze. "Yeah?" He studied her.

"I need—" Brooke fidgeted with her watch, "to head home. Remember, I have an early shift at the hospital tomorrow?"

Her pulse galloped. She couldn't stay any longer in this home, not when her relationship with Logan wasn't real. Logan needed to be here with Shelby. Shelby was the person for him, she'd fit.

"Oh." Logan quickly sat up. His lips formed a tight smile. "Right, I completely forgot." He kissed each of the twins on their heads then stumbled to his feet.

Brooke scooted off the loveseat and readjusted her blouse as she stood. "It was nice meeting all of you." She glanced around the room and tried to flash her best smile.

Everyone rose to their feet in a rush. Danielle and Michael each scooped up a baby. Amy and Paul crossed the room.

"Thank you for coming." Without hesitation, Amy pulled her into a hug. "I'm glad Logan found you," she whispered before she let go.

Logan hugged everyone goodbye.

With Lily on her hip, Danielle moved closer to Brooke. "Sorry." She avoided eye contact and glanced down at Lily. "I shouldn't have brought up Logan wanting kids. I apologize if I made things awkward."

Brooke cupped Lily's cheek with her hand and didn't find Danielle's gaze. "It's fine." She brushed the baby's cheek then dropped her hand. "I know you only want what's best for him. Don't worry, I want that too."

"I want my brother to be happy," Danielle added.

And it's not you.

Those were the words left unsaid.

The sting of rejection made her chest tighten. She wasn't even good enough as a fictional girlfriend.

"I know." Brooke smiled and met Danielle's gaze. She pulled back her shoulders and straightened her back. "I want him to be happy too."

Logan finished his goodbyes and came up next to her. He placed a hand on the small of her back. Her body warmed to his touch. He leaned in closer for only her to hear when he said, "Let's get you out of here."

More goodbyes followed, since one didn't seem to be enough for this family. His parents walked them to the front door and watched as they walked to their car. Brooke waved back to them. Logan made it to the car and opened her door. She scooted into her passenger seat.

"I know they are a lot—" Logan gripped the corner of the car door and peered over to his parents' front door. They had wandered back inside. He twisted back at her. He scratched his chin. "Did my sister say something weird?"

"No." Brooke leaned back in her seat. "She was fine. But she did mention how you wanted kids." Then as an afterthought, she added, "I think she doesn't think I fit the bill for you."

Logan groaned and leaned his forehead against his hand.

"I told her I'd only have kids if I found the right person." He popped his head back up. "Sounds like a reasonable answer to me, right?"

"Totally." Brooke fidgeted with the end of her jacket. "I'll never see them again, and I bought you a little time, so you're welcome."

"Thanks." He straightened himself. "Hey, we survived, right? Soon this will be a distant memory for them. And you won't need to worry about my sister who doesn't know boundaries."

Logan might forget her.

His family might forget her.

But Brooke knew Logan was one person she'd remember, forever.

"So true." Brooke placed her hand flat against his hard abdomen and gazed up at him. "And for what it's worth, I had a nice time even with Danielle. But I started to feel guilty lying to them. They really care about you. It was refreshing to be around a family, especially parents who want what's best for their kids. You're blessed with a beautiful family. I hope you can find someone who can slide right into the missing spot next to you."

"Me too." Logan rubbed the back of his neck.

"You—"

A voice from behind interrupted them.

"Logan?"

They peered over their shoulders toward the voice. *Shelby.* She knew it, because she had the look. Brooke's gut clenched. A beautiful blonde with long flowy hair floated on over to the car. Logan's back stiffened. He shifted back to face Brooke, and they locked eyes. Understanding passed between them. Logan let go of the corner of the car door.

He leaned his back against the car. "Shelby, what are you

doing here?" He plunged a hand into his pocket and made no attempts to move closer.

She called it.

Her heart plummeted.

Brooke glanced quickly between Logan and Shelby. And in a snap, hope vanished. The one who got away would win again.

CHAPTER 7

Even years later, Logan knew he could pick up Shelby's voice from anywhere. Crowded restaurant, yep. A sprawling park, absolutely. The whisper in the church pew four rows back, unfortunately yes.

Which was why his body nearly convulsed when she said his name. And he knew then he'd never be free. And he hated her for it.

"Shelby." Sweat slathered his brow despite the wind chill seeping through his jacket. "This is a surprise."

"Yes, a good one." Shelby shoved her hands into the front of her puffy coat. "You look great." Her hungry eyes roamed his body. "Have you been working out?"

"No." His jaw locked and he tried to ignore his mounting blood pressure. "Did Danielle ask you to come by?" His brow furrowed.

"What?" Shelby shook her head. Her blonde hair cascaded down her shoulders and across her back. "No, I was only out for a walk." She peered past him to Brooke in the car.

Shelby looked the same as though she somehow mystically bypassed the challenges of time. His stomach swooned without his consent. He willed himself to stay in the present and remind himself of the pain she caused him. Being attracted to Shelby had never been the issue, her treatment of him had been.

"Do you live around here?" Logan asked.

"I thought Danielle told you." Shelby stepped closer. "I moved in across the street from her."

What?

He nearly peed his pants.

"I thought she ran into you at the grocery store," he countered.

"Yes, true." Shelby removed her hand from her pocket and scratched her nose. "Then we figured out I had moved in across the street. I mean what are the odds?" She smiled.

His mind reeled. How could Danielle have failed to mention this huge bit of information? Every time he went to visit her, he'd wonder if he had a chance of running into Shelby again. Ugh. The thought made him nauseous. He ran a hand through his hair.

"It's my first house," Shelby added.

"You don't say." His back stiffened.

And so, the unraveling began.

"Sorry." Shelby glanced over at Brooke and waved. "We're being really rude. I'm Shelby."

Duh, he'd completely forgotten Brooke had a front row seat to this train wreck of a moment.

Brooke climbed out of her seat and straightened her blouse. "I'm Brooke."

He slid an arm around Brooke's waist and gently brought her closer to his body. "Brooke's my girlfriend."

"Guilty." Brooke placed a hand on Logan's chest and smiled brightly. "Logan is all mine." She scrunched up her nose and gazed up at him adoringly.

"Oh," Shelby blinked. "So, she's real."

His neck ached. He longed to crank it back and forth to relieve the tension.

"Despite what Danielle may or may not have told you," His fingertips dipped into Brooke's waist. "Brooke is real, and we couldn't be happier together."

"Great to hear." Shelby pressed her lips together for a second. "I guess I'd better let you go. It was nice seeing you again. Maybe I'll see you around." Then she swiveled quickly and headed in the opposite direction before he had time to say goodbye.

He stared dumbfounded as he watched Shelby grow smaller and smaller on the sidewalk.

Brooke exhaled. "So, that's the famous ex."

"Yeah." Logan unfolded his arm from around her. Then he rubbed the back of his neck. "That's her. Do you think she bought us being together?"

He hated how much he wanted the answer to be yes. Would he ever be rid of this grip she had on him?

"Totally." Brooke smiled. "You're golden. She was definitely jealous. That's why she took off so fast." She patted him lightly on his chest. "You're welcome."

A calm washed over him and soothed the knot out of his stomach. "That's a relief." He plunged his hand into his pocket and retrieved his keys. "Thanks again. You played the part perfectly."

"I know." Her eyes glinted with mischievousness. "I guess I'm a better actor than I thought."

Logan fidgeted with his keys and stared back in the direction Shelby disappeared. He wondered if she'd replay this conversation on repeat in her mind like he would.

"You're still hung up on her," Brooke stated.

He snapped his head back to face her. "No," he replied far too quickly. His keys jangled in his hands. "Ugh, okay—she's still beautiful, but she's still Shelby."

"Okay—" Brooke paused then slowly nodded. "I'll help you come up with a plan to win her back. We can make this work for you."

"I didn't say that was what I wanted." Logan avoided her gaze as he stared down at his keys. He swung one key around the ring over and over again. "But I'd be lying if I didn't say she still did it for me."

"Exactly." Brooke slid back into her seat and buckled her seatbelt. "Now, let's get out of here. I've seen your parents peek out of the front window three times. We need to go before they start to think there is something wrong. You're into Shelby, and I'm going to help you win her back. Wasn't this the entire reason I came?"

"No." Logan shifted to glance back at his house. Immediately, the curtains swooshed back into place. "I brought you to get my family off my back."

"Right, but now we have a new plan." She playfully nudged him. "Let's go. I'm freezing."

Logan fisted his keys in one hand and shut her door. By the time he rounded the car and slid into his spot Brooke's teeth chattered loud enough for him to hear. He started the engine and cranked up the heat to full blast. They waited as the windows defrosted. She shivered then resorted to rubbing her hands together to bring some heat to her icy fingers.

"Here." Logan cupped his hands around hers. He rubbed his hands over hers, attempting to warm them up. "Your hands are freezing." He commented like an idiot.

"I've always had cold extremities. My mom used to say it was because I was cold hearted."

Whoa, that was some deep layer messed up stuff. He mulled over how to respond. His words needed to incite trust rather than push her away.

"I think your mom was completely wrong." He continued to rub her hands. They warmed bit by bit. "Maybe she was the one who had the cold heart."

Brooke wiggled her hands out of his. "You don't have to

pretend anymore." She shoved her hands into her pockets and leaned back in her seat.

"Pretend what?"

"That we're together," she peered out the passenger side window, "and that you want to touch me."

His stomach twisted. The lines between real and fake smeared together. He liked being with Brooke and enjoyed having her visit his family. He even for a minute imagined them in a real relationship with real feelings. Then, he saw Shelby. Everything tumbled back into place quickly. His years of self-work gone in a snap. He hated himself for it.

He desperately needed to move the conversation in a better direction, but he didn't have the bandwidth to figure out how. Instead, Logan shifted the car out of park and merged onto the road. The sounds of the radio spilled out of the speakers and filled the silent void. A trendy pop song with a catchy beat matched the staccato pump of his pulse. The trees which lined his parents' neighborhood slowly faded behind them and the entrance to the expressway appeared.

"For what it's worth," he broke the silence, "I'm glad you came today." He directed his car onto the on ramp.

She grunted an indistinguishable reply.

He continued, "I'm also positive in about ten minutes Mom will be calling to tell me how much she loved you."

"I don't think so." Brooke folded her arms across her middle. "I saw your entire family watching the exchange you had with Shelby on the lawn. If your mom calls, it will be about her, not me."

"Oh." He scratched at the scruff on his jaw. "You might be right. But I know she'll ask about you, too."

"You're lucky." Brooke shifted in his seat to face him. "You have a whole house full of people who love you and want the best for you. I'm really glad you have them. It was beautiful to see a family who loved one another."

"As much as they annoy me— I know I'm lucky." He merged over lanes then set the car on cruise control. Another spell of silence filled the car. "Do you really think I made Shelby jealous?"

Brooke let out an exaggerated sigh. "Are we back to talking about her again?" She peered out her passenger window again.

"I know." He shook his head. "I'm sorry. It's like my mind gets stuck on this Shelby track. I haven't been on it for a long time, but here I am I see her once then bam I can't shake the idea of her away."

"I get it." She unfolded her arms then clasped her hands together in her lap. "It's hard to let go of the one who rejects us. Maybe this will be your chance to win her back or let her go for good." Her shoulders drooped.

"Or maybe I can make her jealous. I could live with that."

"Okay," Brooke simply replied. "If that's what you need."

"The best would be if she accidentally sees us together again when I go to visit Danielle and Michael's house sometime."

This might work.

"I don't know—" Brooke shook her head. "I agreed to one dinner in exchange for one wedding date. That was the deal."

He saw it play out before his very eyes. Shelby would finally regret her rash choice when she saw him and Brooke being ridiculously happy, she'd finally regret letting him go. Yes, this was his chance to make her feel the sting..

"Please, will you go on another fake date with me?" Logan flashed her a crooked smile.

"Why?" Brooke asked flatly.

"Because we're friends," he offered.

"Right, friends." Brooke rested her head against the headrest and stared out the passenger side window. A long lull weaved through the car. Her jaw tightened a smidge. "I'll do one more fake date for you." She held up a finger. "But it'll cost you."

"Sure, anything."

He straightened his back as excitement raced through him.

"There's some concert tickets I have. I bought them over a year ago, I thought Justin would go with me." Her voice sounded small. "Will you go with me?"

"That's it?" He raised an eyebrow.

"Yeah, we could go as friends."

"I'd love to go with you." He genuinely smiled, because he did enjoy Brooke's company. "Text me the date and time, and I'll ask for the day off."

Brooke retrieved her phone from her purse. "I'll find the email with the information about the concert."

"We could grab dinner before the concert," he offered.

"I'd love that." Brooke scrolled on her phone then tapped. "I'll send the email to you, and I'll research restaurants."

Their exit came into view as the sights of downtown emerged on the horizon. He merged over and exited the expressway.

His phone rang.

Brooke glanced over. "Is that who you think it is?"

"If you mean, Mom, then yes." He slowed the car down near the stoplight at the end of the exit. "I'm positive it's her. I'll call her back after I drop you off."

Then he weaved through the streets of downtown until he stopped in front of her building. Brooke unbuckled her seat belt.

With one hand on the steering wheel, Logan said, "Thanks for coming today."

"You're welcome." She opened her door and climbed out. "I'll see you soon." Her purse slipped, and she readjusted it on her shoulder.

"Yes," he agreed. "Soon."

Brooke shut the door and wandered to the front door of her building. A different doorperson opened the door, and she disappeared inside.

Logan drove home. By the time he parked his car in his underground spot, his phone had dinged ten times. Plus, Mom had called twice.

When he walked across the parking garage toward the elevator, he picked up his ringing phone. "Geez Mom." He made it to the elevator bay and punched the up button. "I'm not even up to my apartment, and I didn't want to answer the phone with Brooke in the car."

"She's perfect for you," Mom gushed.

In the background, Danielle yelled, "Did you finally get a hold of him?"

Mom yelled out, "He finally picked up."

Logan held the phone further away from his ear to save his ear drums. The elevator opened, and he entered. After he hit his floor, the doors swung shut and the elevator sprung into action.

"Put it on speaker phone," Danielle hollered in the background. "I want to hear everything first hand."

"Okay." Her voice nearly blew out his speaker. "Danielle wants me to put it on speaker."

"Yeah, I heard."

He leaned his back against the wall of the elevator and shifted his phone from one ear to the other.

"Get over here Danielle, I'm not waiting any longer," Mom hollered.

"Coming!" Danielle shouted.

Logan smiled to himself, because the ruse had worked. He knew they had taken the bait, hook, line, and sinker. He made it to his floor and left the elevator making his way to his apartment.

"You're on speaker," Mom announced.

"Why is it so quiet?" He landed in front of his apartment. "Where are the twins?"

"Michael and Dad took the girls home to nap," Danielle said.

"Makes sense." He opened his apartment door then tossed his keys onto the tray where he kept them. Then he proceeded to shut the door with his foot. "You called me a thousand times, out with it." Logan plopped himself on his couch.

"We wanted to talk to you about Brooke," Mom said.

"Okay," he tread lightly.

"I thought she was perfect for you," Mom blurted out.

Danielle remained silent which wasn't like her. He waited to see if she planned on adding anything to the conversation, after all, she wanted to be on it.

He shifted on his seat. "Danielle, you're silence on the subject of Brooke is speaking volumes." Then he ran a hand through his hair and down the length of his face.

"We saw you talking to Shelby outside," Danielle stated.

"Yeah, and you *failed* to tell me she moved in across the street," Logan countered.

"Shelby looked good, didn't she?" Danielle said.

Logan didn't respond but he hated that the answer remained a resounding yes. He'd hoped she'd gone off and lost her teeth and let herself go, instead she somehow had managed to get better looking. *She rejected you. She dumped you. She left you broken hearted. Don't go there.*

"We aren't talking about Shelby. I never liked her," Mom interrupted. Then she whispered something to Danielle he couldn't decipher. She cleared her throat. "Let's circle on back to Brooke. Now, she is the one for you."

"I disagree with Mom. Shelby is who you need to pursue."

"Lucky for the both of you, you don't get a say in my relationship choices." Logan pinched the bridge of his nose. "But really Danielle, you could've given me a heads up on Shelby being your neighbor. I might even go so far as to say you maybe told Shelby when to walk right on by to run into me. I smell something fishy with the entire interaction."

"I'm pushy but not that pushy," Danielle scoffed. "That was purely a serendipitous moment."

"It wasn't anything of the sort." Logan raked his hair again. His fingers went numb. "I am happy with Brooke."

"Of course, he is," Mom chimed in. "I've never seen him look so happy."

Mom muttered something else to Danielle. He waited, because clearly, they planned on discussing his relationship with one another and not him. Wait, he reminded himself it was a fake relationship.

"When do we get to see her again?" Mom piped up. "I hope we didn't scare her off."

"I'm not sure," he stalled. "We both have busy schedules over the next few weeks—" His voice trailed off.

"Dad and I don't mind driving into the city for dinner one evening," Mom said.

"I don't know—"

Quickly, Logan tried to figure out when and how their fake relationship could end.

"I want to come," Danielle interjected. "It's about time Michael and I went on a proper date without the twins. The neighbor across the street said she'd babysit for us."

"You mean Shelby?" Logan grumbled. "She's your neighbor across the street, right?"

"Yes, but I don't even know if she can do it. I have a few options. Besides we would be coming into the city, and you don't need to be concerned about who watches the girls."

His jaw twitched. "We're both swamped for the rest of the month. It would have to be next month."

This imaginary date he had no intention of seeing to fruition.

"How about the first week of next month?" Mom asked.

"Maybe."

"I'll take that as a yes until I hear otherwise," Mom said.

"I saw this restaurant on social media I want to try," Danielle added.

"Fine, we'll hash out the details later. I need to run it by Brooke. Talk to you soon."

Then Logan hung up before any future plans with his fake girlfriend could be made.

CHAPTER 8

A week later, Brooke perused the racks of wedding dresses. One dress caught her eye. Little intricate beads covered the bodice then spread down the length of the full skirt. She ran her finger over the beadwork. She wondered if she'd ever have a chance to wear something so beautiful. Her heart ached. A deep loneliness settled inside her. Her hand lingered far too long on the delicate pattern the beads made. Would she ever find someone who loved her enough to marry her? The thought vibrated around in her head as she traced each bead.

"Can I get you something to drink?" asked the voice from behind her.

Brooke flinched. Then she shoved the dress to the left and busied herself with examining the next dress on the rack. "No. I'm fine," she replied with a quick glance over her shoulder at the attendant. "My friend should be out soon. She is trying on her wedding dress for her final fitting. I couldn't help myself from browsing through the dresses here. Not that I'm in need of one."

The wedding dress attendant came up next to her and flipped through a few of the hanging dresses. "These are the newest dresses in the shop." She located the one Brooke had studied.

"This one was a special order from a designer in Paris. You have very good taste."

"Paris?" Brooke stepped back. Her skin itched. She knew she'd never have a need for a dress from Paris. She had been so foolish in looking at them in the first place. "Paris. I'd love to go someday," she added for no particular reason.

Brooke hadn't been anywhere. While many of her classmates in college enjoyed study-abroad financed by their parents, she could barely scrape together enough to save for a weekend in Florida with friends over spring break. Paris, who was she kidding?

"They don't call it," the attendant shuffled through the dresses and pulled one from the rack, "the city of love for nothing." She held it in front of Brooke's body. "I think the dress is perfect for you."

"I'm not in the market to buy a wedding dress." Brooke stiffened in place. Her neck tightened. "I don't even have a boyfriend." She stepped further from the dress until her back hit the hanging clothes.

"Have you ever heard of manifesting?" The attendant placed the dress back on the rack then rifled through a few more. Eventually, she removed another dress and held it up in front of Brooke's body. "I'm a big believer in it."

"I think you're only trying to sell wedding dresses," Brooke muttered.

The wedding dress attendant laughed. "I think you need to manifest getting married." She tilted her head as she examined the dress she placed in front of Brooke's body. "Visualize it in your mind, then boom, someday it'll come true. Buy a dress today and trust me someday your prince will come."

"How many women have you told this to?" Brooke sidestepped around the dress and moved back to the middle of the shop.

"Not many," the attendant traipsed behind her with the dress still in her arms. "But it worked for them."

"How would you know? You only sold them a dress. You don't know if they actually are married now." Brooke crossed her arms and peered in the direction Aubrey disappeared to earlier. She wanted her to make an appearance, fast. The sooner they left this land of sunshine and rainbows the better.

"The cost of wedding dresses will only continue to rise. Buy a dress today and lock in the price."

This lady needed to learn to read the room.

Brooke put a finger under her collar and tugged. "I'm not buying a dress, even if that is your hard sell. It isn't happening. I'm having to bring a fake boyfriend to my friend's wedding, so I don't have to feel like a complete loser in front of my ex-boyfriend and his new arm candy. I'm miles away from purchasing anything. I'll take my chances with price fluctuation."

"Okay—" She awkwardly placed the dress back on the rack then straightened some of the dresses next to it. "Have it your way."

Then to her great relief, Aubrey appeared in her wedding dress.

Brooke sidestepped around the wedding dress attendant. "Aubrey!" She squeaked a tad too loud as her gaze roamed Aubrey's form. "You look incredible. I forgot how much that dress highlights your best features." She walked the rest of the way to where Aubrey stood in front of a wall of mirrors, angled in every direction for a perfect view of the entire dress.

"Thanks." Aubrey beamed as her hand ran down the front of her dress. "I love it as much as I remember, and luckily the adjustments they made are perfect." She made an okay sign at herself in the mirror.

Brooke lowered herself into one of the white cushy armchairs in a semicircle facing the wall of mirrors. "Can you take the dress home today?" She dropped her purse by her feet. "Or do you have to come back?"

The wedding attendant from before appeared with a veil in her hands. "Here, let me place this on your hair." She came up from behind and attached the veil into Aubrey's hair.

"Ahh," Brooke gushed. "You look gorgeous. Ian is going to lose his mind when he sees you."

"You think so?" Aubrey twisted this way then the other, getting a full look at herself. "I do love this dress."

"Absolutely, and I can see why." Brooke watched as Aubrey admired her reflection in the mirror.

"If you're happy with everything," the attendant stepped up and removed the veil, "I'll help you out of this dress. Then we'll steam it before you take it home today, and you'll be ready for your wedding day."

"Only two more weeks until my big day." Aubrey took hold of the large bottom half of her dress, lifting it up enough to walk. "It feels surreal."

"It'll be here in a snap." The attendant motioned toward the dressing room. "Let's get you out of this dress and on your way."

Aubrey walked back to the dressing room with the attendant traipsing behind her.

Brooke leaned back in her cushy chair and waited. Her phone dinged, and she retrieved it from her purse. A message from Logan flashed across the screen.

> What time should I swing by for the concert? I checked out the route there and we can take the L train.

Since meeting his parents, Logan hadn't really touched base with her, not like before. Their nightly text messaging and calls had stopped. They had run into each other a few times at the hospital. She guessed the ruse was up, and she reminded herself this would just be until the wedding. Then Logan would drop from her life completely. Brooke figured by now Logan might be reacquainted with Shelby.

Brooke smiled and typed.

Are you sure you are still up for it? I haven't heard from you for a while, and I figured it was off.

It's far from off. I want to go with you to the concert. I was looking forward to it, I've just been busy. Sorry

Busy with Shelby.

Ok

Okay, now when and where do I pick you up?

Great, swing by my place tomorrow at six we can catch the L Train and eat at a place by the concert. Sound good? Or I can text you your ticket and we can meet each other at the venue.

"Who are you texting?" Aubrey asked, appearing out of nowhere, back in her normal outfit.

She plopped herself down in the cushion chair next to Brooke.

"Oh—" Brooke flashed her gaze to Aubrey then back to her phone screen. She watched the cursor dots dance at the bottom of their text chain. "Logan."

"Ahh." Aubrey leaned back in her chair and folded her arms. "I'm glad things are going well for you guys. You deserve it, especially after Justin." She peered out at the racks of gowns.

Brooke hadn't clued Aubrey into Logan and her fake dating agreement. Fake dating Logan meant Aubrey didn't worry about her anymore. She liked that part. And she also knew Aubrey had told Ian about it, who no doubt passed the information onto Justin. A fact she enjoyed a smidge too much.

"Thanks." Brooke kept her gaze on her phone, watching the dots dance at the bottom of their text chain. "He's been a fun distraction from Justin."

Not a lie. And it's just until the wedding, and you'll never need to know about my little arrangement.

A message flashed across her screen.

No, dinner sounds good. I'll swing by at six.

The dots at the bottom continued to dance. Another text shot through.

Another favor—

Oh dear, what do you need me to do now? Make out with you in front of Shelby to make her remember how great you were at kissing?

No nothing like that

Then what? Just ask

Instead of cashing in on my fake date for a night at Danielle and Michael's house. Would you go on a triple date in the city with my parents and sister?

Brooke gnawed on her bottom lip. When she met Logan's family she really didn't think she'd ever see them again. This fake dating was beginning to feel a little too real, but she still needed a date to the wedding. Afterwards, they could part ways as friends.

She typed back.

I could probably grin and bear it. But that means you are paying for dinner before the concert.

A message appeared almost immediately.

Deal. You're the best, Brookie.

Hey, no nicknames. We're nowhere near the nickname level of friendship.

I beg to differ.

No nicknames!

We'll see about that, my Brookie. See you at six.

She shoved her phone back into her purse. Then she peered over at Aubrey who grinned at her.

Aubrey winked. "Don't you just love the beginning part of a relationship?"

"I don't know." Brooke shifted uncomfortably in her seat. "Usually, the middle part is the best. By then the honeymoon stage has worn off, but you still aren't sick of each other."

The endings, she didn't care for those either. They often were too sad and came too soon.

Playfully, Aubrey shoved her. "Hey, Ian and I are still in the honeymoon stage, and I'm marrying him in two weeks. I love it."

"I know." Brooke smiled. "But some of us don't get to live in a fantasy world where we marry the man of our dreams."

"Maybe Logan will be your happy ending."

"Perhaps."

If only she knew the truth, Logan had the hots for Shelby not her. As they were only friends, she didn't dare let herself dream about anything more even if she did like how broad his shoulders were or how he raked his hair when it fell in his eyes.

Aubrey's phone dinged, and she fished her phone out of her purse. "Justin and Ian are a few shops down doing their tuxedo fittings." She scrolled through the message with her pointer finger. "Looks like they're going to stop by since it's around the corner. Then we're headed to dinner. Do you want to join us?"

"Is Justin going?" Brooke fidgeted with her watch, twisting it unnecessarily.

"Yes." Aubrey nodded as she typed something into her phone, partly distracted. "But come, it could be fun—"

"No, I'm good." Brooke forced her hand away from her watch. "That's the complete opposite of what I consider fun."

Aubrey slid her phone back into her purse. "Okay. I understand." She propped her elbow on the armrest of her chair. They sat for a minute in uncomfortable silence, because bringing up Justin always made things weird between them. She picked at a piece of lint on the front of her blouse.

"I sat Justin and you at entirely different parts of the room for the wedding reception dinner," Aubrey said. "You only have to get through the ceremony."

"Don't worry, I'll behave." Brooke folded her arms. "Besides, Logan will be there."

"That's right." The tense lines on Aubrey's forehead loosened. "You'll have Logan."

Brooke patted her friend's arm. "I won't ruin your big day. I promise."

"I wasn't implying—"

A door chimed, interrupting her. Justin and Ian entered. The door swung closed behind them. Justin caught her gaze. She rolled her eyes and darted her glance back to the center of the room. She could behave, but it didn't mean she needed to look excited about seeing Justin. They walked over to where they sat.

"We finished the fitting." Ian leaned down and kissed Aubrey. "Did everything go okay with the dress?" He brushed some loosened strands of Aubrey's hair behind her ear.

They did appear to be in love. It made Brooke's heart happy and sad at the same time. A twinge of something stung her, and she forced the feelings of inadequacy and loneliness away. Her friend found happiness. Maybe someday she'd find her person too. Isn't that how we continued to hope or believe in love? Brooke had to lean into the hope of someone, because she didn't want to waste her life away with bitterness.

The wedding dress attendant appeared with the long dress bag. "I have your dress right here, freshly steamed and ready to go." She held it out to Aubrey.

Aubrey and Brooke rose to their feet.

"Thanks." Aubrey accepted the hand off of the dress and draped it over one arm. Then she looked at Ian. "You have your car, right?"

Aubrey and Brooke had taken the L train across town to the wedding dress shop. Clearly, Aubrey had failed to mention they wouldn't be returning together.

"Yes." He peered over his shoulder to the exit. "The tuxedo place had a parking lot behind their shop."

"Great." Aubrey readjusted the dress in her arms. "Then we can drop Brooke off on the way to dinner."

"Oh." Brooke waved the suggestion away. "I'm fine to take the train home."

She had zero desire to share a back seat with Justin for the duration of the ride. Even if the car ride would cut her travel time in half.

"Just take the ride home," Justin muttered with no attempt to hold back his annoyance. "I promise not to talk to you. We can ignore each other the whole time, you're good at that." His words had an edge to them.

Apparently, he forgot he left her. But he was good at forgetting, because he had already forgotten their time together. She needed to do the same.

You can't let him win. You can't let him know he hurt you.

"Okay, then I accept." Brooke adjusted her purse strap. "Thanks for dropping me off on your way."

Ian blew out a rattly breath. "Then follow me." He took the white dress bag from Aubrey and waved everyone to follow him.

They left the warmth of the dress shop and weaved around a few shops and down a back alley until they arrived at his car. Gingerly, Ian loaded the dress into the trunk of the car. Then they climbed in. Ian and Aubrey sat up front. Justin and Brooke settled into the back seat. Luckily, when Ian started the engine, the radio blared and filled the car with its obnoxious noise. Brooke appreciated Ian didn't turn the volume down. Even he seemed to know this car ride would be awkward for everyone.

Brooke gazed out her passenger window and stared at the tall skyscrapers as they weaved through the city. She didn't glance at Justin once.

But then Justin interrupted the silence, he whispered, "Do you have a date for their wedding?" He leaned across the empty seat between them, making himself far too close.

Brooke flashed him a pointed glance. Then she shifted and scooted her body as close to the window as possible. "Why do you care?" She hissed as she peered back out the window. "You don't get to worry about me anymore."

Her blood simmered a touch below the boiling point.

"I feel bad— I don't want you to have to go alone."

"I see," she muttered low enough so Aubrey and Ian couldn't hear. "By some miracle you've seemed to find your conscience again. If you, for some unknown reason, need me to set you free from guilt, just know I'm fine."

"Great to hear," he muttered. Justin adjusted the sleeves of his jacket. Then whispered under his breath, "Will you ever not hate me?"

"I don't hate you." Brooke shifted and faced him. "Dislike you, yes, but I decided a long time again not to waste my time hating anyone. But why do you care?"

"I just do." His voice sounded small.

She found his response unrecognizable from his normal overly confident demeanor.

"If you must know," Brooke sat up straighter, "I'm going with Logan to the wedding."

Justin lifted an eyebrow. "Dr. Schofield?" His lips pinched a bit. "The new general surgeon?"

"Yep." Smugly, Brooke smirked. "The very one."

"Are you two dating?" Justin wiggled around in his seat. "Since when?"

"You promised me no small talk." Brooke saw her street coming into view. She spoke over the radio and leaned between the two front seats. "You can pull up to the curb after this light."

"You've got it." Ian eased through the intersection then stopped at the curb.

Brooke unbuckled her seatbelt and climbed out of the car. "Have a great night everyone. Aubrey, I'll see you tomorrow at work." Then to her great satisfaction, she shut the door and walked to her building. This time Justin got to be the one with all the questions and none of the answers.

CHAPTER 9

Logan walked briskly from the hospital to Brooke's apartment. His long and stressful day had him in a weird headspace. One of the surgeries had numerous complications. While it ultimately turned out okay, the entire experience had left him anxious. He knew Brooke loved this band, and he didn't want his off mood to dampen the evening.

Her apartment came into view. George was stationed outside again. Logan waved then fetched his phone out of his pocket. He shot Brooke a quick text to let her know he had arrived as he neared the lobby door.

As he slid his phone back into his pocket, he greeted George. "Good evening."

George smiled when he recognized him. "I see you're back to take Brooke out. I knew you had a good head on your shoulders."

"Thanks." Logan shuffled his feet and looked down at them. He hated lying about their relationship, but he genuinely considered Brooke to be a friend. "But we're only friends."

"Sure." George winked then opened the glass door into the building. *"Friends."*

"No, it's true." Logan didn't even know why he felt the need to explain their arrangement to him. "But I enjoy hanging out with her."

"Hanging out," George repeated like it was a four-letter curse word. "And your generation of men wonder why they are single and unmarried."

Logan rubbed the back of his neck. "I don't wonder that." He passed through the open door and into the lobby to wait.

"See, even worse." Then George closed the door and returned to his post outside.

The elevator doors swung open. Brooke stepped out. With a peacoat jacket slung over her arm, she wore dark jeans, and a black button-down blouse tucked into it. A shiny gold necklace and the bangles on her wrist made her practically sparkle. Her cute boots racketed against the tile floor of the lobby. He stared in awe. The familiar uptick of his pulse made his breath hitch.

For a brief second, he glanced down at his outfit. He wore a simple henley long sleeve navy tee, black puffer jacket, and jeans. For a split second, he questioned everything."Wow," he finally voiced. "You look incredible."

She halted in front of him. "Thanks." Her cheeks splashed with red, making them adorably rosy. She shifted her coat from one arm to the other. "You look great yourself."

"No, I don't." He forced a laugh. "I came straight from the hospital, and this was what I had left in my locker that was half way presentable. Believe it or not, I mainly wear scrubs or workout clothes to and from work."

Brooke bit her bottom lip. "Was it a long day?"

"Yeah." He sighed and ran a hand through his hair. "But I'm happy to be here with you."

She scrunched up her nose. "That bad?" Her gaze scrutinized him again.

"I almost lost a patient during surgery, but it ended up being okay." He rubbed the back of his neck. His blood pressure rose a bit as he recalled the harrowing experience. It was part of the job, but it didn't mean it didn't affect him. "The whole experience shook me up a bit."

"I can only imagine."

He dropped his hand. "If I'm being honest, it made me question my abilities as a surgeon." Logan wondered why he was revealing everything to Brooke, because normally he bottled everything up.

"Ahh." She nodded then stepped closer to him. Her hand grazed his arm until she squeezed his bicep. "I'm sorry. It's never easy when things like that happen, but I believe you're an incredible doctor and surgeon. Things happen, you're only human. I think giving yourself grace is essential."

"That is easier said than done." His arm warmed through the layers of his coat. He wondered how long her hand would remain on his arm, because he liked the feeling of her closeness. Her fruity perfume made his head spin. He gulped trying to remind himself he had unresolved feelings for Shelby. Didn't he? What he wanted and what he had muddled together in a jumbled mix. "I'll try to take that advice to heart."

"You don't have to come with me tonight. You can be off the hook and head home." Brooke squeezed his bicep again then let go. "I totally understand if it's too much."

Logan wrapped an arm around her shoulders, tugging her closer until their hips touched. "Are you kidding me?" He glanced down at her. "I've been looking forward to spending the evening with you all day."

A surprise look flashed across her face. "Really?"

"Absolutely. We're friends, right?" He removed his arm from her shoulders. "Now let me help you into your coat." His head nodded toward the glass door. "Or I think George will think less of me, because he's being eyeing me since I came in. I can't let him down."

Brooke laughed. "He's a bit protective of me." She handed him her coat. He held it out for her to slip her arms in. "But he knows about our little arrangement."

"Ahh," he commented.

"I even showed him the list of rules."

With the coat on, Logan used his hand to untuck her hair from where it hid beneath her collar. The silky strands glided through his fingertips, and he had to pull away to keep himself from letting his hand linger too long.

"He didn't seem to believe it." Logan stepped back and plunged his hand into his pocket. "Not even when I told him we were only friends."

"Friends—right." Brooke fidgeted with her purse. "Absolutely. I didn't think this was a *real* date."

"Then we are on the same page," Logan offered.

"Yep." Her lips formed a tight line. "Even if George thinks differently."

Brooke strode to the front door, and Logan jogged to catch up with her and snatched the door open before she grasped it. She passed through, and he followed behind. Chilly winter air nipped at his skin, so he plunged his hands into the pockets of his puffer jacket.

"Hey, George." Brooke buttoned up her coat and popped the collar. "I hope you stay warm tonight." She shoved his hands into her coat too.

George held up his gloved hands. "My wife bought me these new gloves. They're keeping me extra toasty this evening. Where are you two headed?"

"To a concert," Brooke shuffled back and forth to stay warm, "at the Chicago Theater."

"Don't let me keep you from *hanging out.*" George found Logan's gaze and rolled his eyes. "Have a nice time."

Dumbfounded, Logan left George at his post and followed Brooke toward the entrance of the L train. They climbed on when it arrived. Being the evening commute time, the train was crowded. They had to stand, but Logan didn't mind. It allowed him to be extra close to Brooke without crossing any boundaries. Brooke held onto a bar while Logan nabbed a free overhead strap. His lungs filled with her intoxicating scent and pushed away the weird smells of the other passengers.

"Tell me about this band. I've heard of them, but I don't know much about them."

Brooke's eyes sparkled. "Then you're in for a treat. The first time I heard them was in a small club in NYC. A bunch of my college roommates and I went on a road trip during fall break my junior year. My friends and I stumbled upon the band one evening, and I loved them. Since then, I've been a fan, and they've grown super popular. Instead of basement clubs, they're selling out huge concert halls."

He loved the way she lit up talking about them. The L train slowed to a stop. Passengers squeezed on by to get off and more came on, making him inch even closer.

"Why do you like their music so much?" he asked. "Is it the genre?"

"It might be," she paused. Her eyes scrunched up around the edges. "But I think I love the band because I listened to them during some of the darker and harder times in my life. I left home at eighteen. I was glad to be out of there, but it didn't mean I wasn't lost and lonely. Luckily, I became close with my college roommates. The music resonated with me, and it felt like the songs were written only for me. I think that's what good music can do for a person."

She looked so beautiful when she spoke. He stared at her for a moment, before remembering it was his turn to share. "I agree. Music can truly transform you to a different time and place."

Brooke nodded. The stuffy air of the train made him unzip his jacket.

"Did you ever go home while you were in college?" Logan asked.

"No." Brooke met his gaze. "I never went back. Then I heard through the grapevine that my mom moved without telling me and changed her number. Or more likely she didn't pay the phone bill and her cell phone was disconnected. I didn't know it at the time, but when I left I would never see her again. She died half a decade ago, overdose. I only know about it because I ran into a person I knew from high school in the city. They thought I already knew." She blinked a few times like she needed to fight the moisture gathering in the corner of her eyes. "I don't like talking about it. It hurts too much." A few tears spilled down her cheeks.

"I'm sorry." Without thinking, Logan brushed them away with his forefinger but let his hand linger as it cupped her neck. "I think you are so brave. You might even be one of the bravest people I've ever met."

Brooke scoffed. "I highly doubt that." Her voice cracked a tad.

"It's true." He forced himself to drop his hand and widen the gap between them. "But, enough about that. I want you to tell me more about this band."

"Anyways," she cleared her throat, "I think you'll recognize a few of their hit songs. They play regularly on the radio."

"I can't wait," he smiled.

Brooke tightened her grip on the bar. "Me either." She smiled then shifted to let someone push through and around them.

They rode the rest of the way to the Chicago theater. Unfortunately, with the crowds it took them longer than expected to get across town. By the time they arrived, they had missed their dinner reservation.

"What do we do now?" Brooke gnawed on her bottom lip. "I know you have to be starving. You came straight from work."

"How do you feel about taco trucks?" He rubbed the length of his jaw.

"Sounds good to me." Brooke tucked some loosened strands of hair behind her ear. "I love tacos. They're my favorite food."

"Come on." He held out his elbow for her. Brooke wrapped her hands around the crook of it and huddled in closer to him to stay warm. Her closeness made his stomach swim. The more time he spent with her, the more he liked her. But then like a pesky rat, Shelby popped back into his mind. He nudged his shoulder in the direction they needed to head. "I remember the street up here is usually lined with food trucks on the night of concerts."

They walked up a block and around the corner. Sure enough, they found the row of food trucks tucked into various spaces along the curb. The tantalizing aroma made his mouth water. A small line formed behind one of the taco trucks, and they joined the end of it figuring it must be the best one, due to the crowd. Soon, they ordered and received their food. With no tables or chairs to be found, they decided to lean up against a building and eat their food standing up.

For a few minutes they happily ate, and then Brooke wiped her face with a napkin and asked, "Have you seen Shelby again?" The question caught him off guard, and he nearly choked on his bite of taco. He coughed then pounded his fist against his chest. Brooke raised an eyebrow. "Are you okay?"

Logan crouched down and picked up his soda by his feet, taking a long swig. "My food went down the wrong pipe." With his throat clear, he set the soda back down and stood again. "No, I haven't seen Shelby."

"Why not?" Brooke took another bite of her taco. "You're telling me you haven't wanted to text her?"

"I didn't say that." He attempted to eat another bite of his taco. "I want to text her, but I haven't figured out how to go about doing it."

"She wants to go out with you." Brooke wiped her face with napkin. "Stop dragging your feet and text her. Trust me. Women want the guy to make the first move."

"We certainly have unfinished business, but it doesn't

necessarily mean I care to dip my toes back into the water when it comes to her. Shelby broke my heart once. I don't think I could handle it if she did it again. But then the not trying— well that eats me up inside too."

She shot him a pointed look. "I understand first loves are hard to get over. They linger with you far after they are gone. Many people marry their first loves, because being in love is intoxicating. And once it's no longer there, it's like a gut punch. Then you question if you'll ever find anything that good again. The problem with first loves is you compare everyone that you meet for the rest of your life to that person."

"Spoken like a woman who has experienced the same thing?" He raised an eyebrow. "What about you? Who was your first love?"

"Oh, some guy in college." Brooke brought up her foot and propped it against the wall. "He doesn't matter now, but I was hung up on him for a good year after we broke it off. I thought I'd never love anyone as much as I loved him. I figured I'd have to settle for a person I loved second best."

"What about Justin?" Logan finished his food and tossed the wrappers into the trash. "Did you love him too?" He picked up his soda from the ground and sipped.

"I was in love with the idea of him." Brooke bent down to fetch her soda then shifted to face him, leaning her hip against the building. "I hate admitting that. It makes me sound so desperate."

"How so?" He sipped again.

Brooke sipped her soda. "I wanted to be in love. I wanted to be with someone. So, I decided he was good enough. Honestly, as more and more time passes, I realize I never loved him, and he never loved me. We were simply place holders for one another until something better came along. Sad but true."

"At least you know now it wasn't meant to be." Logan finished his soda and tossed it and his other trash into the bin. "I hope you find love, real love someday. You deserve it."

"Thanks." Brooke finished and threw it away too. "I hope you find it too, if not with Shelby, then someone else."

"Thanks." He smiled.

Brooke checked her watch. "We'd better head to the theater or we'll miss the openers."

"Then let's go."

They weaved through the people walking on the sidewalk then made their way to the line already in front of the theater. Twenty minutes later they were in their seats only a few rows from the front.

"These seats are incredible," Logan commented after they sat down.

"Thanks." Her cheeks reddened enough for him to notice even with the dim lighting. "I bought them as a birthday gift to myself, a bit of a splurge."

"Sometimes you have to treat yourself."

"I know, if I didn't, then most of my birthdays and Christmases would pass with little fanfare."

Before Logan responded, the lights in the theater dimmed. The openers made their way onto the stage. Everyone in the theater erupted in applause. Brooke leaned forward on her armrest and listened with rapture. He found himself far too aware of her nearness. Her signature sweet scent radiated off her. A few times their shoulders bumped or fingers knocked. Being a fake date, he resisted the urge to take her hand or wrap his arms around her shoulders. *Friends, friends, friends.*

When the main band came on stage, everyone in the audience rose to their feet to clap and dance to the beat. Brooke sang along to the words, and he found himself mainly watching her watching the band. A few times she playfully shoved him to get him to dance. Eventually, he loosened up. By the final song, he joined in with Brooke and sang the words of the familiar melody.

When the curtains dropped back down, ending the night, he wished for it to linger a bit longer. And to his pleasant surprise, he realized that he hadn't thought about Shelby once.

People shuffled out of their seats. They were smack dab in the middle, and they had to wait for the seats to clear before moving. Brooke dug into her purse and removed a hairband as they waited.

"Here, can you hold this for me for a minute?" She held her purse out to him. He clutched it against his chest. "Thanks." Then she proceeded to gather her sweaty hair up into a loose knot on top of her head. Once in place, she secured it with the hairband and dropped her hands down. "Much better." She smiled, making her eyes glimmer under the lighting of the theater lights.

He forgot about her purse in his hands as he stared back at her. "Gosh, you're beautiful." He blurted out without thinking.

"Oh," Brooke removed her purse from his arms. "Thanks. I don't think I've ever been given that type of compliment when I'm this sweaty." Then she shot him a crooked smile as she put her coat back on.

"That's a shame." Logan retrieved his own jacket from the back of his seat and slugged it on. "I loved watching you tonight. I think that was the best part. You lit up each time the band played one of the songs you liked."

This didn't feel like pretending, and Logan didn't care to fight his growing attraction for her. But then he had no idea what any of it meant. Shelby popped back into his mind.

Her cheeks splashed with color. "Come on." She gripped his elbow. "Let's get out of here." Then she motioned for him to exit.

They filed out of the row and then out of the theater. A crowd gathered outside of the L train station, and they waited to catch the next train back to her apartment. The temperature had dipped even lower. A chill nipped at him. They both shuffled their feet to stay warm. Brooke's teeth chattered, and she rubbed her gloved hands together.

"Here, let me help you stay warm." Logan stepped closer and covered his gloved hands over hers. He rubbed them between his hands. "My mom used to do this for me when I was little."

Brooke peered up at him. "Lucky."

"I know."

And he meant it. Some didn't have a loving family with a whole gaggle of people who loved him. Brooke didn't, but he hoped in the future with some other guy she could have a second chance at a family.

For a minute, Logan rubbed her hands. Her teeth continued to chatter.

"I've always been a bit of a wimp when it comes to the cold." Brooke locked eyes with him. "It doesn't matter the season. Summertime my hands and feet are ice."

Logan dropped his hands and wrapped one arm around her shoulders, slowly tugging her closer. Without prompting, Brooke placed her arm around his waist. His body warmed from hers being nearby.

"I wouldn't mind your cold hands," Logan enjoyed her being tucked in against him, "you can place them on me anytime you want, wherever you want."

"Umm." Brooke laughed. "Is that an invitation?"

"Sure." He shrugged. "But only if you want it to be. I guess the ball is in your court."

"Okay, noted." She wrinkled her nose and her lips twitched. "But if you must know the verdict is still out."

"Let me know when it's in." His fingers itched to brush the hair that had fallen in front of her eyes away from her face.

For a second, the world stilled. And he had no idea what any of it meant. His steady heartbeat sounded in his temples. Gosh, he wanted to kiss her.

She gulped, and Brooke replied, "I will."

The L train came. Logan dropped his arm from her shoulder and found her hand. He led her through the crowd to the entrance of the train. They made it on, and the train lurched forward. Enough people exited at the last stop, so they walked on the moving train to some seats at the back. Then they sat down next to each other.

His pulse thundered in his ears. "What if we date for real?" he blurted out.

"What do you mean?" Brooke tilted her face and studied him. "What about Shelby? I think you need to see if there are still feelings there. Date her then we'll talk."

"I don't need to do that. I already know what I want."

"You say that now." She gnawed on her bottom lip and clasped and unclasped her hands together. "But I think you have some unresolved things with her. I saw the way you looked at her."

He shook his head. "I didn't look at her in any particular way, but I certainly like looking at you."

Brooke squeezed his knee. "Go out with Shelby. See where it goes. Then we'll talk. I think you're caught up in the moment from the music and the concert."

"I don't think so."

"Go out with Shelby." Brooke insisted way more than he liked. "Then we'll see." She squeezed his knee one more time before removing it. Then she peered out the window. The lights of the tall buildings glimmered against the backdrop of the dark sky.

He knew she was probably right, no matter how much he hated it. Nothing would move forward until he finally put these lingering feelings for Shelby to bed.

CHAPTER 10

Brooke strode down the hallway of the hospital, nearing the end of her shift. Her feet ached and head throbbed. The late concert from the night before meant she was running on pure adrenaline. Her mind replayed the conversation she'd had with Logan on the train. As much as she wanted to jump at the chance to date him, her head told her to hold up. She saw how Logan looked at Shelby. The tension between them could've been cut with a knife. No, it was better this way. He needed to close that chapter of his life before they'd ever have a shot at starting something.

She rounded the corner to the nurses' station where she found Aubrey shoving a granola bar into her mouth.

"Hey." Brooke set down the files in her hands on top of the station. "Are you almost off or only beginning?"

Aubrey swallowed. "Halfway." She ate another bite and chewed. Once done she asked, "How about you?"

"Only," she double checked her wrist watch, "twenty minutes left." She opened the top file folder. "I'm tired. I went to a concert last night with Logan. I didn't get back until after midnight."

"Logan, you say." Aubrey shoveled the last bite of granola bar into her mouth then tossed the wrapper into the trash can. "How is *that* going?" She waggled her brows.

"We're only friends." Brooke made a note on the patient file then tossed it into the bin to be entered into the computer. "We like to spend time together." She shrugged and shot her a *what can you do* expression.

"I see." Aubrey snatched the file from the bin then slugged herself into the chair behind the computer. She wiggled her mouse around. "Friends—"

"Yes," Brooke hissed as she made a note on the next patient file.

Then out of nowhere, Logan landed beside her. "I thought that was you." With a smirk, he casually leaned his hip against the nurses' station desk. His body was intimately close to hers. Close enough, she smelled the scent of soap. "It's nice to see you again so soon."

"Oh, hi." Brooke nearly dropped her pen but straightened it in the nick of time. "Are you following me?" she teased.

"I mean I can if you want me to." His curious gaze made his eyes flicker. When she didn't respond, he glanced at Aubrey behind the desk and dipped his chin at her. "Hey, Aubrey. It's good to see you. How are the wedding plans going?"

Aubrey smiled, leaning forward. "Brooke went with me to my final wedding dress fitting. According to the wedding planner, everything is set to go."

"They say as long as you have a dress, a groom, and a date, that's all you need."

"I think I have heard that before." Aubrey continued to type on her keyboard. "You're still good to come with Brooke, right?" She finished typing and placed the closed file into the outgoing bin.

"I wouldn't miss it," Logan shifted to face Brooke and winked, "for the world."

Heat splashed Brooke's cheeks. If she didn't know better,

she'd think Logan was flirting with her instead of being friendly. A part of her might even believe he wanted to spend the evening as her actual date. But she knew better. Their arrangement kept the lines of fake and real plain as day.

Suddenly a buzzer went off, Aubrey tapped the flashing button and stood. "That's me. I'll see you both later." She wagged her fingers at them.

Brooke watched Aubrey disappear down the hallway before she twisted to face Logan. "I'm off in fifteen minutes, you?" She clicked her pen closed and pushed it into the front of her lab coat pocket.

"I'm done. I came from my last surgery." He hesitated for a second, looked down at his feet then back up at her. "Want to grab dinner at the sandwich shop around the corner?"

Dinner. This eerily sounded like dating, but then she reminded herself last night she had told him to date Shelby first and then they could talk. One dinner with a friend couldn't hurt, right?

But she knew she was in deep. She could admit to herself that her feelings for Logan were one hundred percent real. Her heart picked up speed anytime he came near. Friends, yeah, she didn't want to be friends. She wanted to kiss him in the rain or in the moonlight, or anywhere for that matter. Brooke wanted to go with him to Sunday dinners at his parents, babysit the twins to give Danielle and Michael a night off. Geez, the list went on and on. But it didn't matter what she wanted, she had to live in the reality of what was.

"Sure." Brooke plunged one hand into her lab coat. Luckily, she had on a nice dress and cardigan underneath her lab coat. It didn't fall into date attire, but it also didn't lean into disheveled either. "I'd love that."

Logan grinned. Then he slapped the top of the nurses' desk. "I'll go change out of these scrubs and meet you in the hospital lobby. See you soon." Then he pivoted and left.

Her simmering blood pressure slowly subsided as he slipped into the elevator at the end of the hallway. Then she placed the completed files into the bin that needed to be entered into the computer. A few minutes later, she ended her shift. After a trip to the locker room, she removed her lab coat, touched up her makeup, and gathered up her coat and purse.

Twenty minutes later, she arrived in the lobby. She spotted Logan waiting in one of the chairs with a phone glued to his ear. As she approached, he said into his phone, "She's right here, let me ask her." He covered the phone's mouthpiece with one hand and lowered it from his ear. "It's my mom. Does Sunday night work for dinner?"

"Dinner?" Brooke didn't have it in her to truck it outside of the city to sit in that lovely home and lie to those people yet again. "Again?"

Logan leaned in closer and whispered, "My parents wanted to come here with Michael and Danielle to have dinner in the city with us, remember?"

"Oh," Brooke adjusted the jacket slung over her arm. "Right. Let me check my schedule. I think I work the morning shift, but I should be off by six or seven." She plunged her hand into her purse to fetch her phone. Logan chatted with his mom as she pulled up her calendar. "I'm off at six," she announced.

Logan gave her a thumbs up as he listened a bit more. Finally, he said, "Mom, Brooke said she's off at six." His gaze caught hers as he listened to his mom's reply.

Brooke patiently waited as he wrapped up his conversation, putting on her jacket.

He hung up and slipped his phone into his pocket. "We're set. Danielle is insistent on some restaurant she heard had good reviews."

"I don't care where we go." Brooke adjusted her purse strap. "I'm more worried about faking it again as your girlfriend for the evening. I hate leading your family on."

"If it was up to me, I'd be dating you for real."

The words landed in the tight space between them. He shot her a challenging stare, like *your turn*.

She pinched the sleeve of his jacket. "Come on." Brooke led him toward the sliding glass doors. "You promised me food, and I get a bit testy when I haven't been fed."

"I like testy women." Logan laughed. "But I guess I have my marching orders. Let's get out of here."

They walked for a minute down the sidewalk, weaving between the people walking past. Winter wind seeped through her jacket. The L train rolled on by over the track above them.

"What will you tell them once we, quote, break up?" Brooke gnawed on her bottom lip.

He slowed his pace then halted in front of the tiny deli. "Maybe," he held the door open for her and motioned for her to enter, "we won't have anything to tell."

They slipped inside. The deli had a few two top tables. A short line formed behind the cash register to place their order. They joined the end of the line.

"Like I said last night, go out with Shelby and then we can talk."

"I'm not going out with her," he practically growled.

Brooke shrugged. "Fine, then we'll continue to fake this thing."

"I don't need to go out with Shelby, because," he placed a hand at her waist and gently directed her closer. Close enough, her hand naturally landed in the middle of his rock-hard chest. Logan cleared his throat, "I feel something real when I'm with you. I haven't stopped thinking about you since last night, and you can't tell me that doesn't mean anything."

Her throat was constricted. She forgot how to think because of the intensity of his stare which made her stomach swim. Sweat gathered at the small of her back.

When she didn't reply, he squeezed her waist, "Tell me you don't feel this too."

"I—I—" Brooke stammered.

"Next," the voice behind the cash registered announced so loud it made her flinch.

The people in front of them in line had already paid and left. Logan dropped his hand from her waist but let his hand trail down her arm finally interweaving his fingers with hers. He drew her forward to the register. Her body complied like she was in a daze. They ordered some turkey sandwiches, chips, and sodas. After Logan paid, they sat down at one of the two top tables with their food.

He didn't hesitate to peel back the paper wrapper of his sandwich and take a bite. Her hand shook, and Brooke fumbled with the package of her chips. Logan appeared unfazed by his confession while she reeled with the desire to date him but was hesitant due to his unfinished business with Shelby.

"I do feel something when I'm around you," Brooke confessed as she opened her bag of chips. "And, if I'm being honest, it terrifies me." She hesitated then popped a chip into her mouth.

"I know." Logan ate another bite of his sandwich then washed it down with a long sip of his drink. "But you can trust me."

"What about Shelby?" She retrieved another chip from her bag.

He set his half-eaten sandwich back down on his wrapper and wiped his face with his napkin. "I'm here with you, aren't I?"

"Yes." She fidgeted with the straw of her drink.

"And I'm here, because I want to be. If I wanted to see Shelby, I would, but I don't want to."

"But, you might change your mind."

"Like how Justin changed his mind about you?"

Brooke nodded the tiniest amount.

Logan placed a hand over hers and squeezed it. "I won't change my mind."

Desperately, she wanted to believe him. To think this time would be different. This time could be the real thing, but her head screamed *no way*.

"You can't promise that."

"Why don't you give me a chance to show you I mean it?" Logan squeezed her hand again. "Could you do that for me?"

"I'm not sure." Brooke peeled off the paper of her sandwich and avoided eye contact.

"Please," he pleaded. "I know you're scared, because I am too if I'm being honest. But I like you Brooke, and I'd like to date you." He stared back with such earnestness her heart softened.

"Fine." Brooke bit into her sandwich and chewed.

He beamed. "Great." Logan grinned and tossed a chip into his mouth. Then he waved a hand. "Now that we've gotten that out of the way, tell me about your day. Anything interesting happen? Weird cases?"

She ate a few chips as she contemplated her dilemma of being cautious or optimistic about her future with Logan. Logan waited. Brooke brushed some loosened strands of hair out of her eyes.

"I had a patient who came into the ER with a pencil struck right dab," she tapped the middle of her forehead, "in his forehead."

Logan laughed. "What happened?"

"Apparently, he and a kid had had a fight at school. The kid threw the pencil at him, and it landed in his forehead."

Her shoulders relaxed. The tension in her neck dissipated. She ate some of her sandwich.

Logan shook his head. "They're lucky it didn't take out an eye."

"Oh, for sure."

"I'm surprised," Logan popped a chip into his mouth, "I didn't hear about it."

A dab of mayo from her sandwich dribbled onto her chin, she

used a napkin to wipe her face. "The plastic surgeon removed it, but luckily the kid only needed a few stitches. How about you? How was your day?"

"Decent." Logan drank his soda then set it back down. "But it's much better now." His shimmery gaze made warmth flood her stomach.

"Mine too," Brooke smiled then ate another bite of her sandwich.

They finished eating then gathered up their trash and threw it away. When they exited the deli, the brutal icy temperature made her shiver. She dug a scarf out of her purse and wrapped it around her neck.

As they made their way to her apartment, Logan's pinky finger wrapped around hers. She peered down at their fingers then back up at him. "Thanks for taking me to eat." Then she squeezed. He shifted his fingers over and fully interlaced his hand through hers.

Her heart stopped.

This felt different.

New.

Real.

Even possible.

Logan brushed some loosened hair off her forehead and tucked it behind her ear. "Anytime." He kissed her on her temple. "I hope you don't make me wait until Sunday to see you again. My family will be there, and I won't get to be alone with you."

"I have a busy week. I'm helping Aubrey with some last-minute things for the wedding in the evenings. I don't think I'll have time before then."

"Are you," he cast her sideway glance, "playing hard to get?"

Brooke laughed. "I wish I even knew how to do that, but no, it's the truth."

"Then, I'll have to enjoy whatever time I can get with you."

Her apartment came into view. George wasn't in his usual

post outside the building. She wondered if he'd gone inside to the station behind the lobby desk. They arrived in front of her building. Brooke peered inside the glass door, but George wasn't inside either. She turned back to face Logan.

He stepped closer to her, placing a hand at the dip in her waist. "Thanks for coming with me to dinner."

Her breath hitched in her chest. The tangy smell of his aftershave filled her lungs making her head swim. If she didn't know better, she'd think Logan might kiss her. And, she wanted it, bad. Her fear of Shelby and the future dissipated. She didn't care, not now, when a kiss might be on her otherwise deserted wasteland of dead relationships horizon.

"Thanks for inviting me." He moistened his lips.

Neither moved, almost as a dare. The first to move would lose, in this imaginary game she played with herself. Slowly, she placed a hand in the center of his chest, he tightened his hold at her waist.

"I'll see you Sunday?" Her voice sounded breathless even to herself.

"Yes." In one swift movement, Logan swirled her around and backed her up to the wall of her apartment building. She obeyed. Her back eventually rested against the smooth brick. "Unless I can manage to sneak in a time to see you before then," he said.

"Oh," she found his gaze, "that's wishful thinking on your part."

"I have my ways." His eyes glinted with the light from the streetlamps overhead. "I'll figure something out."

Brooke scrunched her nose. "Will you now?" she teased.

He wrapped his arm fully around her back, bringing her closer until their hips touched. Her heart nearly exploded as her pulse thundered behind her ears. His gaze flickered between her lips and eyes then back again. WHAT WAS HAPPENING?

Her mind reeled. Last night, she told him to date Shelby.

Then, snap, she could only think about kissing him, even if it made everything muddled and messy.

"What would you do if I kissed you right now?" He brushed some loosened hair over her shoulder, leaving a long trail of heat down it.

A tremor made her knees unsteady. "I'm not sure." Her voice shook.

"Would you push me away?" He cupped her neck. His fingers glided through her hair.

"I wouldn't." She gulped. *Take a chance. It's only a kiss not a proposal, not a promise of anything, it's just a kiss.* "I'd kiss you back," Brooke finally confessed. Her gaze held his steady.

"Not for fake?" he tilted his head and studied her.

"No." She shook her head ever so slightly.

Her hands had a mind of their own and found their way to the collar of his shirt and tucked up underneath it.

"Not as friends?" he pushed further.

"Did you want to kiss as friends?" she questioned.

Her pulse thundered in her ears.

"I want to kiss you for real." He landed one hand flat against the wall by her head. "I want to kiss you now." His body pinned her in the very best way.

"Great. Then we are in agreement." Brooke tightened her hold of his collar. "Kissing is good."

He shifted closer. His breath tickled her neck. Then before his lips touched hers. He whispered, "Perfect." Then Logan skated his lips across hers.

At first graze, his lips were featherlight, almost undetectable as he tentatively tasted her. She sighed and relaxed against the strong grip of his arm which supported her. Thoughts of his reunion with Shelby whizzed through her head, but she pushed the unhelpful idea away. Logan wanted to kiss her, right? Her fingers grazed his neck as he deepened the kiss. He tasted sweet and tangy.

Cars honked. The L train rolled overhead. A group of wild teenagers made an annoying ruckus then loud whistles as they trekked on by. But none of it truly registered, not when his arm held her steady, not when her heartbeat rang in her ears and her chest thundered, not when his lips memorized the curves of her face. Nah, it was only them. This was a kiss that made one forget. This was a kiss that made people believe in something bigger than themselves. This kiss righted the wrongs of the past, and the possibility of a heartbreak in the future.

Her lips parted as his tongue plunged inside. His finger brushed the length of her jaw. The fabric of his collar slipped through her fingers. Brooke retightened her hold.

She wondered why they had waited this long. If they had started here, they never would have pretended anything. No, this, them, wasn't fake at all. This was the most real thing she had ever experienced.

His signature spicy scent mingled with the cool night air. Though her body shivered, she was warm all over. He deepened their kiss while she memorized the feeling of his body pressed against hers. The train rolled over their heads again, making their bodies vibrate.

Then a loud but familiar boisterous laugh out of nowhere made her tug her lips from his. In a daze, Brooke peered toward the interrupting sound. Her gaze landed on George. He smirked and wagged a finger at them. Logan loosened his grip, straightening himself. Brooke pushed off the wall of the building.

"Nothing fake about that kiss," George hollered in their direction with a look of triumph. "I'd say I have a sixth sense for that type of thing."

"No." Instead of cowering, Logan's lips broke out into a wide smile. "You were right. How could we have ever doubted you?"

George waved a dismissive hand. "I'll let you two love birds get back to it." He slipped back inside the building.

Brooke watched as the door shut behind him. "I guess there's no going back now."

"Nope, only forward." He wrapped his arms around Brooke, pulling her into a tight all-embracing hug. His breath tickled her neck as he whispered into her hair, "I can't get enough of my Brookie."

Brooke loosened their embrace enough for her to gaze up at him. "What have I told you? No nicknames," she teased.

"Come on, not even for me?" He gave her a puppy dog look.

"Fine, I'll take it into consideration."

He kissed her on the temple. "Sounds like a win to me."

Brooke laughed. "You keep telling yourself that."

"I will, Brookie." Logan stole a quick peck. "I will."

CHAPTER 11

In a daze, Brooke slipped into her apartment building. Behind the lobby desk, George let out a long embarrassing whistle. Heat splashed her cheeks, and she fidgeted with her hair.

"Stop." She waved him off then fully planned on walking as quickly as possible to the elevator bay. "You're embarrassing me."

He held his arms out wide. "Did I call it or did I call it?" George leaned back in his chair and cupped the back of his head with both hands.

"Fine." Brooke whipped back around and stomped over to the lobby desk. Her heels clacked against the marble floors. "You called it. There, are you happy?"

George grinned. "Of course I'm happy. That's all I've ever wanted for you. Just wait until I tell my wife about this. This has been the most entertainment either of us has had in years."

"How pathetic," Brooke leaned a hip against the lobby desk, "for me."

"I like this one better than the other one." George leaned forward and cupped his hands together on top of the desk. "I have a good feeling about him."

"Hold your horses." She straightened herself. "I think it's far too early to predict if this will work out or completely blow up in my face."

"Nah." George shook his head. "He likes you. I can tell. Justin never looked at you the way this one does."

Brooke ignored his comment about Justin. "I'm going out to dinner with his family again on Sunday. Any advice?"

"Yes, please don't order a pasta dish with red sauce." He wagged a finger. "You don't need a big splatter on your shirt to ruin your evening."

"Okay." Brooke laughed. "I'll keep that in mind. Anything else?"

"Nah, a dirty shirt will be your only obstacle to avoid. I'm sure they already love you."

Logan's mom might, but Danielle was probably a different story.

"I appreciate your confidence in me. Have a nice evening." Brooke waved goodbye.

She rode the elevator up to her apartment, and her bone-dead tiredness resurfaced. Her eyelids flickered open and closed. Being with Logan had distracted her from reality, she was going on very little sleep and had another full day tomorrow.

After her shift tomorrow, she and Aubrey had an appointment to taste a new wedding cake. The original cake maker had left suddenly for a family emergency and wouldn't be able to bake it. Luckily, Aubrey's wedding planner arranged for her to meet with someone who could follow the chosen design last minute. They only needed to decide on the cake flavor.

Brooke shot Aubrey a text before going to sleep and confirmed the location of the shop. Promptly, she drifted off to a dreamy sleep thinking about one guy and one guy only.

~

After work, Brooke caught the L train to the bakery on the other side of the city. At her stop, she climbed down the stairs from the station, the delicious and tantalizing aroma of the bakery guided her the rest of the way. By the time she arrived at the place, her stomach growled, and mouth watered. She entered and the bell on the door announced her arrival.

The tiny bakery had a beautiful display of cakes and cookies in glass display cases. She found Aubrey in the little two-top nook, facing the street. Slowly, she slid into the empty seat across from her and unwrapped the scarf from her neck.

"This place looks amazing." Brooke gripped a glove between her teeth and removed it. "If it tastes as good as it smells, then your cake is going to be perfect."

"Really?" Aubrey wrung her hands together. "I almost lost it when the wedding planner told me the cake was up in the air, but she assured me she sent them the photo of what I wanted. They have a quick turn around and promised to match what I selected."

"I'm sorry Ian couldn't be here." Brooke wrinkled her nose. "But I'm always up for cake." She flashed her an enthusiastic grin.

Aubrey waved it off. "Ian doesn't care what we get, which is why I needed your opinion."

"I'm in." She removed her jacket and placed it on the back of her chair. "Plus, I'm starving so bring it on."

The baker appeared from the back of the store with two plates with small slivers of cake in various types. "Here we are." They placed them on the table in front of each of them. Then they pointed out each type and the ingredients. "I'll give you a few minutes to try them. If you can't decide on one flavor, we can do a different cake for each layer of the cake."

The baker returned to behind the glass cake display.

Brooke scooted the plate closer to her and cut into the first sliver of cake which looked like red velvet. "What did you pick for your last cake?" She tried the first bite and sighed as the moist texture of the cake touched her tongue.

"I think," Aubrey nibbled on a bite, "Ian liked chocolate, and I liked the almond vanilla."

"This red velvet," Brooke shook her fork at it, "is out of this world good." She dug in again and ate another bite.

"The one I'm eating is good, too," Aubrey remarked.

A phone dinged. Brooke set her fork down and retrieved her phone from her pocket. A message from Logan displayed on the screen.

"It's mine," she announced with her eyes glued to the screen.

"Mm," Aubrey said.

She tapped on the screen to read the entire message.

I can't stop thinking about that kiss last night. I think that was the hottest kiss I've ever had in my life.

Her cheeks burned. Brooke used the back of her hand to cool them off one at a time. Then her finger whizzed across her phone.

Really? I thought it was okay.

She gnawed on a fingernail hoping he understood her flirting. Her stomach twisted as she watched the cursor dots on their text chain dance.

Okay? Ok. Fine, I guess I'll have to kiss you again with the promise of improvement. I'm very good at receiving critical feedback.

A laugh escaped her. Fire mounted in her gut.

Uh, oh. That sounds almost like a dare.

Tell me where you're at, and I'll come kiss you senseless and bring my grade up from okay to fantastic.

"Who are you texting?" Aubrey's voice interrupted her. "You can't stop smiling so I'm guessing, Logan."

"I'm not smiling, am I?" Brooke peered over at her.

"Like a fool." Aubrey licked the frosting off her fork. "So, spill it."

"We kissed." Brooke shrugged then buried her head back down over her cell phone.

"What?" Aubrey shrieked. "And you didn't text me last night with the details? Come on that's what I live for."

"It's new. I don't want to jinx it." Then Brooke held up a finger. "Give me a second to text him back then I'll spill."

Brooke tapped out a message to Logan.

I'm tasting wedding cakes with Aubrey on the other side of the city. I probably won't be home until later.

I don't mind. Text me when you're headed home. I'll meet you at your place and bring dinner.

How can a girl resist that type of offer?

I know, right?

I'll text you on the train.

She slid her phone back into her purse and picked her fork back up.

"Details." Aubrey raised an eyebrow and waited. "I need details."

"What do you want to know?" Brooke cut into the white cake with coconut frosting.

"Everything."

"Then buckle up, you're about to go on a wild adventure."

Brooke then spent the next ten minutes filling Aubrey in on everything. The fake dating, meeting his family, Shelby, and their kiss which might change everything. By the time the baker whipped back around, they had finished the cake. Both agreed the chocolate and almond vanilla were the best. Aubrey put in the order for a doubled flavored cake.

"When do you see his family again?" Aubrey asked as she wound her scarf back around her neck and stood.

"Sunday." Brooke pushed in her chair and put her jacket back on. "Only this time we won't be pretending." She let out a sigh and slugged her purse over her shoulder. "I'm worried. You know my family history. Justin's family never liked me. I'm sure once they get to know me more, I'll be the last person they want dating Logan."

"I'm sure if you make Logan happy, then that's what his family will want for him."

"I think his mom likes me, but his sister wants him back with Shelby," Brooke revealed.

"The ex?" Aubrey questioned.

Brooke nodded and weaved around the table to the door. Aubrey followed behind as they filed outside. Dark sky surrounded them and forced her to button up her jacket and tighten her scarf.

"I'm sure the sister will get on board." Aubrey put her gloves on. "Once she feels you out a little bit more, she'll see how terrific you are."

"I hope so."

They walked toward the L train. Aubrey was headed in the opposite direction but from the same station. A train rolled overhead making the staircase vibrate as they climbed up to the platform. Before they parted ways, Aubrey asked, "Are you going right now to see Logan?"

Her lips curled as she fought off a smile. "He's bringing dinner over to my place. I'm texting him once I get on the train with my ETA."

"Then I won't invite you to dinner." Aubrey hesitated as she bit her bottom lip. "I'm meeting up with Ian. Justin and his girlfriend will be there."

"Hey," Brooke stepped closer, "you don't have to tiptoe around me anymore. You can tell me your plans without worrying about hurting me. I'm over Justin. If these past few weeks have taught me anything, it's how wrong he was for me."

Aubrey's chest heaved as she blew out a rattly breath. "That's a relief." She motioned for her to hug her. Brooke welcomed the embrace and hugged her back. "You're a great friend. I didn't want to lose you over this thing."

"I know." Brooke loosened their embrace, taking a step back. "I'm not going anywhere. Now, get out of here before you miss the next train." She shooed her away.

"Have a nice time with *Logan*." Aubrey winked then disappeared into the crowd as she took the path that weaved around to the other side of the track.

The train rolled up next to her platform, and Brooke made her way on with the other late-night commuters. No empty seats were available, so she gripped onto a pole and managed to balance her cell phone to send Logan a text.

I'm en route. I'll be there in about thirty minutes.

A text came through almost immediately.

I'll be ready and waiting.

You realize how bad that sounds, right?

Her cheeks flushed. She unbuttoned a few of the buttons on her coat as the air within the train cab grew stuffy. A tickle of sweat ran down her spine.

What's wrong about being ready to see you again?

You know what I meant.

No, I don't. I'm going to need you to spell it out for me.

She giggled to herself.

I'll see you soon.

Then she slipped her phone back into her pocket and tightened her hold on the pole. In her little love haze, nothing brought her down. A couple kissing elbowed her in the back, another man yelled at her when she inadvertently stepped on his foot, but nothing could dampen her bright mood. In a few minutes, she'd be seeing Logan. Maybe her luck was turning around as well.

CHAPTER 12

A jittery jive ran through Logan as he paced the sidewalk in front of Brooke's apartment. The bag in his hand slipped, and he straightened it. Since last night, his thoughts only focused on Brooke and their kiss. Shelby, who? If things continued to progress in this direction, he could only imagine where they would be this time next year. Whoa, calm down, he reminded himself.

George poked his head out of the front door of the apartment building. "Do you want to come in from the cold?" He paused and waited for him to answer. "Your pacing is making me nervous."

"Oh," he shifted the bag of food from one hand to the other, "is it that obvious?"

"Son, even a baby could pick up on your anxious energy." George waved him over. "Come on in, and let's have a chat until Brooke arrives."

"Umm." He didn't really want to have a chat, but he didn't think he had a choice in the matter either. "Okay, but she should be here any minute."

"And I'm off in five, so— come in out of the cold." George held the door open for him.

Logan passed through it. "Thanks," he commented. "I guess I am a bit wound up. I keep telling myself not to mess this up. My usual *don't be an idiot* pep talk isn't working."

George chuckled as he closed the door and motioned for him to follow. He snatched a chair from the lobby and dragged it over next to the lobby desk. "Sit." He patted the chair then slid into his seat behind the desk.

Logan obeyed, placing the bag of food down at his feet. In an attempt to appear casual, he propped his ankle on his opposite knee. "Is this where you threaten me with a shotgun if I ever do anything to hurt Brooke?"

"Do I need to give you that speech?" George raised an eyebrow.

"No." Logan shook his head. "You don't. I know how special she is."

"Good." George pulled himself closer to his desk then rearranged some loose papers on top. "You seem smarter than the last guy, so I'm rooting for you. I'd like to see her happy. You know she didn't come from the most ideal circumstances, but she worked hard, putting herself through college then medical school on her own. That shows how much grit she has. A woman like that is one you want to keep."

"She's mentioned a bit about her parents, her dad abandoning her and her mom being an alcoholic and drug addict. I don't know much more than that."

He wished he did, but he picked up on Brooke's hesitation to share more about her less than flowery childhood. Also, he sensed she didn't like to dwell on the past. He wished he had the same bandwidth to do that very thing.

George paused then flashed his gaze to the lobby door then back to him. "Her mom was verbally abusive. Brooke's life was riddled with the consequences of being around an addict. Then to make matters worse, her mom had a whole slew of boyfriends in and out her life that didn't make it any easier. You know that's why she wanted to become a pediatrician, right?"

"I see."

He began to see how much he still needed to learn about her, how many layers of Brooke he needed to peel back and discover. This was a privilege he knew most probably didn't get. Logan hoped it was something Brooke would show him.

"She wanted to help children, since she was a child who desperately needed help but didn't receive it."

His heart warmed. "I love that about her."

Then she pushed through the lobby door. Her cheeks were flushed, and her eyes were vibrant and alive. The beauty of her made Logan's breath hitch in his chest. How had he managed to kiss her? His younger self would be so proud. He stumbled to his feet, snatching up the bag of food as he stood.

"Brooke," he said with a tremor in his voice.

"There you are." Slowly, Brooke unbuttoned her coat as she trekked across the lobby. "Hey there, George. Were you keeping him company for me?"

"Something like that." George straightened himself. "There may or may not have been a mention of a shot gun."

"Geez." Brooke half chuckled and half rolled her eyes. "I can only imagine what you said." She stopped in front of Logan and tilted her head to meet his gaze. "Hey, you."

Molten lava filled his gut. He attempted to swallow. "Hey back." Then he leaned in and kissed her gently on the temple.

"What do you have in there?" Brooke peered down at his bag of food. "I'm starving."

"I picked up some Chinese food." He rubbed the back of his neck. "I hope that's okay."

"Perfect." Then she went up on her tiptoes, leaned in and kissed him gently. "I'm glad you're here." She smiled, making his knotted ball of nerves disappear.

"Me too."

George cleared his throat. "Well don't keep the guy waiting. Go eat."

Brooke laughed. "Come on." She tugged his free hand. "See you soon George." Then she led him to the elevator bay.

Once alone behind the closed doors of the elevator, Logan gained his courage. He wrapped an arm around her waist and brought her closer. "I can't stop thinking about you."

"Interesting," Brooke smirked. "I haven't thought about you once," she teased.

Then she rested her hand on his chest.

"Is that right?" Logan kissed her lightly.

"Umm, maybe." She pulled away enough to glance up at him. "But if you keep doing that, I might start thinking about you a little bit more."

The elevator dinged open, and they shuffled off it. He filed behind her down the long hallway.

"Just keep in mind," she led him to her apartment, "this is the nicest apartment I've ever lived in, so if you make fun of anything I'll be devastated." She slipped her key into the door then pivoted to peer back at him.

"I hope," he leaned his hip against the wall next to the door and crossed his arms, "you don't think I'm someone who would ever tease someone about where they live. I'm not that guy."

"I know." She turned the key. "I guess it's my insecurities bubbling up again, but you'd be surprised what people say." She pushed open the door and held it open for him to pass through. "The places I lived in when I was a kid were horrible, run down apartments with leaky roofs, rusty pipes, and people yelling way too loudly in the hallways. This is finally a place I'm proud to show people. Justin always complained about how small it was." She removed her key from the latch.

He walked into the apartment. "Justin sounds like a total tool."

Brooke laughed. "No argument there." She closed the door

behind them and came up beside him as she tossed her keys on the bowl on top of the long credenza.

His jaw clenched as he thought of Justin. What kind of person made fun of where someone lived? *A jerk, that's who.*

"I'm beginning to believe he was a quote, *tool,* too." Brooke gathered up her hair and tossed it over one shoulder. "I don't know how I didn't see it until now."

"I'm nothing like him," Logan added.

"I know," she said softly. "That's why I like you."

He smiled as he peered out at her apartment. It was small but there were large floor to ceiling windows which looked out over the city.

"This is incredible." He walked the few paces across the living room and dropped the food on the small table to enjoy the scene out the windows. "What a view. My apartment faces another wall. I can only see the other residents in their apartments and nothing else. But this—" he glanced over his shoulder. Brooke wrung her hands together as she came up next to him, "might be the best view I've ever seen."

"I thought so." The deep lines on her forehead eased. Brooke pointed. "I love seeing the Chicago River. It sparkles in the evening. See—"

He wrapped an arm around her and drew her closer. "It does glimmer." The lights of the city reflected in Brooke's gaze. "A lot like you."

Geez, he sounded cheesy, but he couldn't help himself. He didn't know what was happening, but he knew he couldn't stop it even if he wanted to. Brooke mattered to him. Now that he had her, he never wanted to let her go. For a minute, they stared out at the view together. Their steady breathing competed against the sounds of the city on the street way below.

Then his phone rang and broke their blissful spell.

"I hope," he lowered his arm from her shoulders and retrieved his phone from his pocket, "this isn't the hospital."

His gut twisted as the familiar name flashed across the screen. Why in the world would Shelby be calling him? He regretted keeping her number in his phone from high school. He should've deleted it a long time ago. But this meant she never deleted his either.

"Everything okay?" Brooke scanned his face then her gaze dropped to the phone in his hand. "Oh, Shelby is calling you." She gnawed on a fingernail. "I didn't realize— I thought—and I shouldn't have."

"We don't talk." He sighed and ran a hand down the length of his face. "I didn't even know she still had my number or that I still had it saved. I have no idea why she is calling."

"Then you'd better pick up," she said matter-of-factly.

Logan sighed and punched the accept button. "Hello?" Logan plunged his free hand through his hair then rubbed the length of his jaw.

"Hey, Logan."

"Yeah." A tremor made his hands shake.

"This is Shelby."

"I know." He forced his shaky hand into the pocket of his pants.

Then he waited.

Brooke left his side and walked over to the table and dug into the to-go bag, placing the cartons on the table. She busied herself with opening and closing some cupboards, retrieving plates and cups.

"I'm babysitting the twins, and I can't get a hold of your sister or your parents. Lily has a fever. I didn't know who else to call. I'm not sure how high is too high. I'm a nurse, but I deal with adults. This is a small infant, aren't fevers in them much more serious?"

Since when did Shelby babysit the twins? His mind tried to play catch up. A creaking drawer in the kitchen made him peer over his shoulder toward Brooke. She snatched two forks out of it and walked them over to the table. She appeared seemingly unfazed by his conversations with his ex-girlfriend.

"I'm with Brooke. She's a pediatrician. Why don't I have you talk to her? She would be better equipped to help you than me."

"Oh, umm. I guess—I mean you're a doctor too, I'd rather talk to you."

Logan ignored her and held the phone against his chest. "Lily has a fever. Shelby is babysitting. Do you mind talking to her for a minute to evaluate how bad it is?"

Brooke finished setting two place settings on the table.

"Sure." She weaved around the table as she motioned for him to give her the phone. "I'll talk to her."

He halved the distance to her. "Thanks." Logan slipped the phone into her hand. "I appreciate it."

"No problem." She squeezed his bicep and smiled. Then she placed the phone to her ear. "Shelby, this is Brooke."

Then she stepped away and walked over to the windows which overlooked the city and river. He only heard her end of the conversation as she asked a few questions. Logan didn't know what to do, so he paced the length of the living room while he waited.

"Okay, we'll come right now. Don't worry, babies get fevers a lot and most of the time it isn't serious." She found his gaze and continued, "It's no trouble. We're coming. See you soon." Then she hung up and held his phone out to him. He strode to her and snagged his phone back. "Shelby seemed hysterical about the whole thing. I think Lily is fine, but I told her we would go over right now to help. I instructed her to give Lily some baby Tylenol, and we'll be there soon to relieve her."

"Are you sure?" He raised an eyebrow. "I can go by myself."

"Did you not want me there?" Her voice was calm and even. But her gaze roamed over him.

"Of course I want you there." Logan rubbed the back of his

neck. "But I also know you've had a long day and driving an hour roundtrip wasn't on your to do list tonight."

"I don't mind." She wrung her hands together. "What's the point of being a pediatrician if I don't make house calls for the family? Am I right?"

He scooped her up into a tight hug then kissed her. "You're the best." He smiled down at her.

"I know," she laughed. "But I don't mind hearing you say it out loud."

They quickly repacked up their dinner and took it with them with the hope they would have a chance to eat it at Danielle's. Thirty minutes later, they pulled up. Logan killed the engine.

"I still don't know why anyone isn't picking up their phones." He had tried calling both his parents, Danielle and Michael multiple times on the drive there. "And my parents never go anywhere so I have no idea what's going on with any of them."

Brooke cupped his elbow. "It's fine." She unbuckled her seatbelt. "We're here. Let's go relieve Shelby, and I can figure out what's wrong with Lily."

With heavy-laden steps, Brooke followed Logan up the path to his sister's house. Perspiration gathered on her brow despite the cold. She reminded herself she had nothing to worry about. Logan liked her, but a part of her worried about him seeing Shelby again. Often people don't know what they want until they are fully confronted with it. Desire was tricky like that.

Logan tapped lightly on the door. Then he rubbed the back of his neck with one hand. The guy looked anxious. He double checked the front of his shirt then smoothed it out. Brooke tried to fight the sinking feeling deep in her gut. This had better not be their end when they had only begun. But something told her to brace herself for the worst.

A minute later, the door swung open and revealed Shelby with a screaming Lily on her hip. "She's hysterical." She bounced the infant up and down, but Lily only screamed louder.

"Where's Amelia?" Logan peered past Shelby into the house.

"Luckily," Shelby continued to bounce up and down, "Amelia is still asleep in her crib."

"Here." Brooke opened her arms to take the infant from Shelby. "Let me have her."

Shelby shoved Lily into her hands. Then she pushed loosened hair with the heel of her hand out of her eyes. Some had fallen from the thorny knot on top of her head.

"There, there," Brooke whispered. She leaned her forehead against Lily's own. "Her temperature is high. What time did you give her the fever reducer medication?"

"Right after I called." Shelby sighed and put a hand on her hip. "So, it's been maybe thirty minutes?"

Brooke met Shelby's gaze. "Hey," she shifted the screaming infant from one hip to her other then squeezed her bicep. "You did great."

Then Shelby dropped her face into her palms and cried. Logan's eyes widened then shot Brooke a *what do we do* glance. She nudged her head toward Shelby and tried to convey silently for him to comfort her.

"Come on," Logan finally said. "Let's go back into the living room. You can grab your things and then Brooke and I will take it from here. Any luck in getting a hold of Danielle and Michael?" He gently steered the sobbing Shelby down the hallway.

Brooke closed the front door with her foot then spoke calmly to Lily as she slowly meandered down the hallway toward where they disappeared. When she entered the living room, she stalled in place. Shelby wept in Logan's arms. He gently patted her back.

They locked eyes over the top of Shelby's head.

He mouthed, "I'm sorry. I don't know what to do."

Shelby clung to his shirt. The fabric twisted against her grip. "I'm terrible at this," she wailed.

"No, you aren't." Logan patted her back some more. He rolled his eyes at Brooke, but it didn't help. The familiar feeling of rejection eked back into Brooke's being, while Logan said, "I need to try my sister again." He plunged his hand into his pocket and loosened their embrace.

Lily continued to cry in Brooke's arms. "Where's the bedroom and bathroom the babies use?" Brooke asked while her heart broke a little.

She wondered why she had opened her heart to Logan when it clearly belonged to Shelby.

Logan pointed. "Down the hallway, you can't miss it."

Without hesitating, Brooke wandered down the hallway to the bathroom. Luckily, she found the tub had a baby seat still inside. First, she double checked Lily's temperature then checked her ears with the otoscope she'd brought along. Sure enough, Lily had a double ear infection. She stripped Lily down and filled the tub with cool water to help bring down her temperature. Then she placed the screaming infant into the baby seat and called the pharmacy for an antibiotic prescription while she crouched down next to the tub.

The medicine would be ready in thirty minutes, and hopefully if they managed to get a hold of Danielle and Michael, they could fetch it on their way home. How long she had been alone with Lily she didn't know.

Then Logan strode into the bathroom. "Everything okay?" He opened a cupboard in the bathroom and removed a hooded towel.

Lily continued to scream.

"Double ear infection, poor thing." Brooke pulled up the latch to let the water drain. "I called in the prescription. Any luck with your sister?"

"She finally called back." He came closer with the towel in his arms. "And is en route home and about a half hour away."

"Can you get her to pick up the prescription I called in on her way back?"

"Sure." He came closer with the towel in his arms for Lily.

"And Shelby?" Brooke lifted Lily out of the tub and placed her in the towel that Logan held out for her. "Is she still here?" She kept her gaze on Lily and avoided eye contact with him.

He swaddled Lily tightly in the towel. "Oh, she's still here. She's refusing to leave even though I told her to go."

"Wonderful," Brooke said through a crooked smile. "This is going to be interesting."

Lily calmed down in Logan's arms. He leaned in closer to her, kissed her on the forehead and whispered softly, "They are coming baby girl. I promise." Then he buried Lily against his chest. Her eyelids fluttered open then closed a few times before she finally succumbed to sleep.

The scene made Brooke's insides melt. For a moment, she forgot about Shelby. This guy knew the way to a woman's heart.

"She," Brooke stroked the top of her curly hair and lowered her voice, "has to be in so much pain. I'm glad she fell asleep."

"Me too." Logan smiled back at Brooke then kissed her on the cheek. "Thanks for tonight."

"Anytime." Heat flooded to her core.

"Not to be the bearer of bad news but this little one doesn't even have a diaper on." Logan's eyes widened. "How do we get her diapered and changed without waking her up?"

"Is she going to be okay?" Shelby's voice broke the spell of tranquility as she popped her head into the bathroom.

Lily let out a shriek. "Well, she's up now." Brooke stroked Lily's cheek once.

"I'll go get her dressed. I know where Danielle keeps some extra clothes and diapers in the closet so we can at least keep one of these babies asleep." Logan shimmied out of the bathroom, making a wide step around Shelby. "I'll text Danielle, too, about the medicine."

"I'll help," Shelby announced as she scuttled after him, leaving Brooke alone.

Brooke forced herself to take a settling breath. Then she wiped up the water that dripped onto the bathroom floor and gathered up Lily's used pajamas to place in the hamper in the corner of the room. Once done, she turned off the light and decided to return to the living room to wait. She figured Logan would return in a few minutes but almost fifteen minutes ticked by with no sign of either Shelby or Logan.

A garage door screeched open and seconds later Danielle burst into the living room from the door off of the garage. Brooke stood and walked toward her, meeting her halfway.

"I have the medicine." Danielle shook the paper bag in her hand. "Where is Lily?"

Michael trekked in and removed his jacket. "How is she doing? Sorry we ruined your evening by making you come. Apparently, the theater we were in was a big dead zone. Our phones were on roaming, and we didn't even know it. Plus, Danielle's parents were with us, what a mess."

"Yeah, it wasn't good." Danielle set the bag down on the sofa and removed her jacket too. "But, where's Lily?"

Brooke wrung her hands together. "Logan went off to change her. Shelby followed him but that was fifteen minutes ago. I didn't want to wander around your house looking for them when I don't know where anything is located."

Danielle snatched the medicine off the couch and rushed from the room down a hallway Brooke didn't know.

"So," Michael rocked back and forth on his heels, "I guess I should go check on that, too."

"Go, go." Brooke waved her off as her stomach twisted into a nauseating knot. She imagined Shelby and Logan making out in a dark closet and any second, they would reappear holding hands together. "But please send Logan my way when you find them."

"I will." Then Michael disappeared down the same hallway.

Once again, she found herself alone and out of place. Ten more minutes went by. Brooke wondered what could possibly keep Logan from at least checking on her. Then she heard the front door open along with some muffled voices then it closed shut. Footsteps creaked down the hallway and into the living room.

Logan stopped at the threshold into the living room and leaned against the wall. He looked pale and refused to look at her.

"Something happened, didn't it?" Brooke stated in an even voice as she tried to not spiral.

"Umm." He scratched his chin then rubbed the back of his neck looking incredibly guilty. "I—I—" he stammered.

Brooke didn't need him to go on. It was written all over his face. Shelby wanted him back, and now Logan questioned everything, especially them.

CHAPTER 13

To say the drive home was a bit awkward was the understatement of the year. Logan tapped his hands against the steering wheel as he watched the exit signs fade into a sea of black through his rear-view mirror.

"Is the temperature okay in here?" Logan asked. The silence made his skin itchy. He moved to adjust the temperature up a bit to fight against the outside cold.

"I'm fine." Brooke stared out her passenger side window.

Fine. The universal word in a woman's vocabulary which meant the complete opposite.

"I appreciate you coming with me." His clothes suddenly made his skin itchy and restrictive, he wished he had turned down the temperature rather than up.

"I know," Brooke said without glancing his way.

His mind scattered, Logan forgot how close he was to the city.

"Don't miss the exit." Brooke pointed at the approaching off-ramp only yards away.

"Right." Logan changed lanes rapidly and exited the off-ramp. "Thanks."

He drove through the streets of downtown Chicago toward

Brooke's apartment. "We never even ate." Logan tapped the heel of his hand against his forehead. Their food, no doubt, was still sitting on his sister's kitchen table, long forgotten. "You have to be starving."

Brooke shrugged.

"Do you want me to drive around and find a food truck?" Logan offered.

"No." She shook her head then clasped and unclasped her hands in her lap. "I want to go home."

Logan nodded, taking the upcoming left which turned onto her street. He pulled up to the curb in front of her building.

"Here you are." Logan stopped the car.

She unbuckled her seatbelt and opened her door before he even put the car into park.

"Hey," Logan cupped her elbow which halted her in place. She finally twisted to face him. "I didn't kiss her if that is what you were wondering."

"Well, that's a relief," Brooke said, deadpan.

"But—" Logan scrubbed a hand down his face.

"But?"

He exhaled. "Shelby did want to go out with me again. She said it might be good for us to catch up and see if things are really done between us. She regrets leaving me like she did."

"That's what I thought." Brooke scooted out of her seat and stood. Then she peered back into the car. Her hand gripped the corner of the door, making her knuckles turn white. "Text me if you're still up for faking it at Aubrey and Ian's wedding." She didn't wait for a response but shut the door and wandered into her building.

Logan slumped in his seat as he watched her disappear inside. How had he managed to make such a mess of things? Up until tonight, he didn't care to see Shelby ever again. He liked Brooke, but he'd be lying if he didn't admit seeing Shelby messed with his head. The bottom line was he didn't know what he wanted anymore. And he knew if he didn't figure it out soon, he stood to lose everything.

He drove the rest of the way to his apartment. Then he proceeded to have a very fitful night of sleep. The blaring ring of his cell phone awoke him the following morning.

Groggily, he swiped it from his bed stand and saw Danielle's name flash across the screen. He bolted up right and accepted the call. "Is everything okay?" He asked as he rubbed his eyes with a closed fist. "Is Lily doing better?"

"Lily is fine." Danielle paused, a wail sounded in the background, and he heard her ask Michael to come in and assist her with the twin. "The medicine seems to be working. Her fever has broken. I think by tomorrow she'll be fully on the mend. Thanks again for your help." Then almost as an afterthought she added, "and Brooke's."

His elevated heart rate slowly pumped back down to normal. "Any other reason you are calling me at this unearthly hour on the one day I don't start until noon." He didn't even attempt to hide his annoyance.

"Sorry, we've been up all night. I don't have much concept of time right now."

"No, duh." He waited.

He knew Danielle was itching to ask about Shelby, but he wasn't offering any information. Frankly, he didn't even know what he wanted to do. Things were new with Brooke too. His emotions seemed to be on a teeter totter going back and forth. Then before he fell asleep last night Shelby had already sent him a text message. He hadn't responded, because he didn't know what his heart cared to do.

"Shelby texted me and let me know you chatted."

"My, you've been busy." His jaw clenched. Why did Danielle think she had a say in his relationship?

"She offered the information," Danielle explained.

"And you couldn't wait to call me," Logan countered.

"I want you to end up together," Danielle stated. "Sue me."

A symphony of baby cries cut through their conversation. "Thanks for calling. I'll let you get to those babies." Logan hung up without waiting for her to respond.

What if he lost Brooke in the process of seeing if there was anything with Shelby? The thought made his stomach churn and bile tickle the back of his throat. Ugh, Shelby. The past still remained the same, Shelby dumped him then hightailed it out of town without a thought. Shelby could've contacted him anytime, but she didn't. He let the idea marinate. Instead, she waited until he had a successful job and a girlfriend—wait was Brooke his girlfriend? He paused for a minute and let the idea of Brooke as his girlfriend settle. Losing Brooke, he could fathom it.

Then as if Shelby knew his mind, a text came through from her even though he ignored her first attempt to contact him.

I'll be in the city today to meet up with an old friend. Do you have time to grab a drink this evening?

Logan groaned and flopped backwards onto his bed. His indecisiveness would be his ruin. Did he want to risk things with Brooke? No. He scrolled up to his text chain with Brooke and held off on answering Shelby. Instead, he typed out a message to Brooke.

Thanks for coming with me last night. I'm sorry for how things ended. I don't need to go out with Shelby to know I want to explore things with you. When can I see you again?

After he sent the text message to Brooke, he placed the phone on the bed beside him. His body jumped with nervous energy. He forced himself to get out of bed and pace the small space of his bedroom. Then he tried to remember if Brooke was at the hospital or home today. Why hadn't he listened closer when she told him her schedule earlier in the week?

His phone dinged. Logan nearly toppled over as he slid across his bed to snatch up his phone.

So, what do you say? For old times' sake.

He rubbed the back of his neck and toggled back to the text thread with Brooke. The message had changed from delivered to read, but she hadn't responded. Resolved, he typed out a message to Shelby.

It was nice to see you last night, but I'm with Brooke. I'm really happy with her, and I don't want to do anything to jeopardize our relationship.

The cursor dots of the text thread with Shelby danced at the bottom of the screen. Then they started and stopped so many times, he wondered if she'd simply never respond. Finally, a message appeared on the screen.

I understand. I'll see you around.

Okay.

He exited out of the text thread and breathed a sigh of relief. Tension in his shoulders made his neck ache so he cranked his neck back and forth to lessen the pain. Did he still have the possibility of salvaging things with Brooke? He sure hoped so.

Then his phone dinged again while simultaneously ringing. Brooke still hadn't responded to his message. Instead, Danielle sent him a text message while Mom called him. He knew Danielle only wanted to rail into him about Shelby, so he opted to answer the phone.

"Hey, Mom," Logan answered. "What's up?"

"Oh, honey, I'm checking to see how everything is going, especially after last night when you and Brooke had to drive out to check on Lily. Tell Brooke thank you for us."

"I will." Logan braced himself for what was coming. "Was the concert at least nice?"

"Yes," Mom said, then she spoke for the next five minutes about the songs, instruments, and musicians.

After Logan listened, he asked, "Mom, was there another reason you called?"

He already knew the answer was a resounding yes.

"Ahh, yes," Mom paused, "I wanted to make sure you're still with Brooke, that's all."

"Who told you we weren't together?" he hissed.

"Danielle mentioned you're going to go out with Shelby."

"Unbelievable," he muttered.

"But I worry you might throw things away with Brooke. I think she makes you happy."

He stilled. "You like Brooke better?"

"It's not my life—" her voice faded off. "I don't want to interfere."

"Wrong, you called me to do exactly that." He rubbed the back of his neck. "Now spit it out."

"Fine," Mom huffed. "I like Brooke better. Anyone who dumps my son then leaves without even an explanation is off my list. Shelby is only interested in you now because she's divorced, alone, and finally realizes what a fool she's been. But a mother never forgets how someone treats her child."

"Okay." His phone kept buzzing with incoming text messages from Danielle. "Then can you get Danielle off my back, she keeps pushing me to go out with Shelby, but I'm not interested."

"I'll talk to her. You know they were friends back in high school."

"I know," he sighed. "Still, I need you to talk to her for me. I don't have the time or energy to deal with her. I need to call Brooke, things didn't end great last night, and I need to hopefully fix things."

"I'll get Danielle to stop," Mom sighed.

"Thanks."

Logan said goodbye to Mom and ended the call. A long string of text messages had come through from Danielle. He chose not to respond. The one person he wanted to hear from, Brooke, remained radio silent.

He inwardly groaned as he trotted into his bathroom to shower. The entire time he showered he devised his plan on how to fix things with Brooke. He only hoped it worked.

CHAPTER 14

After the house call for Lily, Brooke stopped responding to Logan's text messages and placed them on mute. She didn't have the emotional bandwidth to be tossed back and forth while he figured out things with Shelby. She only hoped he still planned on holding up his end of the bargain by coming with her to Aubrey and Ian's wedding.

But Brooke never went to dinner with Logan's family. She wasn't sure if they cancelled or went ahead without her, or if he took Shelby, which meant him coming to the wedding was most likely off. She busied herself with work and pretended like the wedding date wasn't approaching.

Two days before the wedding, Brooke ate junk food with Aubrey as they watched a chick flick. She hadn't explained what had happened with Logan. Instead, anytime Aubrey brought up the subject, she maneuvered the topic of conversation back to some part of Aubrey's wedding plans. It worked like a charm.

"What's Ian doing tonight?" Brooke popped a handful of M&M's into her mouth.

Aubrey bit off a chunk of her red vine licorice. "Some sort of top golf thing. I think it was a last-minute bachelor party."

Last weekend, the women had headed to a cabin of Aubrey's parents up in the woods. They had a great time utilizing the hot tub and hanging out. It meant she was out of cell phone range which made her enjoy the time even more.

"Isn't it a little cold for top golf?" Brooke plunged her hand into the shared bowl of popcorn.

"It's one of those inside, digital ones," Aubrey explained.

"Ahh, cool." Brooke snuggled back under her blanket, finding the most comfortable position. "Sounds fun."

"I can't believe I'm getting married on Saturday," Aubrey remarked. "It seems a bit surreal. I feel like we've been talking about it forever. Boom, it's finally here, and now I don't know what to do with my wide range of emotions."

"What emotions are we talking about here?" Brooke shoved another mouthful of popcorn into her mouth. "Happy? Scared? Nervous?"

"I feel mostly excited." Aubrey picked at the end of a licorice piece. "I'm ready to be married and start the next chapter in my life. Ian even talked about buying a house outside of the city. Then it makes me realize everything is changing, in a good way, but still, I'll be someone's wife. Life will be different. Better, but different."

Brooke's stomach twisted. She tried not to think about being left behind. Everyone always left her. What made her so dang unlovable? Would anyone ever find her interesting enough to stick around for?

Her throat grew tight as tears tickled the corners of her eyes. She cleared her throat and blinked the emotion back down. "I've heard there are some great suburbs around here." Brooke tried her best to keep her voice upbeat and happy. "It certainly would be nicer with kids to have more space. I know Ian is anxious for you to start a family."

"I know." Aubrey ate her licorice slowly. When she finished, she snatched another one out of the package. "I want those things too. I want a picket fence, a big yard, and kids. But mainly I want Ian."

"See?" Brooke smiled brightly. She playfully shoved her. "You're going to get everything you ever wanted. I'm happy for you. Plus, I think the suburbs could be fun."

"Liar." Aubrey released their embrace. "Nobody wants to live in the suburbs."

Brooke shrugged. "Some people do. Logan's family seems to like it."

Frankly, she didn't know the first thing about families or suburban life, but Logan's family made it appealing. To have a home, community, and neighbors who knew you and supported you, who wouldn't want that. Maybe even someday she might receive those things for herself.

They ate for a minute in silence, munching on the popcorn. "Logan is going to meet you at the wedding, right? I want you to get ready with me in the bride's room."

"Um." Brooke hadn't contacted Logan about the wedding plans. Actively avoiding him had become a bit of a dance for her. He had texted her a few times since that evening with his niece, then she ignored him completely and didn't read anything he wrote. Since then, she figured he was happily dating Shelby, but she still needed him for this one last fake date. Then they could both go their own ways. "I can tell him to meet me there."

"Great." Aubrey smiled and waved a piece of popcorn at the screen. "What are we watching anyways?"

Brooke laughed. "You've Got Mail. It's a classic."

"Oh, Tom Hanks and Meg Ryan. I thought we were watching Sleepless in Seattle, and I kept waiting for the funny banter between Meg Ryan and Rosie O'Donnell. I was beginning to be a bit disappointed."

"You're in luck." Brooke stopped the movie and toggled to another streaming service and pulled up Sleepless in Seattle. "I happen to be the proud owner of digital copies of both of the movies. What part did you want to watch specifically?"

"The part about how it's hard to get married when you're older." Aubrey chomped off another bite of her licorice.

"I know the exact spot." She queued it up. "And frankly I find it eerily true."

Aubrey whacked her on her arm. "Whatever, you have Logan now."

"Right," Brooke muttered. "How could I forget?"

Then she pressed play, and they watched the iconic scene together.

Later that evening, after Aubrey headed home, Brooke mustered up the courage to text Logan about the wedding.

> I wanted to double-check that you're still okay with going to Aubrey and Ian's wedding on Saturday? I know we haven't been in contact, and I still owe you, but I need the favor if you're willing to come.

She sent the message and then walked her empty popcorn bowl to the kitchen. Then she forced herself to gather up the trash and toss everything into the garbage. Anxious energy pumped through her veins, but she didn't allow herself to check if he had read her message or not. Instead, she focused her attention on cleaning up her apartment. After fluffing her couch pillows, vacuuming the rug, starting the dishwasher, and wiping down the kitchen counters, she still hadn't heard from Logan.

She wondered if she needed to frantically browse through her contact lists to find a date last minute. Then her phone vibrated in her pocket and her heartrate sputtered. With a tremor in her hand, she dug her phone out.

> Of course I'll be there. Just text me the details. I can't wait to see you.

Heat flushed her cheeks. What did his text even mean? Did he want to see her so he could fill her in on his new relationship? Or did he genuinely miss her?

I'll text you the address of the church. You'll need to meet me there. I have to get there early to get ready with Aubrey, and I won't be able to see you before the ceremony.

She gnawed on her lip then shuffled her feet as she typed out the address of the church and sent it to him.

No problem. I put in the time off. I won't even be on call. I don't have anything else going on. I can't wait to talk to you. We have a lot to catch up on.

Her stomach dropped. A tickle of sweat ran down her temple. Then she knew the glimmer of hope she held onto dimmed.

Great see you then.

She tossed her phone onto her couch and groaned into her palmed hands. Just until the wedding, she reminded herself, then she'd be free of the idea of them.

CHAPTER 15

Logan double-checked the address of the church on his text thread with Brooke. When he confirmed the church with Gothic Revival architecture was indeed the place he needed to be, he circled until he found a parking garage. His insides did a somersault as he exited his car and straightened his suit jacket. He hadn't seen Brooke in nearly three weeks, and he missed her and ached to lay eyes on her. Once he did, he planned on convincing her and showing her how much he wanted to be with her, and not Shelby. But chances were slim, she hadn't responded to any of his text messages. Tonight felt like an olive branch even if it was under false pretenses.

The foyer contained a beautiful array of floral arrangements which made the space drip with the tantalizing aroma of roses and lilacs. An easel had a huge engagement photo of Ian and Aubrey for people to sign in lieu of a book. Logan added his name to the photo then took his seat at the back of the church. He recognized a few doctors from the hospital but didn't know them personally.

Slowly, the pews filled up. The string quartet at the front of the church played a light melody of a classical song he knew but couldn't name. Ian took his place at the front of the chapel. The back doors of the chapel swung open, and the people of the wedding party started their way down the aisle. Logan craned his neck in search of a glimpse of Brooke. Justin walked down the aisle first with the woman he escorted then a few more couples from the wedding partied followed, finally Brooke made her appearance on the arm of another groomsman.

His heart nearly stopped at the sight of her. Her hair was half up and half down, curled then twisted into a hairdo he imagined had taken hours to prep. The long silky coral dress hugged her perfectly. Never in his life had Logan been more jealous of the man she held onto as she walked down the aisle. Their eyes locked as she passed his pew. A zing shimmered down his spine.

Without a thought he mouthed, "You look beautiful."

Pink splashed her cheeks. Brooke's eyes crinkled around the edges as she smiled back. She continued past his pew. The wedding party arrived at their positions at the front of the church. Then the music changed to the traditional wedding march and those in the audience rose to their feet. Aubrey appeared at the back of the chapel doors and entered on her father's arm. Slowly, she walked down the aisle then joined Ian at the front of the chapel. An officiant began his remarks, and the audience sat back down.

Logan didn't remember a word from the ceremony. A few blissful times his eyes met Brooke's as she stole a few glances in his direction. He never took his gaze off of her, because he'd never seen someone so beautiful in his entire life. The tide shifted between them, he could feel it. A glimmer of hope made him believe tonight, things could be different if he changed them.

By the time the ceremony ended, he itched to touch her, talk to her, hold her. When the ceremony ended, the chapel erupted into a busy chaotic herd of people trying to leave through the back doors at the same time. When he reached the exit, Brooke had already faded into the crowd. He didn't have any choice but to wait for her to show up at dinner.

A dinner reception was set on the back lawn behind the church following the ceremony. When he found the tent set up on the wide grassy lawn with tables fanned out around the dance floor, Brooke still hadn't appeared. Space heaters kept the area surprisingly warm. He forced himself to find his seat at the table with his name card next to hers.

Guests slowly slid into the empty seats of the table. He made quick introductions with those who sat, but his mind was elsewhere. Brooke ran rampant through his psyche making it impossible to concentrate on anything else. Then moments before they announced the arrival of the newlyweds, Brooke slipped into her seat.

Out of breath, she said, "Hey." Her hair had loosened from the half up and half down hairstyle. She tucked some fallen strands behind her ears. "I'm glad you found the table okay. I've been busy having photos taken with the wedding party."

Their eyes met. "I figured." The dancing candle centerpiece lit up her gaze with fiery perfection. "You look beautiful." He took a shaky breath then immediately sped forward, "I'm glad you reached out. I thought I was off your list after you ghosted me. I hope we can go back to being in each other's lives."

"I needed some space, but I think I'd like that too." Her cheeks reddened. "Thanks for coming." She darted her gaze away from him and peered at the others at the table.

His fingers twitched with anticipation of touching her. "I wouldn't have missed it."

"I know." Her gaze turned flat. Her back straightened as she leaned back against her chair and glanced away. "A deal is a deal, right?" Brooke removed the napkin ring from the napkin on the plate in front of her. "But I backed out on the dinner with your parents, so I owe you."

"No, you don't." Logan brushed her shoulder with the back of his thumb knuckle. "I wanted to come."

"You wanted to pretend one more time?" Brooke set the napkin ring next to her plate then placed the napkin on her lap.

"No, that's not it at all. We don't have to play this game anymore." Logan shifted closer to her. "Brooke—" He stroked her arm again with his finger as he tried to find the right words.

Then a voice over a loudspeaker interrupted him. Everyone clapped. Logan had no choice but to listen and clap along with everyone else. He hated how things hung in the balance. A quiet corner and a few minutes was what he needed to explain to her his true feelings. But tonight, this moment wasn't it. Ian and Aubrey made their appearance and sat at the head table with their parents.

Logan removed his napkin ring and placed his napkin on his lap. The servers placed the first course in front of them, a bowl of creamy potato soup. Luckily, the others at the table fell into conversations with each other and didn't find the need to open the table up to a group conversation. He ate his first bite of soup but tasted nothing.

"I feel like I haven't seen you in forever, catch me up with what's going on in your life," Logan said.

The spoon in Brooke's hand stilled, she shifted to face him. "Aren't you," she raised a skeptical eyebrow, "the one who said you have so much to tell me?"

"Ahh." He forced himself to take another bite then wiped his face with his napkin. "I might have exaggerated how much I needed to tell you. Mainly, I wanted to say—"

Then he was interrupted again by someone at the loudspeaker. The universe seemed to be on some kind of mission to keep him from saying what he came here to say. Justin, who apparently was the best man, made a few remarks about the happy couple.

"Aren't you the maid of honor?" Logan whispered.

"No." Brooke shook her head. "It's Aubrey's childhood friend which I'm completely relieved about, because it means I don't have to make some speech. I've never been one for public speaking."

Justin finished his rambling address which garnered a few laughs though Logan's jaw only locked when he looked at him. The maid of honor followed and everyone clapped. Then the servers immediately served the main course of chicken and pesto pasta. They ate for a few minutes. It was much too loud with the music playing, and the setting wasn't right for a deep conversation.

A woman stopped by the table as they finished their entrees, "Brooke?" They twisted in their seats toward her. "I thought that was you."

"Cece," Brooke exclaimed as she jumped out of her chair. They hugged. "I didn't know you were coming. It's good to see you. How is the hospital in New York working out?"

"I love it there." Then Cece whispered to Brooke, "You need to introduce me to your friend."

Brooke's face splashed with heat, but she squeezed his shoulder. "This is umm—"

He didn't waste any time rising to his feet. "Hi, I'm Logan." He shook hands with Cece. Then he wrapped a protective arm around Brooke's waist. "I'm her boyfriend."

"You don't say." Cece smirked while her eyes dilated a smidge. "Way to go Brooke, this guy is a total upgrade from loser face. Aubrey told me what happened, ouch." She motioned with a thumb in the direction of Justin laughing a tad too drunkenly with a group of friends. "You're way better off."

"I know." Brooke snuggled up to Logan and placed a hand on his chest. Then she lovingly gazed up at him and remarked, "Logan's wonderful. I'm a lucky gal."

Cece smiled. "Do you happen to have a brother?"

Logan laughed. "Sorry, only a sister."

"Dang." Cece shrugged. "It was worth a shot."

The two old friends chatted for a minute about Cece's new position as head of Pediatrics at a hospital in Manhattan. Logan listened intently, adding a few remarks to help show his interest in their conversation. Then the music in the background stilled. They announced the bride and groom's first dance.

Cece hugged Brooke. "It was great seeing you." Then she leaned in and whispered but loud enough for him to hear, "Your new guy is hot and nice, do yourself a favor and hold on to him."

"I'll try," Brooke replied.

"I'd better get back to my table." Cece stepped away then glanced in his direction. "It was nice meeting you."

Logan smiled. "Likewise."

They sat back down and watched for a moment as Ian and Aubrey danced far off on the dance floor.

"Cece seems nice," Logan said as he readjusted his tie. "I'm sure working in Manhattan is exciting."

"She was a great co-worker, but I'm happy for her and her promotion." Brooke leaned back against her seat. "As for Manhattan, I think Chicago is a big enough city for me."

"Yeah?" His ears perked up. "Could you see making Chicago home?"

"Maybe," Brooke shrugged.

Their gaze caught. His breath hitched.

"I mean what is home anyways?" Brooke gnawed on her bottom lip.

"I think it's where you make it, but I'm partial to Chicago."

Brooke peeled her glance from him. "I've never really felt I had a home anywhere, but Chicago is growing on me. I think with time it could become home. I figure it's as good as place as any to settle down."

Those in the room erupted into applause as the song and dance ended. The announcer opened up the dance floor to everyone else. A soft smooth slow song came out of the speakers.

Logan watched for a minute as others joined in with the happy couple. Then he pushed back his chair and stood.

"Dance with me." He held out his outstretched hand.

Brooke tilted her chin up and met his gaze. Her hair had loosened even more, practically fallen out of the updo. The silky strands cascaded over her shoulders. She yanked the last of the bobby pins out of her hair. Then she shook her hair and used her hand to fluff it out.

"There." She tossed the bobby pins onto the table. "My head was killing me from how tight the hairdresser did the top part." Her hand smoothed out it out a bit more. "Does that look okay?" She scuttled out of her chair.

"You look perfect." Logan wrapped an arm around her waist and gently brought her closer. "Now come dance with me."

"Right," Brooke paused, "is this for pretend? Because I think Justin is far too drunk to notice."

"What?" Logan faltered. "No. I want to dance with you, not for pretend, not for anything other than I want to be close to you."

"Do you?" Brooke tilted her head and examined him. "I can't decide what is real and what isn't."

"I want to dance with you." Logan's chest tightened. He wished he had the words to better convey the myriad of emotion trapped inside of him. "That's what is real."

The song changed from a soft melody to a fast, upbeat one. His chance to slow dance withered away, and he hated it.

"Fine." Brooke snatched his hand. "Looks like they are onto the fast songs. Are you ready to show me your wicked dance moves?"

Logan cringed. "I'm such a dorky dancer."

Brooke crinkled her nose. "Which is something I'm sure I'll find endearing."

She weaved them through the throngs of people and made their way over to where her friends danced. Those on the dance floor bopped and swayed. Brooke continued until they landed next to Aubrey and Ian dancing. The iconic YMCA song blared, and Logan let himself get lost in the joyful spirit of dancing. Brooke glimmered under the twinkle lights which hung over the area. She looked beautiful and free as she laughed along with her friends. The song ended then a long slew of faster songs followed. Logan shucked his jacket off and tossed it on a chair nearby. Brooke's tight curls loosened even more, and he resisted the urge to run a finger down the length of the smooth strands.

Then as luck would have it, the DJ played a slow song again. Couples paired off and Brooke glanced around at everyone but at him.

Logan held his hand out to her. "Don't make this weird."

Brooke took a step closer to him and gently placed her hand into his own. "I'll try not to."

He brought her close, wrapping his arm around her waist. At first, she kept her body stiff and two inches apart. But as the soothing music played, her tight muscles relaxed. To his delight, she rested her head against his shoulder. Logan closed his eyes for a moment as they swayed to the melody. He let himself revel in the feeling of her body relaxing softly against his. The smooth curves of her hips fit perfectly next to him. Her tantalizing aroma filled his lungs, hints of lavender and vanilla. The scent made his head spin.

He tilted his chin down. Their gaze locked with one another. His heartrate racked up to a staccato beat. Her lips twisted into a twitching smile while her eyes crinkled around the edges. She studied him, and he wondered if she felt this momentum too, this building tide which would eventually have to break.

She moistened her lips. Logan's breath hitched in his chest. He brought his face closer to hers, but he forced himself to stop before their lips could gaze each other's. The ache to kiss her rattled him.

"Should I kiss you now?" he whispered.

His gaze roamed her face.

Ever so slightly, almost indistinguishable, she nodded. Logan cupped both sides of her neck. His thumbs brushed the length of her jaw. Then he let his lips collide with hers. Brooke melted into him. Her hand crept to the middle of his chest and soon her fingers fisted a handful of his shirt. His insides melted into a velvety smooth wave he wanted to ride forever. Their kiss was warm and gentle. It was filled with the possibilities of a future. All the waiting, wanting, only further laced the layers of heat between them. How much time passed, he had no clue. A few times he felt the bumps and brushes of other dancers, but Logan lived in a world where only he and Brooke orbited. This world he never cared to leave. This time he would never walk away even if she pushed him.

Their kiss deepened. Their shared breath warmed them despite the lowering temperature. Tonight, he held the one thing he cared to have, and he had no plan on letting go or being the first to tug their lips apart. For as long as Brooke would allow him to kiss her, hold her, he'd enjoy the beauty of being in the present.

Soon, the song ended. The DJ changed the song back to a fast song. Brooke broke their lips an inch apart. "I guess we'd better stop now." Her lips were raw and red. "We're probably making a scene and there are children here."

"Huh?" In a daze, Logan tried to find his place back on solid ground. He loosened their embrace and ran a finger under her bottom lip where her lipstick had smudged. "Whatever you say." He smiled and kissed her at her temple.

Some of the people on the dance floor bumped into them, he guided her away from the crowd to the outskirts of those dancing.

"Ugh, you still have Shelby." Her words broke the trance. "We shouldn't have kissed. I don't know what I was thinking." She gnawed her bottom lip.

"What?" He dropped his hand from around her waist. "No. I'm not with Shelby."

The mention of her made his gut twist. When would Shelby finally be out of his life forever?

"But you went out with her," she fidgeted with the buttons on his shirt, "right?" Then she tilted her chin up to meet his gaze.

"No." His jaw tightened. "Why do you keep pressing me on this? I told you I want to be with you. Why won't you believe me? Didn't that kiss tell you everything you wanted to know?"

Logan forced himself to take a long calming breath.

Brooke stepped back. "Your sister thinks you should be with Shelby."

"But I want to be with you." Logan rubbed a hand down his face. "I don't care what Danielle wants or thinks."

He didn't want Shelby, maybe at one point he did, but not now, not when he'd had another taste of Brooke.

"I asked you to go out with Shelby. I need to know that chapter of your life is closed." Brooke widened the gap between them and wrung her hands together. "I can't handle it if we start to date and you change your mind."

"I won't change my mind." He attempted to reach for her, but she stumbled a step back out of his grasp. "It's not like that. Shelby, well— there's—"

Her flat expression made his stomach plummet. "Just go out with her."

"I'm not going to go out with her," Logan said as he shoved his hands into the pockets of his pants. "I want to be with you and not for pretend, and not just until the wedding."

The DJ interrupted their conversation with the announcement, "Everyone grab a sparkler, the newlyweds are about to leave."

"I need to go. This was a mistake." Brooke backpedaled and bumped into another guest. "Oh, sorry," she said as she weaved around them.

Then she twisted on her feet and drifted into the crowd of people moving toward the exit to line the path for Ian and Aubrey's departure. Logan didn't see the point in going after her. He tried and failed to convince her he wanted so much more. So, he watched her drift away and then he turned around and left.

CHAPTER 16

"So, where is Romeo?" Brooke flinched as Justin sidled up next to her in the long line of guests holding sparklers to give Ian and Aubrey their fairytale send off. "I thought I saw him head to his car. Is he coming back?"

Was this guy still talking?

"I could ask you," Brooke peered around the crowd, "the same thing. Did what's-her-name need to go home and get her beauty rest?"

Gosh, she hated him. What had she ever seen in him?

Justin smirked. "I mean she is beautiful, but nah, she's here, taking a load off. Her feet were aching from her four-inch heels."

Brooke had admired how long and lean Justin's girlfriend looked in her shape-hugging, gem-colored cocktail dress and her heels with the special red bottoms. She'd fit right in with Justin's family.

"Ahh," Brooke managed. She peered down the long row of guests. Their sparklers lit up the dark sky. The city lights made it impossible to see the stars. "I bet."

"So, you never answered about your guy ditching you." Justin smugly waved his sparkler.

Brooke could only think about punching him in the face.

"He didn't ditch me. He was on call." Brooke gritted her teeth. Two minutes around Justin, and he already managed to get under her skin and then the lies spilled out. "Emergency surgery. You know how it is."

"I do." Justin looked pleased with himself. Unfortunately, he continued, "I'm glad you found someone, that means I'm off the hook for feeling guilty. What's the saying? It's all water under the bridge."

Maybe for him.

"Sure." Brooke forced a tight smile. "Whatever you say."

Then like a Greek goddess of the night, Justin's girlfriend emerged from behind, tucking her hands around his elbow. "I was looking for you everywhere." She ignored Brooke until she shifted and gave her a once over.

Her gaze formed tiny slits as she shot Brooke a death stare. If looks could kill, Brooke would've withered into a pile of ash on the spot.

"I'm glad you found me." Justin peered toward the end of the tunnel of guests. "There's the happy couple." He pointed to the opening where the newlyweds emerged.

Aubrey and Ian had changed out of their wedding clothes. Aubrey had put on a loose and flowery dress in coral. Ian sported a casual sports coat and slacks. They were headed straight to the airport to catch the red eye flight to Aruba.

The long line of guests erupted into applause and cheers as they meandered through the tunnel of people. When Aubrey passed by her, she stopped her by placing a hand on her shoulder. Their eyes met. "Have a great time," Brooke shouted over the roar of the guests. "You look so happy."

Aubrey smiled. "I am," she shouted back.

Brooke dropped her hand.

Aubrey continued through the throngs of people to where their car awaited. When they arrived, everyone watched Ian help

Aubrey into the passenger seat. Then he rounded the car and climbed in. Soon the car peeled out of the parking lot and merged into the sea of traffic on the city street.

An emptiness washed over Brooke as she had no choice but to head back to where she'd left her things. She skillfully avoided Justin and his new woman as she trekked across the lawn to the reception area. Her sparkler neared the end of its burning life. Once it burned out, she tossed it in a trash bin.

She gathered up her things to leave, but then she remembered she had driven over with Aubrey in the car which now was headed to the airport. In her mind, she had planned on Logan dropping her off at her apartment. The thought of taking the L train home made her heart sink. Loneliness seeped into the very fiber of her being.

To make matters worse, she ran back into Justin and his girlfriend on her way out.

"You headed home?" Justin loosened his grip on his girlfriend's waist. He peered around then finally asked, "Did you need a ride?"

"I'm okay." Brooke clasped the front of her jacket closed.

The coolness of night had been fought off by heaters surrounding the tables and dance floor. Now, they had run out of gas and she was no longer in the cozy reception tent. The night air was cold and made her shiver. She tried her best not to let her teeth chatter and shifted uncomfortably on her feet. Why hadn't she remembered to bring a pair of comfortable shoes to wear home?

"We can give you a ride." Justin unrolled his arm from his girlfriend's waist. "It's on the way."

She'd rather eat dirt than get into a car with them.

"No, thanks." Brooke crossed her arms in an attempt to stay warm. "I have a few more things I promised Aubrey I'd do before I left."

Brooke remembered she had offered to return Ian's tuxedo. She needed to head back to fetch it.

"We could wait," Justin offered.

Why was Justin being nice? Guilt?

"No. I'm fine." Brooke moved to leave. "Have a nice night. It was nice seeing you again."

Then she didn't wait, instead she booked it across the lawn toward the bridal suite, a room off the chapel of the church, where Aubrey said she would leave their things. Once inside the comfort and quiet of the small room, Brooke collapsed against the back of the door, sinking down it as though the day had drained the strength from her bones. She had pushed Logan away, and she only had herself to blame.

Her mind reeled as she replayed their kiss on the dance floor. The light brush of their lips, the feeling of strength in his hands, and his manly scent filling her lungs. If that was the last kiss they ever shared, at least it was a memorable one.

Logan wondered if he should whip back around and head back to the wedding. The light up ahead turned red and forced him to come to a stop. He tapped his hands on the steering wheel and matched the random beat of some song he'd heard a hundred times but couldn't name. *Go back, go back, go back.* The words vibrated in his mind and competed against the thump of the song's beat. *And say what?*

Green light, Logan eased off the brake and shifted his foot to the gas. If he headed back now, he could catch Brooke before she left, maybe even give her a ride home. *But she told you to leave.* Yeah, that was right. Leave and call Shelby? Why? He thought the kiss they shared said everything he cared to get across and more. Kissing Brooke, well, he didn't have enough time to unpack how mind-blowingly good they were together.

They fit. Why didn't she understand he knew what he wanted?

His phone rang, blasting it through the Bluetooth speaker of the car, silencing the music. Danielle's name flashed across his dashboard. He groaned. If he didn't answer, she'd only call again and again until he picked up.

He slapped the answer button on the dash and hissed, "I hope you're happy."

"Geez, take it down a notch," Danielle replied.

Logan passed through another light. Then the next light changed from green to yellow. He made the last second decision to slam on his brakes and wait. His blood simmered a touch below exploding.

"Brooke told me to go out with Shelby and figure out if there is something there. She told me she won't go out with me again until I do." He raked a hand through his hair.

"I always liked Brooke," Danielle calmly replied.

"What on earth are you talking about?" The light turned green. Logan peeled off the line and passed through the intersection then turned right onto the street which led to his apartment. "You've been pushing me to date Shelby."

"I like that Brooke recognizes that you have unfinished business with Shelby. If you go out with her then decide Brooke is for you, I'll be happy to see you end up together."

"Danielle," his jaw twitched. "You're going to pay for this whole thing."

"Nah, you'll thank me later when you end up with the right woman."

His building came into view. He turned into the driveway which led to the communal garage below it.

"Which is who exactly?" Logan pressed the garage button on his car visor and waited as the large garage door to the parking garage opened.

"Umm, I'm not sure yet, but at least you have two very solid leads which is more than you had a few months ago."

"I might end up alone," he countered.

"Or you might end up with the right woman."

"This is not how things play out in romance movies."

"It's exactly how they play out." Danielle cleared her throat. "Now call Shelby, take her out and then either close the chapter or open it back up."

"Fine." He gritted his teeth then parked his car. "I'll reach out to Shelby."

"Perfect."

For everyone but him.

CHAPTER 17

Logan adjusted the lapel of his sports coat and knocked on the door of Shelby's house. His heart pounded in his chest so loudly it made his temples pulsate. His thoughts were scattered but kept drifting back to Brooke. He hadn't talked to or heard from her in over two weeks, and his fingers twitched at the idea of holding her again. But here he was picking up another woman for a date after agonizing over what to do for too long. How had he managed to make a mess of everything? Why had he listened to everyone else but the voice in his own head?

The door swung open, revealing Shelby. She had dressed to kill in a form-fitting crimson cocktail dress.

"Hey." Shelby smiled brightly. Tension in his shoulders eased slowly out of his body. "It's good to see you again."

"Yes." He stepped closer and leaned in for a hug. She moved into his arms. "I'm glad we are doing this."

"Me too." She squeezed him again then broke their embrace. "Let me grab my coat."

Shelby disappeared inside. Logan peered over his shoulder across the street to his sister's house. He spotted her staring at him through the front living room window. Instead of growing angry, he waved. His sister darted away and closed the drapes in a hurry. He shifted back to face Shelby's front door. She appeared a minute later with a coat slung over her arm.

"Do you mind helping me into this?" Shelby asked as she locked her front door.

"Sure."

"Thanks." Shelby handed him her coat. He held it open. She slipped her arms inside then readjusted her hair that had tucked inside the collar. "Okay. I think I'm ready."

"Great." Logan motioned for her to go first.

They wandered down her walkway to where his car was parked at the curb.

When she arrived at his car door, Shelby swiveled to face him. "So, where are you taking me?"

Logan scratched his chin. "A restaurant Danielle suggested. She said your favorite food is sushi. That's certainly a change. If I remember correctly, Hawaiian pizza used to be your favorite." He cocked an eyebrow.

"Yeah," she gave him a playful shove, "but I was like seventeen. I'm happy to say my tastebuds have matured. I've ventured beyond takeout pizza."

"There's nothing wrong with Hawaiian pizza. I still get a hankering for it every now and then, and whenever I do order it, I tend to always think of you."

Heat rose up his neck. The words had tumbled out without him thinking. They weren't untrue. He did think about Shelby every single time he ate Hawaiian pizza, but he hated how much he thought about her. If he had a choice, he never wanted her to grace his thoughts with longing again. Most likely, Shelby hadn't thought about him once until she returned to town divorced and alone.

He fumbled for the passenger car door, opening it for her. She slipped around him and slid into her seat. Then she gazed up at him. "I think about you every time I eat Snickers bars. You used to pound them after your sports games."

His lips twitched. "I haven't eaten a Snickers bar in years."

The thought made his mouth taste like lead. Shelby forgot she mocked him once for eating them so quickly. She pointed it out and laughed at him. A memory he had tucked away tightly, and it had only wiggled to the surface at her prodding.

"Too bad, they are one of my favorites."

"Ahh," Logan managed.

He shut her door then rounded the car. A flash of memories from the past came roaring back. Snapshots he had long forgotten, ones which added up to Shelby being overly critical of him. She always had a way of making him feel like nothing. But through the softening lens of time, he had forgotten these parts, until now.

The frigid air nipped at his skin and managed to cool off his flushed neck and cheeks. When he slid into his spot behind the steering wheel, he knew this entire evening would begin and end with the same foregone conclusion. Brooke is who he wanted sitting beside him, but he started the engine to let the warm air from the vent defrost the windshield.

Let's get this over.

"I still can't believe you're a surgeon," Shelby said, breaking the silence.

Logan shifted in his seat to face her as the windshield cleared. "Why? Is it so unbelievable I made something of myself?" He tried his best to keep his voice even and undeterred, but he hated how her doubt made him feel small. Like he only mattered now, due to his profession, and not before when she ditched him for something bigger and flashier.

"Honestly," Shelby scrunched her nose, "and don't take this the wrong way, but I always figured you'd end up never leaving town, flipping burgers at McDonald's."

His jaw clenched. He didn't take her words the wrong way, in fact he took them exactly for what they were. Comments she had made from way back when flooded his mind. And none of them were good.

The windshield cleared of fog enough to drive. He forced himself to take a deep settling breath before he tugged the car away from the curb. "I guess you were wrong." Logan eased onto the street.

The words landed and silence filled the car.

Shelby huffed. "There's no need to get defensive." She whipped her hair over one shoulder. "Even you have to admit you were an idiot back then."

"How so?" Logan flipped on his blinker. "What would have given you the indication that I didn't have high aspirations for my life? I had good grades. Please enlighten me."

This evening was a mistake. He hated himself for being persuaded to go out on this date. Sure, Brooke wanted him to. Danielle had certainly championed it, but he hated how many years he had yearned for a woman who was nothing like the person he imagined in his mind. Years wasted with longing when he should have been wise enough to step back and come to see her breaking up with him had been a blessing. A blessing which kept him from spending years with the wrong person.

"I don't know—" her voice trailed off. She peered out her passenger side window. "I never thought you would have it in you to go do that much schooling. I figured you'd drop out and move back home and live in your parents' basement."

The words stung. But the truth stared back at him. Shelby never believed in him, and he needed to be with someone who would love and champion every part of him, someone like Brooke.

"But I did make something of myself despite your utter lack of confidence in my abilities. And now you're interested in me." He made a sharp turn into the parking lot of the restaurant and found a spot two rows back. "I wasn't enough for you then but now—"

"I'm sorry I brought that up." Shelby squeezed his bicep. "I think you're getting me wrong. This doesn't need to be some harsh rehash of the past. I'm impressed with what you have accomplished. Isn't that enough?"

"Maybe it isn't." He unbuckled his seatbelt and shifted to face her. "Is that why you dumped me? Because you didn't believe I had a future?"

"No." Shelby dropped her hand from his bicep. "I dumped you, because—" She shook her head then fidgeted with the ends of her hair. "It was a long time ago. The past is in the past."

"I've wondered for years. One minute we're dancing at prom, planning our lives together, and the next minute you dumped me. Then you fled town with no explanation." He shifted to get a better view of her. "You didn't even respond to any of my calls or text messages. How could that not affect someone?"

Shelby spun some hair around one of her fingers. "But it was years ago."

"And yet here we are." Logan rubbed the back of his neck. This entire evening had been a huge mistake; one he promised to never make again. This was the first and last time he let his family interfere with his relationships. And this is the last time he ever wanted to think about Shelby. Maybe this date was a good idea. "Honestly, you owe me a reason. So, I'll wait."

Shelby took a deep breath then ran her finger across the condensation on her window. "I made out with Grant Sullivan after the final basketball game."

His blood ran cold. Grant Sullivan. They had been best friends through high school, but Grant pulled away from him toward the end of their senior year. He turned down several invitations Logan offered to hang out. The missing puzzle piece dropped into place.

"You had gone to some sort of family reunion that weekend."

Shelby traced some more on the window. "I don't know why I kissed him. I always knew he had a thing for me, and so when he walked me to my car and leaned in, I kissed him back. It wasn't a huge deal. I had already decided we were done."

"So, everyone knew but me." Logan stared out the windshield. "Thanks for telling me."

"Really?" Shelby questioned with far too much hope in her voice.

"Yeah, thanks." His neck ached. "I can lay that part of my life to bed."

Shelby shifted closer and leaned over the center console. "Does this mean you're ready to give us another go?"

"No." Logan fidgeted with his keys then removed them from the ignition. "I never said that." He sighed. "I know we're better off as friends."

"Because you're in love with Brooke?" Shelby offered.

Love. The word ricocheted back and forth in his mind. He waited for the panic to set in, the urge to argue with her, but instead he let it land and settle. Did he love Brooke?

"I might be." He folded his arms and leaned his back against the seat.

"I knew it." Shelby shifted. They stared across the parking lot toward the restaurant. "I saw the way you looked at her. You used to look at me that way, and I was too dumb and naïve to appreciate it."

Logan didn't argue. Instead, he started the engine and said, "I think I should take you home."

"Yes," Shelby said. "Please take me home."

CHAPTER 18

The right side of Brooke's stomach throbbed. Her late-night Taco Bell run had come back to bite her. Sweat lathered her brow and trickled down her temples. She halted in the hospital hallway then placed her palm flat against the wall and forced herself to take a few deep breaths as the pain increased.

A nurse walking by stopped next to her and asked, "Everything okay?" She placed a gentle hand on her shoulder. "You look really pale."

Brooke peered up at her. "I'm not sure." Another wave of pain hit. "I think I might have food poisoning." She breathed in and out, in and out.

"Come on." The nurse held a hand out to her. "Let's get you to the nurses' station, and I can at least check your vitals."

"I think I'll be okay." A sharp stabbing pain made her suck in breath. "Actually—" Her words came in short spurts. "I might need—something is wrong."

The nurse wrapped a supportive arm around her waist and helped her walk to the nurses' station. Her vision blurred while her knees started to buckle. Brooke gripped the top of the nurses' station to keep herself upright. The nurse reached for the thermometer behind the desk to check her temperature.

"I don't know—" Brooke tightened her grip on the desk. Wave after wave of pain made her groan. "This might be—"

Then Brooke hit the floor, and the world became black.

How long she was out she had no clue, but Logan's voice pushed through her psyche. "Hey, are you okay?"

She tried to open her eyes, but the blinding lights overhead made her head throb.

Why was he here? This must be a very bad and strange dream. The cold linoleum pressed against her back made her shiver. Slowly, she forced one eye open. Logan's face filled her field of vision.

"Hey," his voice was soft and steady. He brushed her arm with the pad of his thumb. "You're coming out of it. That's good."

"Logan?" Her temples pulsated and the stabbing sensation in her gut made her wither in pain. "Something is wrong." She closed her eyes again.

Everything hurt.

"I happened to be walking by when I saw you hit the ground."

"Ahh." She gripped her stomach. Her eyes remained clenched shut. "What are the odds?"

Logan brushed her hair off of her forehead. "I'm glad I'm here. Describe your pain for me."

"I think I have appendicitis." Brooke cradled her side and moaned. "I think I need surgery. I thought—it was—bad Taco Bell."

Brooke felt Logan's hand move gingerly to her right aching side. He pressed only slightly.

"Ahh!" Brooke thrashed around on the floor in pain. "Stop, stop, stop," she hollered.

Logan sprang into action and shouted instructions to the

nurse. Within moments, he and the nurse helped her onto a hospital bed. She moved in and out of consciousness. The world spun while she fought to stay awake, but the pain made her want something entirely different. She wanted to fall into a deep sleep where the pain would no longer register.

Memories came in quick spurts while they pushed her down the hallway on a gurney. Logan held her hand and walked with the speed of the bed. The bright lights seeped through her closed eyelids. Then the world went black, again.

Brooke awoke hours later in a hospital bed. Her head ached. She peered across the small room. Logan was curled up on the single lounge chair in the corner fast asleep. Her side throbbed. Machines beeped. How long had she been out? And what happened? Slowly, her hand moved down to her abdomen. A huge gauze bandage covered the length of it, and she didn't have the strength to sit up.

"Logan," she croaked. "Logan, wake up."

He stirred. Groggily, he swiped at his tired eyes. When his gaze finally locked with hers, he scurried out of the lounge chair and raced over to her hospital bedside. "Brooke, you're back." He interlaced his hand with hers and squeezed. Then he leaned in and kissed her on her forehead. "You scared me. I thought—" His voice cracked.

He brushed her hair out of her eyes and smoothed the top of her head.

"What happened?" She attempted to shift but the pain gripped her. She groaned. "Was it my appendix?"

"Yes." Logan patted her hand he held with the opposite one. "It burst. You had to have emergency surgery. It was scary there for a minute. I thought—but you're okay. You'll be fine. The infection hasn't spread. You should be cleared to go home in a few days."

"Did you perform the surgery?" Brooke tried her best to process everything, but her temples pulsated.

"No, it was a conflict of interest." He squeezed her shoulder. "My fellow surgeon did it, but I scrubbed in on it. I wasn't going to leave you. I've made a lot of mistakes that I need to make up for. I let other people influence how I felt, but I know how I feel now. I want to be with you."

"Let's talk about this later." Brooke leaned her head back against the pillow. "My head is very fuzzy."

A knock at the door interrupted them. Aubrey came barreling into the room with a huge bouquet of flowers. "Don't you ever scare me like that again!" She rushed to her other side and placed them on the side table before taking her other hand.

Brooke smiled. "I think I only have one appendix, so I think you're good."

Logan laughed.

"When did you get here?" Brooke asked.

"Logan," Aubrey glance between them, "called me before you went into surgery."

Brooke found his hand and squeezed it. "Thank you."

He winked. "I know she's your family." Logan squeezed back.

"You're one hundred percent right." Aubrey put a hand on her hip. "Promise me no more passing out."

"I'll certainly try my best." Brooke offered a crooked smile.

"I almost forgot," Logan's voice trailed off. He scratched the scruff on his jaw. "My parents are in the waiting room. They've been there for hours and won't go home even when I've told them to. They said they aren't leaving until they can visit you and make sure you're okay. Can I have them come in?"

"Sure." Her heart warmed. "But can you hold them off for ten minutes while I talk to Aubrey?"

"Absolutely." He kissed her at her temple and squeezed her hand once more. "I'll take them to the cafeteria to eat then bring them in."

Logan exited and left her alone with Aubrey.

"So, how bad was it?" Brooke tried to readjust herself in the bed but grimaced as pain made it not possible.

"It wasn't good that's for sure." Aubrey lowered herself in the chair next to her bed. "When they got you open, your appendix had already ruptured. Luckily, they removed it and started you on some heavy antibiotics. I've never seen Logan look that out of sorts. He loves you by the way." She shot her a pointed look.

Her eyelids grew heavy. Sleep called her name. "I think I might love him, too," Brooke mumbled as her eyes closed. "I'm tired—" Her voice drifted off.

"I know." Aubrey patted her leg and stood. "Now, sleep. The rest you'll figure out later."

CHAPTER 19

Logan wandered to the small waiting room on Brooke's floor. When he entered the room, he found his parents alone. Mom read while Dad worked on a crossword puzzle in the stray newspaper left behind from someone else.

"Brooke's up." Logan collapsed into the hard plastic chair across from the itchy plastic sofa they shared. "Her friend Aubrey is with her now."

"Glad to hear it." Mom placed her bookmark inside her book and closed it. "How's she doing? Better yet, how are you doing?" Her gaze roamed the length of his body. "You look awful."

"I'm sure I do. I feel terrible." Logan leaned forward in his chair. "But I'm relieved she's doing okay. Her body is responding to the antibiotics. In another twenty-four hours, she should be in the clear. She's lucky." Then as an afterthought, he added, "I'm lucky."

"What a scary experience." Dad folded his newspaper closed and tossed it on the side table.

The events of the last day came rushing back, Brooke passing out, her being rushed into surgery, then him scrubbing in on the surgery. As the surgeon cut into her abdomen, Logan kept thinking how Brooke didn't even know he loved her. She meant everything to him, and he needed the opportunity to tell her.

"I'm okay, but it was a bit traumatic for me to see someone I care about be so vulnerable." Logan exhaled then ran a hand down the length of his face. "I'm in love with her. I know that now more than ever. I only hope she'll return the feeling someday."

"You need to tell her." Mom squeezed his knee. "Then everything will fall into place."

Dad nodded. "You can't ever go wrong with telling the truth."

"I regret listening to Danielle." His shoulders drooped as he rested his forearms on his thighs. "I shouldn't have let her mess with my head about Shelby. Deep down I knew she was wrong for me, but I let myself be swayed."

"Trust me, I had a few choice words with your sister on that one," Dad muttered.

"They were friends in high school." Mom folded her arms. "I think in her way, Danielle thought she was being helpful. Your sister only wanted to see you happy, even if she is completely off about who is right for you."

His eyes burned. "I might have lost my chance." He was so tired.

Dad hummed. The look on his face didn't exactly invoke more confidence in him.

"Hush." Mom gathered his face into her hands. "You're going to make everything right. You watch."

"I appreciate your faith in me, but I've made a mess."

"Enough, you'll fix it. You were always up for a challenge when you were a kid." Mom removed her hands from his face and stood. "Come on, take us to see Brooke."

Dad stood too.

"Okay." Logan rose. "Let's get something to eat, and then I'll take you in to see her." He personally couldn't remember the last time he ate.

Logan led his parents to the cafeteria. They chatted over some bagels and pastries. Enough time passed, he returned to Brooke's hospital room with his parents in tow. He knocked lightly on the door and entered, they found her sleeping.

"I don't think we should wake her," Mom whispered. "She looks peaceful."

Brooke stirred. "I'm awake." She shifted and opened her eyes. "I think the pain meds kicked in, because I'm feeling better but sleepy." Her hand roamed over her hair, smoothing it down. "But thanks for coming, Logan said you wouldn't go home until you confirmed I was still in one piece."

"We were worried about you." Mom strode to her bedside and cradled her hand between both of hers. "I've never heard Logan as distressed as when he called us to tell us you were headed into surgery."

Dad moved behind Mom and placed his hands on her shoulders. "We're glad you're okay."

"Luckily, Logan happened to be there when I hit the ground." Brooke pressed the button on her bed to raise the head up then winced as it moved. "But, you really didn't need to come. Logan and I are—" She halted then paused.

"You mean a lot to Logan." Mom squeezed her hand. "So, that means you mean a lot to us too."

Logan itched to tell her exactly how he felt about her. "I was afraid—I didn't want to lose you." He walked around the hospital bed to the side opposite his parents.

"I'm still here," Brooke replied.

Then they stared at one another. For a second, he forgot his parents were in the room, because without further thought he leaned in and kissed her gingerly on her lips. "I'm still here, too."

Dad cleared his throat. "Honey, I think we should let Brooke get her beauty rest." He wrapped an arm around his wife's shoulders. "We can catch up with her another time."

"Yes." Mom dropped her hand. "You still owe us dinner in the city. We'll put something on the calendar the minute you're feeling up to it."

"I'd love that," Brooke smiled.

"Welcome to the family." Then Mom leaned in and hugged Brooke.

Brooke shot Logan a confused look over his mom's shoulders.

Logan shrugged.

"Come on." Dad directed Mom toward the door. "I think Logan and Brooke have a lot to discuss without us here."

"Fine." Then Mom moved to the exit but shifted back and wagged a finger at them. "But dinner." Then she pointed at him. "Call me."

"Of course."

They left the room. The clicks of the machines in the room sounded.

Brooke yawned. "What was—your," she yawned again, "mom saying?"

"I think," Logan fluffed her pillow, "you should sleep. We'll have plenty of time to discuss everything when you're recovered."

Brooke yawned again then shifted against the pillow and lowered her hospital bed with the button. "Sleep is calling my name." She closed her eyes. "But please don't go—" Her voice drifted off, "I don't want you to ever leave—"

Logan leaned in and smoothed out the loosened hair over her forehead then kissed her on it. "I won't leave, I promise."

Then he went and flipped off the lights then settled into the lounge chair beside her bed. He listened as her breathing slowed and evened out, only then did he drift off to sleep himself.

CHAPTER 20

Sunshine trickled through the hospital window and hit Brooke's face. Drowsy, she swiped her eyes and slowly gained her bearings. *Hospital, surgery, appendicitis*. She stretched then winced. Her abdomen still stung with the slightest shift. But nothing compared to the pain she'd experienced before she passed out.

Across the room sat Logan. Their eyes locked. "Hey." She pressed the button on the bed to raise it to sitting position. "You're still here."

"Hi, sunshine." Logan scuttled out of his chair and rounded the bed and sat on the edge of it. "You're back in the land of the living." He found her hand and gave it a reassuring squeeze.

"I'm still not feeling a hundred percent." Brooke knew she looked like a hot mess. Slime coated her teeth. She scrunched her nose to the feeling of grease slathered across it. Her hand attempted to smooth out her dirty and dingy hair. "I can't remember the last time I showered."

"Unfortunately—" he squeezed her hand, "I think you'll have to wait another twenty-four hours to shower. You still can't get the incision wet."

"Ugh," she groaned. "I look and feel disgusting."

"I think you look beautiful." He had a doe-eyed look.

"You're lying." Brooke's lips twitched. "But I appreciate it."

"It isn't a lie." Logan scooted closer to her on the bed. "I always think you look beautiful."

"Again," she wagged a finger. "Lies, but since I'm at an all-time low, I'll accept your attempt at boosting my spirit."

Dr. James barreled into the room interrupting them. "Everything is looking great." She had a stack of papers in her hands. "I put in for you to be discharged tomorrow afternoon."

"Really?" Brooke exchanged a look with Logan then peered back at the doctor. "So soon?"

"Your infection is under control, your incision is looking good, I figure you'd prefer sleeping in your own bed over this one as soon as possible," Dr. James said.

"True," Brooke agreed.

"Are you the significant other?" Dr. James asked.

"I'm the boyfriend."

Boyfriend, Brooke liked the sound of that.

"Okay." Dr. James glanced down at the paperwork then back at Logan. "So, I assume you'll be helping Brooke with her recovery."

"Yes, absolutely." Logan stood.

"Then let me go over the aftercare with both of you."

Dr. James reviewed the dos and don'ts after her surgery. Logan listened intently, which she appreciated, because her head throbbed a little and found concentrating extra difficult.

Once the explanation was completed, Dr. James said, "I understand you both work here, so I hope to see you in the hallways sometime." Then she shoved her hands into her lab coat pockets.

"Yes, likewise," Logan said.

Then Dr. James exited. They watched her leave.

When they were alone once more, Logan said, "I wanted to ask you—"

Then Brooke's nurse entered to check her vitals, then further go over her discharge. Whatever Logan cared to share with her had to wait, because a long stream of medical personnel seemed determined to keep them from discussing anything alone. The rest of the evening and following morning continued in the same manner.

By the next afternoon, Brooke itched to go home and sleep in her own bed without being endlessly interrupted by random people. Logan brought over some comfy sweats from her apartment, and she changed into them before being discharged.

The doctor signed off on her release, and they exited her room to the elevator bay. Eventually, the elevators swung open. A few doctors and staff members tumbled out. Brooke and Logan waited for the elevator to clear before they entered it.

Once in the quiet of the elevator car. Brooke confessed, "I'm sorry I pushed you away. I'm sorry I made you go out with Shelby. Which I'm assuming if you're here, it's because things didn't work out with her. I hope you staying by my side means you want something more between us."

"I do," Logan confirmed. "You know I do." He took her hand and directed their bodies to touch.

She itched to kiss again. Her mind ran rampant with their romantic entanglements, and she wanted to let her body fold against his. She wanted to feel the hitch in her breath, the glide of his tongue, the parting of her lips. Brooke would let him stay for as long as he wanted, hopefully forever.

"Good," she smirked. "Then my brilliant plan worked."

He raised an eyebrow with a smirk. "I didn't know you had one."

"Neither did I. But apparently if you pass out, a handsome doctor might end up saving you." Her lips twitched. "So, thank you."

"I admit it certainly sealed the deal for me." The elevator doors dinged and then swung open.

They left the elevator and meandered across the lobby. When they exited, warm Chicago night air whirled around them. A week ago, an unusual heat wave settled over the city. By next week, it would be gone, and the cold night air would return until summer.

"I ordered us food from the restaurant next to your apartment." Logan's hand found hers. "It won't be a far walk. Maybe an extra fifty feet. Are you feeling strong enough?"

"I'm okay to walk." She landed a short peck on his cheek. "Thank you."

They took an uber to the restaurant next to her apartment.

When they climbed out, and the car drove away, she asked the question itching inside of her, "Do you think Danielle will ever learn to like me?"

He halted, making her nearly stumble against the back of his heels. "She already does, and for the record even if Danielle didn't, I wouldn't care. I'm done with other people telling me who to love and who to be with."

"But she's your sister," Brooke insisted.

"And someday, I want you to be my wife," he stated without hesitation.

"Wife, you say—"

"Wife supersedes sister, always."

"Okay," she softly replied.

His gaze glimmered with the overhead streetlamps and lights. People stumbled out of the shops and restaurants and passed by them on the sidewalk.

"We'll have to see about that." Then Brooke nudged her head in the direction of the restaurant. "Now, enough chatting I'm starving. This is where a package of Oreos would come in handy."

"Oh." Logan retrieved a small package out of his pocket and handed them to her. "These should hold you over until we get real food."

"Oreos," Brooke busted opened the package and ate a bite, "are real food. They're the best food."

Logan smirked. "Right—if you say so." They walked to the restaurant door. He held the door open. "Mom is insisting on this dinner. Are you free any upcoming Sunday?"

"No," Brooke wandered inside the tight foyer of the restaurant. The lights were low and the music a tad too loud. She spoke louder, "I have to work the next three Sundays."

"Then they'll have to wait." Logan checked in with the host and let them know of their order. The host disappeared into the belly of the restaurant and back to the kitchen. He leaned his hip against the counter as he waited while Brooke polished off another Oreo. "We'll go the next time you're free."

"Are you going to want to move back someday?" Brooke brushed some stray crumbs off her lip. "Live in a house on the same street as your parents and sister?"

"What do you want?" Logan studied her.

"I don't know." Brooke shoved the half-eaten package of Oreos into her pocket. Then she brushed her hands together. "That's why I asked you."

He shrugged. "Where you go, I go."

"Okay." Brooke furrowed her brow. "Meaning?"

"Food's ready," the host announced as they set the bag of food on the counter.

"I'll live wherever you want." He kissed her on the cheek, moved to the counter and paid for the food.

They left the restaurant. The tantalizing aroma of chicken, pita bread, and hummus wafted out of the bag. Another train rolled over their heads as they slowly traipsed the few remaining yards to her apartment.

"In the summer, I want to take you to Indiana Dunes." He cradled the to-go bag in the crook of his arm while he laced his free hand with hers. "It's on the coast of Lake Michigan and is about an hour drive."

"How do you know we'll even be a thing come summertime?" Brooke teased.

"A feeling," he smirked. "I have a sixth sense about these types of things."

Brooke's apartment building came into view. "If we're together, together, why haven't you kissed me yet?" She scrunched her nose.

George waited outside in his usual spot.

Logan stopped. "I was waiting," he twisted to face her, "you know with the whole passing out, emergency surgery, infection and stitches across your abdomen thing."

"I think a kiss would be the perfect remedy for a very long couple of days," she countered.

Then he dropped the bag of food to the ground beside his feet. He wrapped an arm around her waist and gingerly brought her close until their hips touched. "I have wanted to kiss you every second of every hour, since the last time."

"Then it's time you stopped counting." Brooke peered up at him and cupped his jaw. "I sent you away to Shelby. I'm sorry. I was scared. I worried I wouldn't be enough. I didn't want to keep you from happiness. Since my life isn't perfect, and I have a less-than-ideal past, I sometimes question my worth. I had an addict for a mother, a dead beat of a father, and somehow in that dysfunction I managed to put myself through college and medical school, but it doesn't mean the scars have completely healed. But I'd like to try with you. You make me feel worthy. You make me believe in myself and most importantly in love."

Logan grinned. "I love," he kissed her gently on the lips, "every part," he kissed her on her cheek, "of you," he kissed her on her temple.

Then he cradled her head between his hands. "And now, no more waiting."

Then his lips gently graced hers.

~

His ChapStick coated her lips. Her heart sped up when his signature scent filled her lungs. She memorized the feeling of his skin against her cheek, and his scruff against her chin. The kiss was smooth and gentle like they were slowly floating away somewhere warm and incredible. His strong arm supported her waist and kept her upright. Her fingers traced his chest and eventually rested under the collar of his shirt.

He deepened their kiss making her lips part. He tasted as good as she remembered. And she knew he was the person she wanted to kiss again and again until the day she died. Brooke completely forgot about their location in the middle of the sidewalk, in the middle of the city. The sounds of the city disappeared, because Logan made her imagine a life full of good things, great things, and better than there ever was things.

Someone whistled. Brooke pulled away and peered over her shoulder toward George who then pumped his arm in victory. “I’m glad to see you survived!” His voice barreled toward them.

“He let me in to your apartment when I went to get your change of sweats,” Logan revealed.

George whistled again.

“You know,” she fidgeted with the collar of his shirt, “he probably won’t stop until we stop.” Then she peered up at him.

“I know.” Logan grinned, sneaking a quick peck. “But I don’t care.”

“Me either.” Then he leaned in and kissed her again.

CHAPTER 21

On the first Sunday evening they finally had free, they drove out to Logan's parents for dinner. It ended up being easier than them coming into the city. Danielle couldn't find a sitter, so he checked with Brooke, and she agreed going to them worked fine. Logan wondered if the dinner would feel different now that they were actually dating for real and no longer under the guise of fake dating. They agreed that his parents never needed to know about their fake dating phase.

The beginnings of spring made the air balmy and sweet. Logan lowered the windows of the car a few inches to let the tangy air roll through the cab. The wind picked up and made Brooke's hair whirl around her.

Brooke spoke loudly over the roar of the engine. "When do the twins turn one?" They held hands over the center console.

"In a week. Danielle has insisted on a huge birthday bash." Logan changed lanes without missing a beat. "She's renting a petting zoo to come set up in her backyard."

"They do that?" Brooke scrunched up her nose. "I can't remember ever even having a cake for me."

"I'm sorry, that bites, but don't worry that will change." Logan squeezed her hand. "I plan on making sure not a single one of your birthdays ever passes without the most annoyingly perfect fanfare."

"I wasn't—I don't need fanfare." Brooke's cheeks splashed with pink. "Just a cake, a day celebrating with family. That would be enough."

"You mean my family?" Logan glanced quickly at her then darted his gaze back to the highway.

"Yes." Brooke gnawed on her free hand's thumb nail. "But they'll be mine too someday, right?"

The thought made his heart soar. He wanted nothing more than for Brooke to slide right into his family. She was his missing thread and belonged next to him in the fabric of the family.

"You've been listening." He brought their holding hands up to his mouth and he kissed the back of her palm. "I want you to be my family. I want my family to be yours, too."

"Then it's all settled." The exit to his parents' came up next. Brooke pointed at the exit sign. "Don't miss the exit, I've been distracting you with all this family talk."

"Hey," he merged onto the exit, slowing down as he rolled to the stoplight at the end of it. "I like this family talk."

Then he made a right turn and drove at a leisurely pace through the neighborhood to his parents. The sidewalks were lined with blooming trees. A mixture of Eastern Redbud, Dogwood and Crabapple trees made a beautiful pop of spring. Houses were set far back with green lawns and vibrant flowers. He loved coming home, even more, he loved that this time Brooke was coming too.

Logan pulled onto the street which led to his parents. "Mom is already asking if we can come for Easter."

"I'd love that," Brooke wistfully sighed. "I look forward to many of these gatherings. If I'm being honest—I am a bit nervous to see Danielle. I haven't seen her since I went to her house to help with Lily's fever."

"Has it been that long?" He eased the car to the curb and parked. "My sister is fully on board. She even apologized to me, which is huge. I can't remember her ever admitting to being wrong about anything before." He turned off the car and unbuckled his seat belt.

"I know." Brooke unbuckled her seatbelt too. "But she wanted you to be with Shelby."

"Not now." Logan shoved his keys into his pocket. "She texted me incessantly during your hospital stay and called me regularly to make sure you were okay. I thought I told you that."

"You did." Brooke clasped and unclasped her hands together. "She's your sister, is it too much to ask that I want her to like me?"

"She does." He brushed her hair over her shoulder. "Just give her a chance to show you."

"Okay."

Before they even exited the car, the whole crew came tumbling out of the house. His parents each held a twin while Danielle darted across the lawn and opened Brooke's door.

Danielle popped her head inside. "I owe you an apology," she blurted out.

Brooke's gaze darted between her and Logan then back to her. "Umm." She tucked her loosened hair behind her ears. "Really?"

"Yes, I almost ruined my baby brother's shot at happiness."

Danielle grasped Brooke by her hands and yanked her out of the car to a standing position. Logan climbed out of the car and joined them.

"I'm sorry." Danielle hugged her. "I hope you can forgive me."

"Of course." Brooke smiled and patted her on her back before releasing their embrace. "It's water under the bridge."

Brooke twisted and met his gaze. She beamed. Logan winked at her.

Danielle hooked her elbow around Brooke's. "Grab her stuff," she instructed Logan.

"Aye, Aye." Logan gathered up Brooke's purse and shut the car door, and he followed behind them as they walked up the house.

"How are you feeling?" Danielle patted Brooke arm with her other hand. "Is your abdomen still sore?" Her gaze roamed over her. "My brother had better be taking good care of you."

"I'm doing much better." Brooke peered over her shoulder to Logan. "And I've had an excellent doctor taking care of me. He's made sure I followed the aftercare to a T."

"Good." Danielle shot Logan a pleased look. "Then Mom and I taught him well."

"Thanks." Brooke smiled. "I've certainly reaped the benefits of your hard work."

"You should've seen him as a kid." Danielle smirked. "Oh, the stories I have to tell you."

"Ooh, this is going to be fun." Brooke elbowed Logan.

"Hey." Logan broke the two women apart and wrapped an arm around Brooke's shoulders. "Please do not listen to her. I was the poster child for a well-mannered and perfect child."

"Yeah, right." Danielle shook a finger at him. "Didn't you almost burn down the school during chemistry?"

"They managed to get the fire out quickly," Logan countered defensively. "The teacher had it one hundred percent under control."

"What?" Brooke's eyes dilated. "How did you manage to do that?"

"A kid dared me to triple the amount of one chemical. He claimed he saw something about it on one of those true crime stories." Logan winced. "It wasn't my finest hour but believe me when I say it was a one-time thing."

"Yes, because you received in-school suspension and Dad scared you straight," Danielle replied.

"But look at me now. I'm a model citizen. My fire days are long behind me."

"You're hogging her." Amy shouted to them as she rearranged one of the twins from one of her hips to the other. "Get on up here."

"We're coming!" Logan shouted back.

"Mom," Danielle leaned in closer and whispered, "made that jambalaya, she claims is a family recipe. Word to the wise, eat slowly, and take large sips of water to get it down."

"When is she ever going to learn how much we hate that stuff," Logan muttered under her breath. "Good luck to us all."

Brooke chuckled. "Okay," she whispered back. "I appreciate the advice."

When they arrived at the front porch, Logan's parents hugged her while balancing a twin on their hips. Brooke shook Michael's hand. Logan snatched Amelia from Amy and snuggled her against his chest. Amy, Danielle and Michael went into the house.

Paul hung back with them with Lily on his hip. "How are you doing?" His gaze swung to Brooke. "Is your incision healing okay?"

"I'm feeling much better," Brooke said. "Thanks for asking."

"I heard one of my colleagues performed the surgery," Paul said.

"Really?" she raised an eyebrow.

"Dr. Stein who performed your surgery went to medical school with Dad," Logan said.

"Wow, small world," Brooke said.

"He is top notch, and he's been a great mentor to Logan. I'm glad he was there to do the surgery."

"Me too," she said.

They paused.

"Come on now," Paul mumbled and gestured for them to follow him inside. "Amy made her jambalaya." He leaned in a tad closer. "I'm sorry. None of us have the heart to tell her it's terrible."

Brooke laughed. "I promise to keep the family secret."

"That's right," Logan squeezed her hip, "*our* family secret."

"Exactly," Paul said.

"Come on." Logan led her inside. "The jambalaya puke fest is waiting."

Her eyes sparkled back at him. "Bring it on," Brooke teased. "I was made for this."

"You are going to fit right in," Paul said.

Logan drew Brooke close to his side and wrapped an arm around her waist. "I know." He kissed her on the cheek. "She fits, right next to me."

CHAPTER 22

Five months later, Logan loaded up his trunk. After a few failed attempts, he finally managed to fit the beach gear in. Lake Michigan called his name. The sweltering summer air made the idea of walking along the beach at the Indiana Dunes that much more appealing. With their busy schedules, this weekend happened to be the first both he and Brooke had free.

His parents and Danielle and her family were driving out to meet them for the day. The twins were walking everywhere, and Danielle said she could only brave the beach with several extra hands in the mix. Everyone wanted a break from the heat, and he knew a day out of the city was exactly what they needed.

Logan doubled checked everything before he slammed the trunk shut. Brooke entered the parking garage of his apartment building in her swimsuit and beach coverup on. Her beauty still made his pulse simmer and stomach do a somersault.

With a soda in one hand and a hand-held cooler in the other. "I didn't forget the drinks." She took a swig of her soda as she crossed the rest of the garage to where he waited. "My word, is this garage stuffy." She stopped in front of him. "Here." Brooke handed him her half empty soda can then unzipped the small bag cooler. "You look like you could use something cool to drink."

"It's terrible down here." He leaned against the car and swiped at the sweat trickling down his temples. "This garage manages to trap all the heat. It makes me want to move out of the city."

Brooke retrieved a soda then held it out to him. "Here, drink this. It always makes everything better."

"Thanks." Logan took the soda and handed hers back. He popped the top then chugged half the can without stopping. Then he wiped his mouth with the back of his hand. "Gosh, that tastes good." The condensation from the can cooled his fingers.

"I know." Brooke gave him a satisfying smile as she brought her can of soda to her lips and took a sip. "What time are we meeting the crew?"

Over the last several months, Brooke had folded seamlessly into his family. He loved that she liked them as much as he did. And Danielle had taken her under her wing and stayed true to her word about being supportive of their relationship.

"Ten." He closed the trunk with one hand while he cradled the soda in the other. "We wanted to beat the traffic, and Danielle said the twins will probably only last until the afternoon. But we can stay as long as we want. I thought it would be nice to stop for dinner on the way home."

"Perfect." Brooke fanned her face with her free hand. "Let's get out of this stuffy and hot garage."

They climbed in and drove out to Indiana Dunes. On the way, Brooke texted Danielle with their arrival time. His parents were coming with them in their van, but a car accident on the expressway meant they'd arrive about an hour later than them. Logan and Brooke found a sandy spot on the beach, set up their chairs and umbrellas and waited for his family to arrive.

Other people filled in on the sand, but the beach remained calm and peaceful. They held hands as they stared out at the water. The sun rose higher and the water sparkled beneath its rays. Wind nipped at them. Eventually, Brooke dug a hat out of her bag and put it on. Logan readjusted the umbrella to keep them from being fried from the sun.

"I don't ever remember going to the beach with family." Brooke said, breaking the silence. "I can't even say I ever went anywhere fun with my mom. Anything normal—I could get used to days like this."

"Me too." Logan interlaced his fingers with hers again and squeezed. He watched a family play in the waves. "There's so much more I want to do with you, show you. I know things weren't good in your childhood, but I believe I can show you there's a second chance to experience the things you missed."

"I know." Brooke shifted to face him. "I appreciate it."

A brush of wind made the sand dance across their ankles. Gosh, Brooke looked gorgeous. He wanted to show her everything, restore her faith in families. He'd give her anything she named, because he loved her more every day. He ran his thumb in circles over the top of hers.

Logan locked eyes with her. "Marry me."

Startled, Brooke paused. "Are you being serious?" Her curious gaze slid across his face.

"Yes." Logan leaned in closer. "I'm completely serious. Marry me."

Brooke nervously laughed. "Are you proposing to me right now? On a beach, when I have a ridiculous straw hat on?" She shook her head. "Do you even have a ring?"

"No." He dropped his hand from hers and ran it through his hair. "But we can stop on the way back to the city at a jewelry shop. I'll google a place. You can pick out whatever ring you want, because you make me happy. I love you, and I can't imagine my life without you. Please say yes. Please say you want to spend the rest of your life with me."

"I mean—I don't even know what to say." She gnawed on her bottom lip. "I'm worried this is simply you being impulsive."

"I'm being anything but that." Logan brought both of her hands into his own. "I've wanted to ask you to marry me for a good two months, but I didn't want to scare you off. Am I scaring you off now?"

"Surprisingly, no."

"Then marry me and I promise to make you happy. I promise I'll work every day to build something beautiful with you."

"Well," a slow smile crept across her face, "how can I resist that? Yes, I'll marry you."

Logan leaped out of his seat and practically heaved Brooke to her feet. Then he removed her large hat and leaned in and kissed her. His heart soared as he held her close. She tasted equal parts sweet and delectable. He memorized the feeling of her tucked in against him, the length of her jaw, and hair tangled up in his fingertips. Logan knew this time he had it right. A loaf of bread and a package of Oreos had changed the entire course of his life.

Danielle out of nowhere loudly cleared her throat. "Alright you two." They stopped kissing and peered in her direction. Dad and Michael were loaded down with beach stuff while Danielle and Mom each held a twin. "We get that you two can't get enough of each other." Danielle set Amelia down on the sand. "But come on, this is a family place."

Mom smiled. "Please don't stop on our account." She placed Lily on the sand next to Amelia. "I like seeing my son happy and in love."

Brooke chuckled and loosened her grip around his waist.

Danielle removed the bag of sand toys from her shoulder and dumped the entire contents on the sand in front of her twins. Dad and Michael dumped their stuff, and each went to work setting up chairs.

Logan exchanged a glance with Brooke.

Then he blurted out, "We're getting married."

Danielle's mouth dropped open. Dad and Michael stopped their set up and stared.

Mom clapped her hands together. "Oh, my." She raced over to them and threw her arms around both of them. "This is the best day ever."

Dad came over and slapped him on the back. "Congrats, you two."

"Sorry to break up this love fest." They broke apart. Danielle pointed at Brooke's finger. "Where's the ring? I thought that was the biggest part of getting engaged." She placed a hand on her hip. "Come on baby brother, I used to think you were sharp."

"I told Brooke," He tugged her close, "we'll stop at a jewelry store on the way home, and she can pick out whatever ring she wanted. I was worried she wouldn't like what I picked out."

"Ahh," Danielle said knowingly. "I see."

"I have a friend who is a jeweler," Michael piped in. "I can text you his info, he'll give you a good deal."

"Great." Logan kissed Brooke on her temple. "I'd appreciate it."

"Fine, but the ring had better be big." Danielle held out her hand, revealing her sparkly diamond. "It still makes me happy every time I look at it. I know it shouldn't matter, but it does."

Brooke laughed. "I don't care what size it is. Promise."

"No, no." Danielle wagged a finger. "My brother had better not be cheap."

"Hey," Logan said. "I'm right here, and I won't be *cheap*."

"Good," Danielle said like she was satisfied. "Because you deserve it, and more, for taking this guy off our hands."

"Danielle," Logan said with a warning tone.

Then the twins started crying. His family sprang into action and found something different for them to play with. They worked together to set up his family's chairs and umbrellas. Later, once they had eaten lunch, Logan led Brooke down to the water's edge for a minute alone. The water raced over their feet and nipped at their ankles. They stared out at the glistening water.

"I'm sorry I didn't exactly give you a romantic proposal." He ran a hand down the length of his face. "I was caught up in the moment but can do a redo after we buy the ring."

Brooke squeezed his hand. "Absolutely not." She peered over her shoulder back to where his family sat on the sand. The twins dumped buckets of sand on their heads. "I love you. I don't want to wait another minute to have that ring on my finger."

"I love you back. No more waiting." Logan leaned in and kissed her.

A refreshing breeze drifted between them. The sunshine made his skin tickle. Brooke smoothed out the front of his shirt then patted his chest.

Her eyes sparkled with the light of the sun. "It's the perfect day." Brooke tugged her gaze away from him and out to the water.

"Agree." Logan grinned. "The perfect day."

"I'll remember it always."

The water splashed around their ankles. "Me too." Logan kissed her on the temple then wrapped an arm around her waist.

Brooke laughed. "I can't believe they still don't know our whole arrangement was only supposed to be until Aubrey and Ian's wedding."

"I know." Logan chuckled too, then twisted to peer over his shoulder to his family. Then he twisted back. "But I'd like to keep it our secret if that's okay."

"Sure." Brooke wrapped her arm around his waist. "Maybe we hold off and tell them at our golden anniversary. You'd better believe it would bring both shock and awe."

"I love it." His lips twitched.

"Me too." Brooke fingers dipped into the stretch of skin between his swimsuit trunks and his shirt. "But you have to promise me that you'll never let us run out of Oreos."

"Uh, duh." He stole a quick peck. "That's a given."

"Promise to buy me hot French bread when I crave it?"

"Absolutely." He kissed her on her cheek. "I'll eat the rest if you don't finish it."

Brooke rested her head on his shoulder and blissfully sighed. "Then I have a feeling we're going to be just fine."

"I think so too."

MEET THE AUTHOR

Emi Hilton is a California native who was born at March Airforce Base, to an Officer in the US Army Combat Engineer Battalion father and an English Professor mother. Emi followed in her mother's footsteps and graduated from Brigham Young University in English. While in college, she took a year and a half break from her studies to serve as a full-time missionary for her church in the Canary Islands.

Emi writes sweet contemporary romance novels. Her novels, Memories in Morro Bay, Bluebird Sky and Picking Pismo were nominated for Whitney Awards. Her novel, Picking Pismo, won the Christlit Book Award.

When Emi isn't writing, she enjoys training for marathons, fishing off local piers with her husband and three sons, or visiting her other love, Spain.

OTHER TITLES FROM 5 PRINCE PUBLISHING

www.5princebooks.com

Having the Werewolf's Baby *Courtney Davis*

Courting the Lion *S.E. Reichert*

Mistress and Mage *Blythe Brandenburg*

Having the Vampire's Baby *Courtney Davis*

Come to the Cape *Emi Hilton*

Time To Byrne *S.E. Reichert*

Bookish *Bernadette Marie*

Dare You to Choose Truth *Lauren Lipp*

Enlightenment *Nicole Kelley*

All the Little Moments *Savannah Reed*

The Rocking of the Ocean *Barbara Matteson*

New to Newport *Emi Hilton*

Trusting the Alpha *Courtney Davis*

Sweet Summertide *Sarah Dressler*

No Words After I Love You *S.E. Reichert*

Demons and Tea Leaves *Courtney Davis*

Shadow of the Throne *Russell Archey*

Shadow Among the Stars *Courtney Davis*

The Pack *E.C. Saulness*

www.ingramcontent.com/pod-product-compliance
Lightning Source LLC
LaVergne TN
LVHW091045080826
845145LV00002B/635

* 9 7 8 1 6 3 1 1 2 4 3 5 8 *